Movement 1

C000078955

Hadena James

Dreams & Reality Novels
Tortured Dreams
Elysium Dreams
Mercurial Dreams
Explosive Dreams
Cannibal Dreams
Butchered Dreams
Summoned Dreams
Triggered Reality
Battered Dreams
Belladonna Dreams
Mutilated Dreams
Fortified Dreams
Flawless Dreams
Demonic Dreams
Ritual Dreams
Anonymous Dreams
Dysfunctional Dreams
Buried Dreams

The Brenna Strachan Series
Dark Cotillion
Dark Illumination
Dark Resurrections
Dark Legacies

The Dysfunctional Chronicles
The Dysfunctional Affair
The Dysfunctional Valentine
The Dysfunctional Honeymoon
The Dysfunctional Proposal
The Dysfunctional Holiday
The Dysfunctional Wedding
The Dysfunctional Expansion

Nephilim Narratives
Natural Born Exorcist
Oh My Wizard
Demon Boxes

Short Story Collections & Stand-Alone Novels
Tales to Read Before the End of the World
Terrorific Tales
Goddess Investigations

Chapter One

It was opening day of baseball season. Remiel had gotten a box for the game and invited the entire family to join him in celebrating his favorite sport at his favorite stadium. The St. Louis Cardinals opened against the Milwaukee Brewers in Busch Stadium. Despite it being a Thursday afternoon game, we had all come to partake of my uncle's hospitality and generosity.

Even though there had been plenty of food, my father invited Jerome, Helia, Gabriel, and me to dinner at Tony's, a fabulous restaurant way out of my price range. We all accepted and found ourselves at the restaurant a little after 8 p.m., minus my mom and nieces, who had gone home.

The hostess led us to a table in the most private area of the dining room. That gave me a bad feeling.

There was a woman already sitting at the large table. My father introduced us to her. She was a witch named Magda the Red who ran a division of the AESPCA as well as being chair of the Witches' Council. The All-Encompassing Supernatural Protection Agency was the worldwide governing body for the magical. It was broken into divisions and councils. For example, the host I belonged to was governed by the Angel Council, which answered to the Division of Magical Councils.

Magda the Red was tall with long red hair that contained a few streaks of silver. Her jaw was masculine, but the overall effect of her face was quite feminine. Helia and I exchanged glances, both of us not sure what was going on, but I was positive I was going to be angry by the end of the evening. Jerome had been unsure about joining a coven full time and had been inducted into our angelic host instead, at least temporarily. He was understandably wary of covens in general and powerful witches specifically. I had little doubt that Magda the Red was a powerful witch since she sat at the head of the council.

I also got the impression she was incredibly old, not just because of the silver hair, but because she hadn't been introduced with a last name, a sign of serious age among supernaturals. Surnames had only come into being in the last thousand years or so; before then people had first names and titles like the Red. Some supernaturals had taken those titles as last names and some hadn't. My father and his brothers were known by their first names, followed by the title the Archangel. My sister and I had been given our mother's surname, Burns.

We all sat down and were handed menus. I was actually stuffed from the baseball game. Remiel didn't skimp on food when he got a box. and he always made sure the catering was top notch for his guests. I'd eaten a cheeseburger around 4 p.m., before I'd learned my father wanted to take us out to Tony's for dinner. Tony's was an Italian place, and I'd never had a meal there that was subpar in any way. Jerome and I sat next to each other at the large round table, and my father ordered wine for all of us except Jerome, who had just turned 15 in January. He got a glass of Dr Pepper and a water.

My father encouraged us to order food, which we did. Appetizers quickly littered the table, and the staff set stacks of small plates out after handing us each one. I frowned. My father and Gabriel had ordered nearly every appetizer on the menu, which was an indication they were up to something we weren't going to like.

As we made small talk, my Uncle Remiel showed up and I felt myself frown harder as he sat down in the only open seat at the table. With both Remiel and Gabriel, this was bound to be something awful, because my father was bringing in reinforcements.

Helia was just picking at her appetizer plate. Jerome's appetite was never dampened by the antics of my family; he had heaped his small plate with steamed mussels, cheese sticks, crab stuffed mushrooms, and herb bread before chowing down.

After the entrees had been set before us, my father got down to business. He stood and gave a toast to new friends and new futures, both of which made my stomach churn.

"We have a couple of reasons for this meeting," Remiel said after my father finished. "We need both of you girls and Jerome to help us out." *Fan-fucking-tabulous*, I thought, and Remiel smiled at me.

"First things first; there were no angelic children born last year, not a single one. In the last decade, this is the third time this has happened. We have a theory," Gabriel said.

"Who is we?" I asked.

"Well, it started with Jerome," Gabriel said, and we all turned to look at the teenager. He smiled brightly.

"Basically, it is my belief that the reason for the declining birth rates among angels is because of the Angel Council. Balthazar Leopold has been chair of the Angel

Council for close to 200 years, and while angelic birth rates have never been stellar, they've gotten much worse since he took over. Balthazar himself is childless; I think it's possible he's sterile, and it's rippling out to the rest of the angelic population. Especially since angels who have zero interaction with him are more likely to get pregnant," Jerome said proudly and pointedly looked at my sister. Balthazar Leopold hated the archangels and went out of his way to avoid us. I'd never met him face to face, and I was unwelcome at meetings of the Angel Council, as was Helia. My sister had two kids, both born in the last decade.

"Meaning it's time to replace him," said Magda the Red. "I can't help with that except to give an opinion, and it is my opinion that only one person can run against Balthazar and win."

I considered this. The Angel Council was voted on every five years, and of all the council elections I'd lived through, I'd never seen anyone run against Balthazar Leopold.

"It has to be an archangel," Remiel said. "But it can't be one of us, as we started the Angel Council and have all served at different times, so it's time for the next generation to throw their hats into the ring of politics. Soleil would be a disaster; angels are mistrustful of her because of the Stygian connection. However, there is an archangel in our midst who has the ability to gain the trust of other angels while also making them happy. We think she should run against Balthazar Leopold."

My sister's mouth fell open, and she stared wide-eyed at Remiel.

"I concur," I chirped. Helia would be amazing as the chair of the Angel Council. Leopold had dismantled the elections for the council beyond chair and made them appointed positions. As far as I could tell, the people who currently filled the roles did not really do anything, and Leopold collected the dismal salaries of all the positions as well as doing all the work. If Helia could be elected to the chair position, elections for the other positions could be held and the council would operate as it should. If Jerome was correct, then we could get the angelic birth rates from dismal to appalling, and we might get ten or so births a year again. As it was, there were only seven angels in Aurora's class; they ranged from five to eight years old.

St. Louis had one of the two angel schools left in the world, and most of the students were boarding students from other countries and other states. Yet, 38 years ago when I'd started angel school, there had been nearly 30 angels in my class and 12 angel schools in the world. The same was true of Helia's class. However, when I bothered to read the Cherubim Newsletter I received every quarter, it had been impossible to miss the lack of birth announcements.

"Uh, it seems like that is going to take a lot of my time and I have two little girls to raise," Helia protested.

"We considered that, but if you aren't doing every job of the council, it really doesn't require that much time. Maybe 30 or so hours a month," Gabriel said. I didn't say anything, but that still seemed like a lot of time to me.

Then I had a second thought—Helia worked for me as a receptionist. She'd been forced to quit the municipal fines office when she sprouted wings because her wings didn't fit in the little booth she was required to sit in, and the city hadn't wanted to pay to renovate it. Would she need to take time off every month to handle council business? If she did, we'd work something out, because I wouldn't let it take too much time away from Aurora and Ariel, who had been through plenty in just the last six months. Their father's trial for attempted murder, arson, vandalism, and a plethora of other charges was coming up in a few weeks. We hadn't told them about it because I was one of the witnesses for the prosecution. Theodore Mark Reynolds was facing the possibility of life without parole, with a minimum sentence of 20 years. No one could figure out how to explain this to a ten-year-old and a seven-year-old. They knew their father was in jail and they knew why, but they seemed to think he might be released in a few years, something that made them both have nightmares. The therapist had told us to ignore it until after sentencing unless the girls specifically asked about it, so that was what we were all doing, even Jerome.

"If you get elected, we'll settle it to where you can handle council business during your regular work hours," I assured my sister.

"Which is another reason we think you'll be great at the job. You have a support network that most angels don't," Magda the Red said. Supernatural families tended to be distant; children could be thousands of years apart in age, which prevented siblings from forming close bonds. Even the relationships between children and parents eroded with time. I wasn't sure why my family was different, but we were. My uncles and father had remained close throughout the eons, and every new birth in the family was a huge celebration. As the children grew up, everyone was involved in raising them. My uncles had all been involved in my childhood, and they were now heavily involved with Aurora, Ariel, and Jerome, the three youngest family members at this point. When Jerome had a baseball game or something else at school, it was guaranteed that at least two or three of the uncles would show up to support him in addition to my parents, and most of the time, Helia and the girls. My family took the idea that it took a village to raise a child as gospel and fulfilled all the necessary roles.

"You have my full support," I told Helia.

"Which brings me to why you and Jerome are here," Magda the Red said, turning piercing grey-blue eyes on me. I managed, with some effort, not to fidget. Her eyes were intense, serious, and stern. "I'm the head of the Division of Law Enforcement at the AESPCA, and I need an outside investigator to handle a delicate case for me. I had originally intended to talk to you privately, but I know Remiel will find out regardless of my safeguards, and I suspect you would struggle to keep the investigation secret from Raphael and Sophia. It seemed expedient then to make this a joint meeting to discuss the Angel Council with Helia as well as introduce myself to you and Jerome."

"Okay," I said, eyeing her skeptically.

"It's gruesome, so we won't be discussing it over dinner. I will accompany you, Remiel, and Jerome back to your house when we leave," she said.

"Okay," I repeated. I wasn't sure if I liked Magda or not, or if I even wanted to work for her on a special case. Remiel must have read my mind, because Jerome gently slapped my hand under the table and I had no doubt it was from Remiel. They could talk telepathically to each other.

Entrees were followed by dessert, which I didn't need, but ate anyway. The rest of dinner was spent discussing the Angel Council. It was obvious that Magda the Red suspected Balthazar Leopold of corruption on some level, although she never got into specifics.

Chapter Two

True to her word, Magda the Red arrived at my house after dinner. I offered to let her follow me, and Remiel nearly wet himself giggling. The previous October my former brother-in-law had used Stygian fire to burn down half my neighborhood. A week later, my father decided to start a new town. I didn't know a person could strike out, buy land and just start a town, but apparently, he can, and I now had a new modern home in the incorporated village of Angelville, southwest of the city of St. Louis.

The population of Angelville was 109 people—most of them my relatives. Once my father had hired one of my cousin's construction companies to start planning and building the town, my uncles and other cousins had all bought land and had houses built. My sister lived across the road from me, and some of my neighbors who were affected by the fire also moved to Angelville and became my neighbors again. There was also a gas station, a stoplight, and three fast food restaurants—Arby's, Pizza Hut, and McDonald's.

The drive to St. Louis was roughly ten miles, and it was about seven miles to St. Charles. The area had once been farmland that was constantly flooded by the Mississippi River, but in recent years the Army Corps of Engineers had managed to stop the flooding, thereby reducing the productivity of the farmland. Several farmers had decided to sell their massive farms to my father for development, giving him roughly 9,000 acres with which to design an entire village. I was also learning this was not a first for my father. It wasn't even the first time he'd done it in the St. Louis area. My father loved living near big cities; he did not love living in them. He preferred residing in smaller towns and having the metropolis close enough to visit. I was exceptionally pleased that Cassanova's Pizzeria and Bistro was willing to expand their delivery service to Angelville. So far, they were the only ones willing to do it. Pizza Hut just wasn't in the same league as Cassanova's.

It was a 55-minute drive from Tony's to our home. We arrived to find our hellhound, Angel, losing her mind in the front yard and all the lights in our house flashing. Jerome's wards and alarm spells were chirping, screaming, trying to find someone to shoot fireballs at, and generally preparing for war. Also, our front door was banging open and shut, a sure sign of an intruder.

Remiel parked his SUV next to mine in the driveway. Angel ran from the walk just in front of the porch to our SUVs, barking like Armageddon was upon us. Jerome and I jumped out of the SUV as soon as it was parked. Remiel climbed out laughing. I glared at him as Magda the Red walked out onto the porch with my neighbor Abigail, an ancient vampire.

"I didn't think he would have the house warded so well!" Magda shouted to us. I stared at her.

"Did you teleport into our house?" Jerome asked her.

"It seemed like a good idea until I got here," Magda said, holding up a piece of fabric that caused me to look down at her legs. Angel had torn one leg of her pants off at about mid-thigh. The other was covered in slobber and had visible holes. There was also blood. Abigail touched Magda's hair, and I realized it was smoking.

"As head of the Witches' Council, I know you have a file on Jerome..." I started, and then let out an exasperated cry as Magda's hair reignited. Jerome put it out using magic. Abigail was grinning.

"I do," Magda the Red agreed.

"Then why would you even consider teleporting into his house?" I asked.

"I had a moment," Magda said with a sigh. "I thought I could slip in and no one would notice me instead of standing on your front lawn waiting for you."

"Yeah," I sighed. "Now everyone in Angelville is aware someone tried to enter our home."

"Yeah, we all came running when we heard Jerome's alarms go off and felt the small earthquake caused by the wards being tested. If it had been anyone but Magda the Red, the magic would have left them in a bad way. Your protection spells are getting much stronger," Abigail said to Jerome. Jerome nodded and Abigail walked over and gave him a high five.

"We should work on the protections at your house next," Jerome said to her.

"Shall we go inside and disarm everything and get down to it?" Remiel said, wiping at the tears of mirth pouring down his face. Magda gave him a look that I swear would have killed him if he hadn't been an archangel. Jerome and I followed them in, with Angel at our heels. Now that the immediate threat had passed, Angel flopped down onto the floor looking exhausted.

"Did you also not know we had a hellhound?" I asked Magda, shutting the front door behind us as Jerome began turning off the magic protections.

"I knew," Magda said nodding slightly. "However, her file lists her as abnormally small for a hellhound, so I was expecting her to be dog-sized."

Angel is roughly the same size as a black bear, but heavier. Her lean, muscular dog body does not have the fat of a bear, it's almost all muscle. She tips the scales at more than 500 pounds. Considering most hellhounds are larger than polar bears, Angel is abnormally small. I considered pointing this out to Magda the Red, but changed my mind in the hope that the meeting would end sooner if I kept my mouth shut. I definitely didn't like Magda.

"What can we do for you?" I asked.

"I need someone to investigate some murders for me," Magda said, walking into my dining room and taking a seat at the kitchen table. "There have been two in two months. My investigators tell me the murders are impossible, but I've seen the bodies and they are definitely happening, which means they aren't impossible, and my investigators just don't have enough imagination to figure out how it's being done. If the killer sticks to the pattern, there will be another one in three days."

"Three days?" I asked, my heart sinking into my stomach. "It's really hard to stop a murder you know nothing about in less than a week."

"I guess it's a good thing I don't expect you to stop it," Magda said.

"You want the murder to happen?" I asked, raising an eyebrow.

"No, but all the crime scenes are old and while you can see pictures of them, that won't let you feel the magic involved, and I think you need to feel the magic."

"Why?" I asked.

"The person doing the physical killing has to be a demon, which means there has to be someone summoning it."

"Well, I can see why your investigators say it's impossible. Demons don't intentionally kill. Sometimes they accidentally kill, but its problematic. When they do initiate physical violence, it's to maim and thereby create fear, which is what they feed on, but they don't intend to kill anyone because the dead aren't afraid of demons," I said.

"Also, summoned demons do not have physical forms. They have to inhabit hosts," Jerome added.

"That too," I agreed.

"Until two months ago, I would have agreed. In my nearly 2,000 years, I have never heard of a demon intentionally killing anyone. Now, some of the forbidden grimoires in the AESPCA archives have summoning spells intended for that purpose, but it requires the caster to summon a powerful demon, and they usually have enough willpower to resist the summoner's order, leading to a stalemate between summoner and demon. However, I have two heartless, stone supernatural corpses that prove a demon is responsible for the deaths. I took the information to Azrael and he suggested I come to you and Jerome, because if anyone has the magic to solve it, it's you two."

13

"I admit I'm intrigued, but I also admit I'm confused that we aren't the prime suspects," I said.

"You were after the first murder," Remiel said. "But you have a rock-solid alibi for the second."

"I do?"

"Yes, the both of you were detained by the AESPCA that night on suspicion of using black magic to hex someone to death." I frowned at her. March 13 the AESPCA had shown up at our home at about dinner time and taken us into custody claiming someone had filed a report that Jerome and I had hexed them to dance themselves to death. We'd been told the hex was broken, but not who had made the complaint, and after being in custody for nearly ten hours they'd released us with an apology that the complainant got the name of the hexers wrong, which seemed unlikely given the unusual nature of our names.

"You had us detained?" I asked after a moment.

"No, your uncles did," Jerome replied, and we both looked at Remiel.

"We knew you wouldn't use a demon to kill someone and we needed to prove it. It wouldn't do any good for us to provide you with an alibi, no matter how many other witnesses to it there were, so we had the AESPCA detain you that night." Remiel blushed.

"Did you consider what would happen if we were detained and no murder took place?" I asked.

"Yes, but that seemed unlikely," Remiel said. "It's easiest to summon a demon on nights with a new moon. The first murder happened at new moon, March 13th was a new moon, as is April 11th."

"Fine, now to the other question I have; you said you had heartless stone corpses. How do you know they were killed by a demon from that?" I asked.

"Because that's what happens when something Stygian kills the living," Jerome answered in place of Magda the Red. *What?*

"Seriously?" I asked, unable to hide my disdain for the answer. I believed Jerome, because Jerome paid attention to shit I didn't and was probably smarter than me, but it just didn't make sense to me for some reason. If he had said because they turned into a molten puddle of goo, I would have been more likely to accept it.

"The Stygian causes petrification to most living things; it's why living beings don't live long there," Magda said. "We were only able to move things like unicorns, dragons, and hellhounds to the Stygian after Leviathan appeared. Originally, the Third Plane was devised for that purpose, but after Leviathan was...I don't know the word...well, after Leviathan arrived in the Stygian, his ability to create worked in our favor and he did something to those specific animals that allowed them to live in the Stygian. After a handful of millennia there, they went from merely surviving to thriving."

"I see," I said. This was not entirely true, I only sort of understood. I really wanted to ask how someone worked with Leviathan, the hell prince, to alter the DNA of specific animals, allowing them to live in the Stygian. However, I was positive I would get either a really confusing answer or none at all.

Of course, I couldn't totally fault Magda the Red or Remiel for that. In the last two years, I'd begun having long conversations with a couple of demons and hell princes; specifically, Leviathan, Ashtaroth, and Lucifer; trying to better understand the Stygian, myself, and Jerome. Remiel knew about them, as did my father, but we were keeping the meetings and the information I got on the down-low. I had even taken to summoning Dantalian from time to time to get information from him.

Also, I'd learned that human food was a commodity in the Stygian. Demons didn't require food to live, but they ate for enjoyment, and there was food available in the Stygian; both plant and animal based. I could get a ton of information for an Arby's Big Beef Classic with cheese and some curly fries. In January, a couple of large Cassanova's pizzas and a dozen two-liter sodas had gained me some exceptional good will among the demons, and they had done me the favor of scouring the Stygian for dead bodies. They'd recovered six; one of them the missing person I was looking for at the time. I was sticking to using demons sired by Ashtaroth, Leviathan, and Asmodeus because they were the most cooperative and least repulsive.

"Well, if a hellhound was doing the killing, would that turn a person to stone?" I asked.

"Yes, but a hellhound wouldn't remove the heart." Magda told me. "Now, it's getting late—will you take the case? I have all the files assembled for you already; if you say no, I'll take them with me."

I looked at both Remiel and Jerome. The archangel was standing perfectly still, his expression blank. The teen was his exact opposite; he was smiling and practically bouncing out of his chair with excitement. I wanted to say no, just based on Jerome's reaction; it seemed almost ghoulish to me, and I wondered if I was unintentionally leading Jerome down the wrong path. I could take the case and keep Jerome out of it, but it would be a lie and I knew it. Jerome just intuitively knew more about magic than I did. Hell, there were times he knew more about magic than my father and uncles. Jerome was terrifyingly powerful and intelligent when it came to magic. This made him an incredible resource when working on investigations that involved magic, but he was still just a teenager and I felt like a terrible person when I allowed him to help me with work.

"You think on it tonight. You can give me an answer tomorrow because I know you take your responsibilities with Jerome quite seriously," Magda the Red said. "I still have two pieces of business specific to Jerome and the Witches' Council to discuss with you tonight. The first is the Practical Application of Witchcraft certificate. I know Jerome occasionally helps you out at work using his magical skills, which is fine; but now that he's 15, he's required by law to get a certificate to work magic as a minor in a commercial situation. To get the certificate, he simply needs to apply for and pass an exam administered by the AESPCA. Normally, it's moderated by the applicant's council chair and monitored by the AESPCA.

"When a mixed supernatural teen applies for the certificate, it is usually done in the magic they are strongest in. For example, a teen who is both vampire and witch would choose whether to apply as a witch or a vampire. For Jerome, it might be a bit more complicated. On his birthday, the Angel Council acknowledged him as a member of the Throne, which is great; this gives him all the protections and advantages of children of angelic stock and given his DNA, the AESPCA believes he more than qualifies as angel even though neither of his biological parents were angelic.

"Having said that, I met with Valerie Dusdain many times to discuss Jerome as he was growing up, and she was unwilling to allow the Witches' Council to be part of his life, for obvious reasons. He is now old enough to make that decision himself, and he is definitely a capable wizard. We will not be pressing him to join a coven, but for the purpose of his certificate, we would need to know if he wants to join the Witches' Council. If he does, as his guardian you will also be required to join. As a member of the council, we would offer him protections and occasionally require service, much the same as the Angel Council would demand of you, if it were functioning properly.

"This is an open-ended invitation to join, there's no expiration date and you don't have to decide right this moment. By all means think about it and get back to us when you have. I know that personally, I would love to be able to formally introduce Jerome to witch society, and I think he would benefit from it. If he doesn't join, he will be required to pass the practical application exam moderated by the AESPCA and administered by Balthazar Leopold. If he joins both, he would get a dual exam with myself as one of the admins along with Leopold, but I have little doubt Jerome could pass Leopold's exam without any issues based on my experience with him tonight."

"Okay," I said, and looked at Jerome. He'd lost some of his excitement. "Magda the Red, do I contact you at the AESPCA or where?" I asked as the witch stood up.

"Most of my friends call me Magda. My coworkers call me Magda Red, as if Red were my last name. I'll leave you to decide which you prefer, but Magda the Red is a mouthful." She scribbled down a phone number on a post-it note that she pulled out of thin air. She put it on the fridge, and then she left.

Chapter Three

I awoke with a feeling of dread. It was the 9th, and if I decided to take on the investigation Magda Red wanted me to, then in just two days someone was going to die unless I could solve the case and stop it. I sighed twice before even climbing out of bed. It was a Friday morning. Jerome was out of school for a teacher workshop day, and I was planning on summoning demons and asking some questions. If a demon really was responsible for the previous two murders, then other demons should know about it. Most likely it was one of Belial's or Beelzebub's demons doing the killing, but it was probable that one of the hell princes I was willing to work with would know about it, and if they did, their demons would know and for a slice of cheesecake or a milkshake would likely tell me.

If I couldn't get an answer from a demon, I didn't know where to turn my investigation. I had only minor investigative experience and had never handled a murder investigation. Most of my investigations were for insurance companies who thought someone was trying to defraud them, or finding missing persons. In movies, the lives of private investigators were sexy, appealing, and involved too much whiskey, famed jewels, and shootouts. My life as a private investigator was nothing like in the movies. I did a lot of computer work and was constantly amazed by the number of people who committed insurance fraud and posted pictures proving the fraud on social media.

Since the demon boxes investigation last October, my most noteworthy case had been a copycat demon box, which could now be bought online from ForbiddenMagic.com for $20 plus shipping and handling. They also sold shoddy love potions and talismans meant to protect the wearer from nearly anything, including rain, love potions, and demon boxes. And customized charm bracelets.

The Forbidden Magic demon boxes were novelty items that did very little. I'd seen three, and all three had produced demonlings too weak to take possession of the person that opened the box. They got trapped in the house in spirit form and ended up acting like poltergeists. The demonlings were tethered to the demon box, which was rather ridiculous, because the magic tether to the demon box was more powerful than the demonlings themselves, which meant if the demonling did manage to possess someone, they would probably be yanked out of their host if the host decided to leave the house.

I was also certain that ForbiddenMagic.com was run by a teenager or college student, because it could only ship locally. When Remiel and I had investigated and ordered one just to see what would happen, it was dropped off at the wrong address. Literally dropped off, not mailed or shipped. Unfortunately, since whomever delivered the package went to the empty office space next to Angel Investigations, the drop wasn't caught on video. However, we did see a teen on a bicycle ride past twice that night on our security cameras.

I got ready to brush my teeth and texted my business partner Janet to have her check to see if there were any demon boxes back in stock on ForbiddenMagic.com. They seemed to be in stock like three times a month, which was the other reason I suspected it was being done by a teen. They definitely weren't doing a brisk business for the site.

I finished brushing my teeth and headed to the kitchen. Jerome was already in there cooking. I sighed for the third time.

"Morning," Jerome said, as he took bacon out of a skillet.

"Morning, what do you want so bad that you are cooking me breakfast?" I asked the teen. "Oh and did you get taller between going to bed and getting up?" I took a seat, and a cup floated from the counter to me, followed by the coffeepot, creamer, and sugar. All of this was Jerome's doing, because I didn't know how to use magic that way. Jerome had started puberty this winter while we were living out of a hotel waiting for our house to be built. In the space of four weeks, we'd had to buy new pants for him twice because he was growing taller so fast.

"Maybe, but not much, my pajamas are only a little above my ankle bone," he said, and I looked at his ankles. Jerome would not tell me if he needed new clothes or new shoes. He would wear what he had no matter how short or how tight until I noticed and forced him to get new clothes. He stared at the white socks covering his feet. They were crew cut socks, and I sighed for a fourth time. Jerome only wore crew socks when there was snow or when his pants were too short. It wasn't snowing and the weather was unseasonably warm this April, which meant he was trying to hide his ankle bone from my prying eyes.

I spent another few seconds debating whether to take the hard line and make him admit new pants would be good, and decided to ignore it.

"Well then, what is it you want this morning?" I asked, pouring coffee and creamer into my cup. I actually drank coffee for the hazelnut dairy creamer I put in it. Man, that stuff is good.

"Can't I just make you breakfast since I am out of school today?" he asked.

"You could, but usually if you cook breakfast it's because you want something. I would love for you to turn around and tell me you need a couple hundred dollars, but I have this feeling it's about the investigation Magda Red wants us to take up." I sighed for a fifth time. "Also, you need new pants—you're wearing crew socks and it's over 60 degrees out. Do you want to go shopping today or tomorrow?"

"Well then, since you are going to ignore social niceties, do you want me to finish breakfast or not?" Jerome asked.

"Up to you," I said to him. "Kiddo, you don't have to butter me up to talk to me about something, even something dreadful."

"You woke up more churlish than usual," Jerome replied.

"Churlish? That is not a kid's word, that's a Remiel word because he's freaking ancient. Please tell me you know you need new pants and breakfast is because you want Remiel to take you clothes shopping and not me."

"I feel like I probably have another week or maybe even two in these pants. I used the word because it perfectly describes your mood and attitude this morning," he said, floating a plate of bacon and omelets over to the table. He walked behind them and stopped at the fridge to get orange juice and jam. As he sat down, the toaster ejected four slices of toast and he repeated the floating routine to bring them to the table, depositing two slices on my plate and two on his.

"Do you even know what churlish means?" I asked.

"Rude in a mean-spirited way, relating to attitude or behavior," Jerome replied.

"Well, all right, if you think you have about two weeks left before you need new pants, that means you need new pants now, not in two weeks when you wake up and suddenly have no jeans that aren't exposing your ankle and part of your calf. We'll get you some this weekend. So what do you want to talk about that warranted southwestern style omelets and bacon?"

"With as warm as the weather is in two weeks, I hope to need shorts," Jerome replied.

"Yes, but you'll be wearing shorts that hit you mid-thigh and are unfashionable if you don't buy new ones before you need them."

"Yes, we'd hate for me to be unfashionable." Jerome rolled his eyes.

"Are you being bullied at school?" I asked.

"No, I'm being bullied at home, by my churlish guardian who is obsessed with the size of my feet and making sure my pants are long enough."

"You are the only teenager on the planet not obsessed with shoes and fashionable pants."

"You hate to shop."

24

"True, but my father and several of my uncles love it. If Grandpa Raphael was supposed to travel to Zurich and I called him and told him you needed new shoes, he'd cancel the trip and take you shoe shopping, or he'd take you to Zurich with him to go shoe shopping in Switzerland. Meaning you can't blame my dislike of shopping on your unwillingness to buy new clothes and shoes. Speaking of which, you've had those shoes about six months. Do they still fit?"

"Fine, if I admit I need new shoes and new pants, can we move on?" Jerome asked, shoving omelet into his mouth.

"Yes." I nodded, taking a bite of bacon.

"Then I admit, I am going to need both new shoes and new pants soon. It isn't urgent, but by the end of the month, it might be."

"Then I admit I am churlish, partly because I dreamed about your shoes and partly because Magda Red wants me to investigate a murder case."

Valerie had told me Jerome's father had been somewhere in the neighborhood of 6 feet, 8 inches tall and that Jerome had been 33 inches long at birth with huge feet, and she suspected he would be as tall or taller than his father had been. At 15, Jerome was taller than me and wore a size 19 shoe.

In archangel genes, the taller an angel is the more powerful he is, and my father is close to seven feet tall. We were expecting Jerome to be even taller. His genome was about 33 percent angel, which was weird and unexplainable by his bloodline. Our theory was that when Valerie's angelic infused bloodline combined with the

Dusdain family bloodline, which was also angelically infused, it had somehow magnified the angelic genome in Jerome, making him about one-third angel. Specifically, he was about a third archangel and he had genes from each and every one of my uncles as well as a massive dose of my father's genes. This could explain both his height and his power. The Dusdain family line had genes from Jophiel and Zadkiel. Valerie's line had only had Raphael's, but all the brothers had contributed to the divine blessing bestowed on the Dusdain family. Jerome was the first child to ever be born whose ancestors on both sides had received divine blessings to help keep the family's line alive. And he would probably be the last, as most family lines with divine blessings had died out over the eons.

"Now that is out of the way, let's talk. If I join the Witches' Council and allow myself to be formally recognized as a witch, am I betraying my mom?" Jerome asked.

"No," I said after several minutes. "Your mom didn't have you recognized because she was trying to protect you. At this point, everyone knows you're a wizard and a powerful one at that. They know you attend a school for witchcraft and that you have angelic genes."

"Plus, I'm with people who can protect me now," Jerome said sadly.

"Your mom was protecting you and she did a good job of it," I told him.

"I know, but now I have you and Raphael. You can protect me in ways my mom couldn't because she wasn't magical." Jerome said.

"I don't think that's the correct word. Your mom was magical. She might not have had witch or angel powers, but she was still magical. No matter how much a mother loves her child, not many would do what your mom did for you. I don't just mean dealing with her cancer hex, I mean all of it, Jerome. She could have had a much easier life if she had accepted help from the Witches' Council. They might even have been able to remove the hex if she had gone to them shortly after it was first cast, but she knew that would put you in danger, so she didn't."

"Then she made sure I was with a family that loved me and cared for me exactly as she did," Jerome said. "I know starting the adoption process for me while she was still alive was emotionally wrenching for her. It took a lot of strength on her part, but my mom was incredibly strong and special."

"Yes, she was." I nodded. I was still chewing that first bite of bacon, because a lump had formed in my throat and I wasn't sure I could swallow. "I think if you asked your mom, she would tell you to join the Witches' Council now, if you wanted to do it. I think she would point out it is completely your choice and you need to do what is best for you."

"I think so, too." Jerome swallowed hard.

"Jerome if you want to join, do it. If you aren't ready, don't. If you want the practicing magic certificate, we can get it for you as an angel and not a witch to give you more time to think about it."

"Yeah, except that for what I do, I think I would need it in both," he said. "I just want to make sure I'm not doing something my mom wouldn't want me to do."

"You could ask her," Remiel's voice floated to us from the living room, and Angel was suddenly up doing the happy hellhound dance.

"I was expecting you earlier," Jerome said and pointed to the third plate he'd set at the table. I frowned. "Something important happened yesterday and Remiel knew about it; he always shows up the next morning for breakfast when he wants to talk you into something."

"Huh, you're right," I said.

"I overslept; I had a weird dream that I was living in a shoe," Remiel said.

"Have you been standing outside the house listening to us?" I asked.

"No," Remiel answered, raising an eyebrow. I pursed my lips. I wasn't sure if I believed him, since I had dreamed I was living in one of Jerome's soccer shoes and Jerome had grown up to be slightly bigger than the hell prince Beelzebub, who was too big to fit in a standard-sized building.

"You need to take the case," Remiel said to me after several long minutes of silence.

"I am a trainee investigator who has never investigated a murder," I told my uncle.

"True, but you'll have help from me and Magda Red. She suspects it is someone who works for the AESPCA and if she's correct and a demon is involved, you might be the only one who can figure that out." After he finished, I sighed again because I had been thinking the exact same thing, when I hadn't been dreaming about living inside Jerome's shoes. Thankfully, in the dream I hadn't had so many children I didn't know what to do, but

28

I had been struggling to handle about three dozen hellhound puppies.

"The problem as I see it is, if I take the case, I will end up accidentally exposing Jerome to the details and I don't think that's responsible parenting," I said.

"I think I'd keep the gory details away from him, but I don't know that you need to keep the case completely away from him. He's mature for his age, very responsible, and he's interested in becoming an investigator for the AESPCA," Remiel said.

"It could be dangerous."

"You summon demons and hell princes for conversations; I think this danger is manageable," Jerome said. "Also, if you say no and we wake up in two days and you find out there's been another murder, you're going to feel responsible because you could have possibly prevented it. If that happens, you won't just be churlish for a morning, you'll be a nightmare to live with for weeks. I will need to move in with Remiel or Grandma and Grandpa to get away from you."

"No one who knows you or Jerome would accuse you of being an irresponsible guardian, despite Jerome's exposure to unusual things. He's an unusual kid and it's probably good for him to be exposed to things like this. If you want another opinion, talk to Camilla about it. She's going to tell you Jerome is exceptional and resilient and that even if you can't keep all the details from him, you should take the case and help do some good. Because that is also beneficial to Jerome. You forget, until Jerome met you, most of his experiences with adults who use magic were negative and awful. You try to make the world a

better place and inspire him to do the same," Remiel told
me.

Chapter 4 Four

After Remiel's pep talk and breakfast, I called Magda Red from my home office and told her I'd take the case. She told me the files would arrive this afternoon if I would be home. I assured her I would. Jerome sat across my desk from me, gesturing wildly, so before we hung up, I told her Jerome had decided to officially join the Witches' Council and get his certificate for practicing commercial magic in both witch and angel magic, at which point she informed me I needed to start using its formal name or Balthazar Leopold would have a conniption fit. I puzzled over that for a moment, trying to figure out what she meant.

"Throne magic," Jerome said as I puzzled over it.

"What?" I asked, looking at him.

"The proper name for angel magic is throne magic. We had an entire lecture on it in school this past year. There's a movement to convince people to use the proper terms when speaking of angels, angelic groups, and angel magic," he told me.

"Why?" I asked.

"Beats me, I just know it's been demanded by the Angel Council and we had several classes dedicated to it."

"I don't even know what that means," I sighed. "When I was growing up, it was just angel magic and a group of angels has always been called a host."

"I'm just telling you what the council decreed and my witchcraft school honored by teaching all its young witches and wizards the correct terms and making us use them. Also, a group of angels linked together by magic is a host. A random group of angels is called a throne. Angel magic is throne magic and all the choirs are going to start being acknowledged," Jerome told me. I tried not to sigh again. It seemed like random pretentiousness.

Only angels and fairies had subsets among their members. Some fairies were leprechauns, some were elves, and some were trooping fairies—the more stereotypical idealistic fairy who was tall, lithe, pretty, and had gorgeous translucent colorful wings—but they were all fairies and had the same basic magic. Walter's wife Megan was a trooping fairy.

An angel could be an archangel, a cherub, a seraphim, a virtue, or a saint. From what I could tell, this seemed to have more to do with whether a being had wings or not. Cherubs, virtues, and saints were always wingless angels. Archangels and seraphim had wings. Being half angel, half human, I was considered a nephilim. However, I was also an archangel because I had a very strong, innate, and unique power that was not found in other angels and could not be learned. Being an archangel basically meant I had initials after my name should I choose to use them, and I could legally stop using my last name and become simply Soleil the Archangel. I had not ditched my last name, and I didn't use the ArAl designation after it. I had also gotten a sigil that I could use in place of my signature—it was a sad sun with wavy heat radiation lines coming off it. The Angel Council had even thrown a celebratory party that I wasn't invited to attend. I found out about it after the fact in the cherubim newsletter for the next quarter. Apparently, they'd had a celebration for both Helia and I, but our invitations must have gotten lost because neither of us received them.

"I have no idea why I give to the Angel Council when this is what they do with my money," I said.

"Demand we use the word throne instead of angel and throw parties for you that they forget to invite you to?" Jerome asked.

"Exactly, they take five percent of my annual income for that," I said. Technically it was a tax paid to the AESPCA that all supernaturals who lived above poverty level were required to pay. However, a portion of it went directly to the Angel Council, since I was theoretically a recognized member.

I checked the time. I had an exorcism scheduled for 10 a.m. A set of 13-year-old twin girls were definitely possessed, but swore they didn't know how they'd gotten that way. However, their parents had started noticing weird things a few days after a sleepover. If they'd done something at the sleepover to cause possession, it was possible there were more possessed girls who would need to be exorcised.

Unfortunately, promising the girls privately in my office that I wouldn't tell their parents what they had done to cause the possessions hadn't garnered any results. Even having Remiel talk them yielded nothing. This morning's plan had been for me to bring Jerome to the office with me and let him hang out with Remiel for a while before taking him along to the exorcism, because while Jerome's mind-reading skills were not as strong as Remiel's, Jerome was a fairly handsome young man about the girls' age. They might divulge something unexpectedly to a peer that they would keep from an adult. It was a surprisingly effective tool that I'd exploited in the past when working with teens. They were always more worried about getting grounded than whether or not their friends had also become possessed. We had an hour and a half until the exorcism. I got up from my desk and silently walked to Jerome's room.

My parents were convinced teen boys needed a special space just for them. When my house was being designed, my father had created an interior room in the house specifically for Jerome. It had one access point, his bedroom, and no windows. Jerome had a gaming system set up in the room along with a couch, desk, desk chair, and bean bag chairs. It could double as a tornado shelter as well as Jerome's gaming room. I used it to summon demons small enough to fit in the house. Jerome followed me to his game room. It was too early in the morning to get food delivered, so I'd have to IOU food for information from whatever demon I summoned.

As I walked, I thoughtfully ran through the options for demons I could summon. The hell princes were too large to summon into a room; when I summoned one of them, I did it in the barn or the yard. Sometimes I went to the Stygian to talk to them, but that had more risks for me, as Belial wanted my soul. There were plenty of smaller demons I could summon that were sired by the hell princes I had an arrangement with, but demons are like living people; they have personalities, and I liked some demons more than others, even among those I somewhat trusted.

"Dantalian is your best bet," Jerome said as I walked. I nodded. Dantalian was an incubus and powerful enough to be one of Ashtoreth's dukes. Oddly, he found food more satisfying than carnal relations and would give me the most information for food. I could give him a single chicken nugget from McDonald's, and he'd give me every bit of gossip in the Stygian available to him. Since he'd stopped trying to seduce me, I found his personality tolerable. But Dantalian was often the demon I went to for information, and I worried about my dependence on an incubus for information. By the time I reached Jerome's game room, I had decided to summon one of Asmodeus' demons. Xaxelju was a count, giving him access to more power and information than a common demon, and I didn't deal with him often, although Asmodeus had assured me repeatedly that all members of his flock were completely trustworthy. Since Asmodeus was not the hell prince of lies, I almost believed him. Jerome shut the door after he came into the room and took a seat in one of the bean bag chairs.

Nothing impressive happened. One heartbeat it was just Jerome and I in the room and the next a tall, lanky figure with small horns on his head and spikes on his shoulders and back was with us. Xaxelju had once been a fairy named Caladar, and he'd lived for about a thousand years before accidentally blowing himself up. He'd told me he was trying to empty out a leprechaun den when it happened, but that had just raised more questions, like why he was trying to kill a bunch of leprechauns. It had just been easier to let the matter drop. Like all of Asmodeus' demons, Xaxelju is black like tar. His skin is pitch black, but has an iridescence to it that makes it a beautiful sight to see. After we dispensed with the necessary pleasantries, I explained what I wanted to know and he named his price—a monster burger from Hardees and curly fries. I agreed and explained about serving times and the current time in this plane and that I would have to send him the food later today after I picked it up. Xaxelju pursed his lips and closed his large orange eyes for several moments.

"Neither I nor my master know of any demons being summoned to kill people. That doesn't mean it isn't happening. It just means that if it is, it's being kept secret from other demons sired by that demon's hell prince and that it's not one of Asmodeus' demons," Xaxelju said, opening his eyes again.

"Would your master know if the demon belonged to Belial or Beelzebub?" I asked.

"Yes. He isn't loyal to either of them, but he is capable of great civility, and both of those princes would want to brag about it if it were them, because it would boost their standing as well as increase their power base," Xaxelju replied without hesitation. I nodded. I'd had the same thought; any hell prince would use it for bragging material if one of their demons was being summoned to kill. Not because of the deaths, but because of the soul collection that would accompany them. Also, there were roughly 100-200 registered demons on this plane living in consensual hosts; if it was general knowledge in the Stygian, the demons here would also be told about it and they could and would use the information to stimulate the fear response of the living and get that hell prince more power. However, since Magda Red and the AESPCA had managed to keep "Demon Serial Killer on the Loose" off the front page of the St. Louis Post Dispatch, it could not be general knowledge among the demons. I thanked Xaxelju, assured him I'd send the food along when I had it and sent him back to the Stygian. I decided to summon a couple more demons just to be sure Asmodeus wasn't out of the loop. However, Leviathan's spawn, Bretchel, didn't know anything about a demon killer. Neither did the succubus I summoned afterward.

"Do you have any thoughts?" I asked Jerome, who had lounged in a chair while I'd talked to the demons. I checked the time.

"If a demon was doing the killing, at least one of the other hell princes would know," Jerome replied. I nodded. This was one of the things Jerome and I had in common; we both just intuitively understood how the Stygian worked and didn't work. I was still stuck on the fact that murder did not suit the purposes of demons if it was kept secret, as this appeared to be. This made the solution complicated. As I saw it, a person could be removing the hearts while something like a hellhound took the soul of the victim, but it would need to be timed perfectly so that the being didn't turn to stone while the murderer was removing the heart. I was sure a person couldn't survive long once the heart was removed and if the victim turned to stone while having their heart removed, surely that would mean there was a risk of the person's hand also turning to stone. I ran these ideas past Jerome. He frowned for a long time but said nothing, and I ushered him out of the house to get to my exorcism appointment.

Chapter Five

We arrived a few minutes early to the exorcism appointment. The twin girls were possessed by demons from different sires. Katrina, the oldest by seven and a half minutes, was possessed by one of Mammon's demons, while Kalina was possessed by a demon of Belgaphor's lineage.

Demons could not breed in the Stygian. Lucifer had cast a spell to prevent it, so now when supernaturals died, their souls were reincarnated in the Stygian as demonlings with a Hell Prince designated as the sire. This process dictated the powers available to demonlings. For example, all of Leviathan's demons could create or alter nature in the Stygian to some degree. Belial's demons all had his characteristic bloodlust, and all of Ashtoreth's demons were lust demons creating incubi and succubae. When I died, I wanted to come back as one of Leviathan's demons. Lucifer had told me it was unlikely I would come back as a demonling under any of his current hell princes. He suspected my connection to the Stygian wouldn't break upon my death, and I'd come back as a new type of demon, possibly filling the void of a fallen hell prince or creating a power struggle as I rose to become a hell prince myself.

Normally when a group of kids became possessed, it was by demons of the same sire. Having two different demons in twins who were possessed around the same time was proof that this had probably been a mass possession event, and my money was on a party game that went awry. There are hundreds of ways to contact the Stygian and many of them create small portals that demons can travel through. Nearly every demon desired more power and possession was the fastest way to get it. Possession could quickly increase the power of even a demonling, the least powerful type of demon. When the first inquiries into the possession had happened three days ago, the demons in the twins had been demonlings. They were going to go back to the Stygian far more powerful than they had been when they left, and they had only been here a total of just seven or eight days. If it were a mass possession, we needed to get the rest of the possessed exorcised before their demons became counts or something.

That was the problem with teen possessions; teens scared easier than adults and were terrified they were going to get in major trouble for doing something that had led to possession. Furthermore, it was easier to take possession of a teen than an adult. Nearly all supernatural teens would become possessed at least once. They were curious about the forbidden and taboo, even if it would get them into trouble. They used homemade ouija boards and played Demonic Telephone and other games that contacted the Stygian and resulted in accidental possessions, and when angry, they sometimes hexed their enemies into becoming possessed. Teens who hexed someone into possession could expect to pay a fine, have to take a special class about the effects of demonic possession, and to serve a hundred or so hours of community service. Adults could expect a fine and jail time. I'd spent eight days in jail for intentionally having my former brother-in-law possessed due to extenuating circumstances. Jail had been bad for me. Jerome projected his dreams and he'd spent those nights with my uncle Remiel. Remiel let him watch horror movies, so every night a different movie character had shown up in my cell block as Jerome searched for me in his sleep. The first night, it had been the Rockbiter from *The Neverending Story,* and the sheriff's deputies in the jail had tried to shoot the projected character multiple times before I was able to explain to them what it was and why it was there. The second night, he'd sent Freddy Krueger, which had been slightly less unsettling.

The problem with every exorcism I'd ever done is they were nothing like people saw on TV or read about in books. There was no screaming, no shouting, no demonic voices hissing and swearing. I'd seen exorcisms that were loud, noisy, violent affairs, but mine were never like that. I was too powerful for demons to be able to mount a resistance against me. I would touch the person and the demon would be gone in the space of a heartbeat; no mess and no fuss. The most dramatic part would be that the person I was exorcising might faint. It didn't happen every time, but most of the time. The demon left the person weak and when it exited, the person would go limp with exhaustion and pass out. When they woke up, they were usually ravenous and they'd eat nearly all the food in the house. The first few days post-exorcism, the person would sleep a great deal and eat a ton, then life would go back to how it was pre-exorcism. Protective parents would pester me for days after I performed an exorcism on their kids because they wouldn't be convinced the demon was gone and they'd be worried about the excessive sleeping and eating, which they saw as signs the demon was still there. I would explain over and over again that this was normal; their bodies and souls were healing and recovering from the demonic possession, and that I was sure the demon was gone, even if they weren't. Eventually, the more annoying ones would contact another exorcist to schedule another exorcism only to be told by that exorcist that the demon was indeed gone, but it was still going to cost them a consultation fee.

Every time I performed an exorcism, I spent a while trying to think of ways to make it more spectacular to watch, to ensure parents wouldn't pester me afterward. But at heart, I wasn't a performer and I didn't know what parents expected to see and hear during an exorcism that would convince them the demon had indeed been banished from their offspring. Once in a while, I would pull out the demon and let the spirit run around the house a bit before exorcising it, so they could see it with their own eyes, but that was always a risk, because it was possible the demon would take possession of someone else in the house or escape out a window or door and possess the neighbor or someone. I couldn't charge a family for my time if their possession was technically my fault. Not that exorcisms took me very long, which was the other issue. The initial consultation for an exorcism took 30-45 minutes. The exorcism then took about five minutes. Once I finished, I had to file about two dozen reports and that took several hours. However, clients complained about the fees associated with my time, because the exorcism was so short. Thankfully, they complained less when their health insurance paid for it, but realistically, most people believed I was charging them for time I hadn't spent on their case. This was again the result of my being too good at my job.

Last week, I'd done an exorcism on a 17- year-old girl and her parents remarked that her first exorcism, which had been a success, had taken three and a half hours and had been done by an exorcist in training with the Bureau of Exorcism. I couldn't imagine battling a demon in spirit form inside a person for more than about a minute, let alone three and a half hours. I hadn't needed but a few minutes the one time I'd exorcised a hell prince and that was difficult to explain and even more difficult to make people understand. As a result, when I charged them a couple hundred dollars mostly to cover the time I spent on writing the possession and exorcism reports for the AESPCA, health insurance companies, and the Bureau of Exorcism, they demanded an itemized receipt. However, insurance companies loved me. Most exorcists charged by the hour and if they had to spend ten or eleven hours performing an exorcism, the bills climbed to five figures fairly quickly. Since I only needed a few minutes, regardless of what type of demon was inside, my prices turned out to be lower in the long run, although most people thought my charge should be under $50; that wouldn't even cover the staff involved to write and file exorcism and possession reports.

Once inside, Jerome took the twins to the living room to chat and I took the parents into the dining room to explain what I was going to do as well as what they might witness and experience, along with how to file their part of the paperwork and assure them that if they needed help with it, Helia was available. I gave both of them possession protection pendants that Jerome made and had them put them on. The mother struck me as the type to throw a fit and demand a second opinion on the exorcism if she didn't see or experience something, which meant I would pull out the demon and let it loose for a very short time in the house before sending it back to the Stygian simply to let them know they had gotten their money's worth. After the exorcism was complete, I would give them a letter to give to the school that announced their daughters were free of possession and could return to school after they recovered. This was a new thing; schools had started asking for it after the incident with the demon boxes last October. I had argued against the need for them, because the incident with the demon boxes and possessed teenagers were not related. There had only been a few instances of demonic violence at schools throughout my time as an exorcist, and the violence had been limited and unusual incidents that I felt had more to do with the kids involved than the demons—some teens weren't nice people.

I spent about an hour explaining the process of exorcism and answering all the parents' questions. The mom seemed concerned that it was going to hurt and I kept repeating that exorcism hurt a lot less than possession and that if we left the demon in place it would eventually take over the body and destroy the soul. After the fifth or sixth time of her asking about how much it was going to hurt, the father jumped in and told her he'd endured an exorcism as a child and he didn't remember it being very painful, but he never forgot what it felt like to be possessed. This didn't mollify her, though, and I found myself explaining that I had been possessed during exorcism training—it was one of the requirements—and that it hadn't hurt when I had exorcised myself. That raised questions with both parents. Most people didn't realize a powerful enough exorcist could perform a self-exorcism.

"The hospital said Miss Burns is the most powerful exorcist around," the father finally said. I didn't agree with this vocally nor did I nod. I sat in silence, unmoving, not even blinking. I was the most powerful exorcist around. I was a better exorcist than even Uriel or Azrael, who ran the Bureau of Exorcism and had been alive for hundreds of thousands of years. If Jerome hadn't been able to perform exorcisms, I would have said I was the best exorcist in the world, but Jerome could perform exorcisms with a touch like I could. We didn't know if it was because he was a mimic or if it was innate power.

"Mr. and Mrs. Jergens, I know exorcisms are scary and I understand your concerns. Let me assure you, I can and will perform the exorcism faster than anyone else and with less pain and complications. I gave you my qualifications and showed you my certification in exorcisms, but what I didn't show you was that about 18 months ago, the Angel Council and AESPCA recognized me as an archangel. I earned that designation solely based on my ability to summon and exorcise the demonic. It is going to take me less than five minutes to perform exorcisms on both your daughters. I don't know how long ago your exorcism was, Mr. Jergens, or who did it, but I can promise both of you that your exorcism was nothing like the one I'm going to perform today."

"I was exorcised by Uriel in 1811," Mr. Jergens said. "I was a teenager and was hexed into possession by a classmate."

"Uriel is my uncle as well as one of my trainers. He will tell you himself that I am a better exorcist than either he or Azrael or any of his brothers, who have been performing exorcisms since the dawn of their existence. I have exorcised every type of demon in the Stygian, from demonlings to hell princes, and all the exorcisms were quick and far less painful than the possession. When I've finished, you are welcome to have a doctor or nurse verify the exorcism was a success," I told them.

"You must think I am very silly," the woman said after a moment. "But I've never dealt with possession before. I didn't encounter it as a teenager and no one in my family has ever become possessed."

"I think you are a parent," I said. "At least 75 percent of the exorcisms I perform are on teenagers. I meet people with the same concerns as you all the time. Older supernaturals are warier of possession than younger ones, and I don't mean younger as in teens or young adults, I mean supernaturals that were born in the last 100-150 years. During that time, possession has become more frequent due to societal changes and the passing of time. It's only been in the last 200 years that teens have even become recognized as their own age group. Before that, only extremely wealthy teens had time for things like sleepovers and idleness. Now, all teens have downtime to spend with their friends, and that has increased the rate of possession. It's not good or bad, it just is." Mr. Jergens was nodding.

"I see," Mrs. Jergens said. "Yes, I was a couple centuries old before I even heard the word teenager let alone had to deal with teen idleness. My family was not among the elite when I was growing up, and my siblings and I didn't have time for idleness, there was too much work to be done."

"Exactly. Now let's go perform the exorcism. Don't expect it to be stunningly visual. I'm going to pull out the demon, and you'll see it for a couple of seconds before I send it back to the Stygian, but it won't be anything like what you see on TV or read about in books." In books and on TV, exorcisms were hauntingly beautiful affairs with great visual effects and terrifying sounds. I've never seen an exorcism that even remotely resembled the ones on TV. I'd really never even heard of one, although I knew some exorcists had to do magical battle with demons to perform an exorcism and that could take hours upon hours, even those were not visually stimulating.

Jerome and the two teen girls were sitting in the living room totally silent when we walked in. This was the most surprising thing to happen all morning. Jerome was a gregarious young man, both a good talker and good listener—he usually had possessed teens yammering their brains out. It was a bit surreal and I wondered if he'd warned his companions we were on the way and they had clammed up as a result. I walked over to Katrina and bent down, placing my hand on her shoulder and bringing us close to eye level. She met my gaze and I sent a little magic into her, finding the demon. I'd never encountered him before this exorcism, but when I'd evaluated the girls a few days earlier the demon had been a demonling. He'd gained enough power to be a low-level demon now, but he still wasn't particularly strong. I grabbed the demon with my magic, pulled it out and tossed it onto the floor of the living room. When I looked, I was surprised to find a second demonling attached to the first. I blinked. Some demonlings aren't powerful enough to take possession of a person, so to get more power they attach themselves to more powerful demonlings and cause a condition known as dual possession.

Finding a second demonling wasn't the surprising part. The surprising part was that as I looked at the unexpected demonling, I knew nothing about it. When my magic touches a demon, I get information on the demon like their name, their sire, and a rough idea of how long they've been a demon; as well as flashes of their lives prior to death. I got none of that from the second demonling. I looked at Jerome. He stood up and walked over to the unknown demonling, who was struggling to detach himself from the first. His lips were turned down, his forehead wrinkled, eyebrows drawn together, and I realized Jerome was getting nothing from the demonling either, confusing him as much as it confused me.

Jerome had closed the distance between himself and the demonling, and he reached out and grabbed it. It wriggled and writhed in his hand. It wasn't just nearly powerless, it was incredibly young; I would have been surprised if it had been more than a few weeks old. I walked over to Jerome and took the demonling squatter from him. Even holding it and pushing magic into it, I got nothing. No name, no sire, nothing. It was as if I were touching a living being. As I held it at arm's length, I saw it shimmer, and a moment later it went from transparent spirit form to having a physical body. This can be useful because most demon lineages have distinct physical features, for instance, the skin of all of Asmodeus's demons is a black iridescent color, and all of Leviathan's demons have dark purple irises.

This demonling's skin was a pale blue that was almost white and had an iridescent quality to it. It had a double tail, which was an uncommon demon feature, that it wrapped protectively around itself. And it was hornless, another unusual demon feature. Nearly all demons, no matter how small, had horns and only a handful of demons had two tails. He was too unique, in my opinion, and I didn't recognize any of his features as belonging to a particular demon lineage. Jerome must have been thinking the same thing, because a large cage appeared at Jerome's feet. The Bureau of Exorcism had created a demon cage ages ago, made of a special Stygian metal and protected by magic, for housing demons in physical form for the purpose of training. The only thing missing was the stamp announcing the cage belonged to the Bureau of Exorcism, and I wondered if Jerome had conjured this one up or somehow stolen it from the BoE and removed the label. I put the demonling in the cage. Then I returned to the exorcised demon. It was running disjointedly about the living room, as if in shock from being ripped from its host and having another demonling attached to it. It very well might have been, this was its first possession from what I could tell and it had dealt with a squatter. I sent it back to the Stygian with a small push of magic.

I turned my attention to the other girl and put my hand on her shoulder, feeling around for the demon in her. I found it easily enough and pulled it out, tossing it down. Another demon I had never encountered in this realm. It had grown more powerful in the days since my evaluation than the demon in the other twin. This could be because this girl was more afraid of possession, or it could have been because this demon didn't have a squatter. I didn't know for sure. I exorcised it.

"Uh, what is that and what are you doing with it?" Mr. Jergens asked.

"This is a demonling, all demons no matter how powerful they become start out like this one. I am taking this one to the Bureau of Exorcism because we've never encountered it before and the sire can't be identified, which means there might be a new hell prince coming into power," I told him. It was partially true. I was going to take it to Uriel and Azrael. But I wasn't going to turn it over to them. I was going to take it home with me and then when I had a few minutes, I was going to personally escort it back to the Stygian and give it to Lucifer to identify. Only hell princes could be assigned demonlings, and there were currently ten of them, the same ten that had been in existence for eons. If there was a new one coming into power, Lucifer should know about it and be able to help me identify who it was. Then we could figure out what it meant for the Stygian. I had a momentary thought that maybe it was one of Leviathan's creations, but I pushed it aside, trying not to get ahead of myself. If it was one of

Leviathan's creations, Lucifer might not be able to identify it, but Leviathan would.

Chapter Six

"A new hell prince?" Jerome asked as I placed the demonling in the cargo area of the SUV.

"Do you have another explanation? Did you get any information off the demonling?" I asked.

"No," Jerome said. "It's almost like it's not a demon."

"Yeah, I know what you mean," I replied. A knot formed in my stomach. I had another idea about it.

"Oh man, really?" Jerome asked, reading my thoughts. I nodded. If it wasn't a demonling of a new hell prince, I wondered if it might be a cambion. Cambions were half demons and, as far as I knew, only one had ever existed, my cousin Azazael. My uncle Jophiel had a child with a woman named Lilith who he discovered was a demon, back when demons still walked the Earth. They had both spirit forms and physical forms in the Stygian, but only their spirit forms were supposed to pass through the Stygian Divide. It was sort of theoretical because I was capable of bringing demonic physical forms across the divide, not just spirit forms. It took an enormous amount of power to bring a demon's physical form across the divide. However, if it could be managed, then there was the possibility for a cambion to be born. It would almost certainly require a living female and a demonic male because a pregnant demon in the Stygian would get Lucifer's attention.

As far as anyone knew there had never been a demonic birth in the Stygian. Demonic births were an issue for both demons and the living. Since demons were reincarnated supernatural souls, for there to be a birth, a soul had to be available and if there wasn't, someone had to die to make one available. Lucifer's system was preferable; with his magic whenever a soul became available it almost immediately became a demonling and was assigned to a hell prince.

I had serious fucking concerns about this demonling. Cambion were strange. Azazael had a fractured soul, I'd felt it. It was part demon and part living. I was sure this was why Azazael was an evil fruit loop. His soul was entirely his own; it wasn't reincarnated like other demons, but half of it was dead, which allowed him to take possession of the living. I'd only heard stories about Azazael taking possession of the living, but they were terrifying. Half his soul would remain in his body and animate it, keep it going about his normal routines, while the other part took up residence in someone else. Since the living should not be able to splinter their soul into pieces, I felt the cambion existence was a horrific one. But cambions would not have a master they served like other demons, and the living soul would not react to my touch like a demonic one, which is why I was worried this demonling might be cambion.

Jerome called all my uncles and my father and told them it was urgent they meet us at our house within the hour. It didn't matter what they were doing, they needed to come immediately. He made it one massive three-way call on speaker phone. Several minutes of which Haniel and Uriel wasted by arguing with him about how busy their lives were and how they couldn't drop everything on one of my whims.

"I think I pulled a cambion from a teenager today," I said as they argued with Jerome. The argument instantly stopped. The mass call went completely silent for several minutes as I weaved through traffic.

"Surely not," my father finally said, breaking the silence. Jerome confirmed he thought so too and if not that, there was an eleventh hell prince. Everyone was suddenly free to meet at my house. I wasn't sure which idea bothered me more, a cambion or an eleventh hell prince, but neither gave me happy happy joy joy emotions. I felt the knot in my stomach tighten. When we pulled into the driveway, my seven uncles and my father were standing on my lawn. They had been huddled in a large group, excitedly talking to each other, but stopped and turned to look at us when we pulled up. I pulled into the garage, leaving the garage door open for them to enter through. Once everyone was in, Jerome shut the garage door and I opened the cargo door on the back of the SUV. I pulled out the cage with the demonling in it. He was maybe a foot and a half tall and weighed about ten pounds. The cage was heavier than he was. Uriel and Azrael stepped forward to get a closer look.

"He's kinda cute," Remiel said, and everyone glared at him. Remiel was the youngest of all the brothers and everyone tolerated his sometimes strange comments, but at this moment if looks could kill, Remiel would have been dead. However, he wasn't wrong. Demonlings in general are kinda cute. This one was no exception.

Raphael took the cage from me and carried it into the house. He set it on the kitchen table and Uriel and Azrael started commanding the creature to tell them its name and its sire. The demonling looked at them with wide eyes and mumbled that he had no name and no sire. Which was what I was afraid it would say. Demons spoke and wrote in angel language until they learned other languages, and this one wasn't old enough to know any others. Thankfully, Jerome had gotten the brilliant idea after reading The Hitchhiker's Guide to the Galaxy to make a spell that translated the angelic language into English for me. He had even named it the Babelfish Spell, and so despite not speaking Angelic myself, I understood the demonling. My father and his brothers all spoke angel.

Speaking of which, Angel the hellhound padded over to see what the commotion was about. She sniffed the demonling and huffed, then padded back into the living room and climbed up on the couch. When she flopped down on the cushions we all felt the floor rumble, and the demonling suddenly looked scared.

"I think Soleil is right, I think it's cambion," Azrael finally said. Gabriel and Raphael agreed, followed by Uriel.

"Great, where and when was it born, and is there a little boy out there with a fractured soul at the moment, since I have half his soul in my kitchen?" I asked.

"Uh," Raphael said. My uncles all looked concerned and unsure at the same time.

"I don't know," Uriel finally admitted. "It isn't like there are experts on cambions running around."

"We should call Magda Red, she's the closest thing to an expert there is on the topic," Remiel said, and his brothers turned to look at him. "She is, she gave birth to one." It was Jerome and my turn to stare. Magda had given birth to a cambion? How? And when? And why? All flashed through my head. Remiel noticed and smiled at me.

"I thought Azazael was the only cambion?" I asked. Magda Red was old, but not old enough to be Azazael's mother.

"There have been three total; Azazael was the first, Titus was the second, and Leif the Red was the third and final. He was Magda's son."

"Was? Are they all dead?" Jerome asked.

"Yes, cambion go mad," Uriel said. "Titus and Leif both committed suicide, and Azazael is the only one still partially living." The living part of Azazael's soul had been exorcised from his body and both parts had been sent to the Stygian, which is where I had encountered him once.

"Titus was Magda's first husband, Leif's father. He was a cambion who married and had a child with a human, hoping Magda's strong witch lineage and humanity would prevent Leif from going mad like himself and Azazael. It didn't work," Remiel said.

"However, Leif didn't go insane as fast as his father or Azazael. Albeit, I have often thought Azazael was born that way and it simply got worse as he aged," Haniel said. As he spoke, Remiel called Magda Red. He explained the barest bones of the situation; I had found a demonling I couldn't identify and would she please come to the house. A moment later, Magda Red materialized in my house and

Jerome's wards, protective spells, and alarms went nuts. Two heartbeats after Magda Red appeared, she grew a tail and donkey ears. A couple more heartbeats passed and the tail and ears disappeared, but she became covered in grey fur and grew different ears. We all looked at Jerome.

"I've been experimenting with ways to mark people that break my wards." Jerome shrugged. As he finished, Magda shrank to the size of a large loaf of bread. Remiel grabbed her and picked her up as Angel climbed off the couch. Remiel placed Magda, now a rabbit, on the kitchen table next to the demonling. Jerome did something and she sprang back into human form sitting on my kitchen table.

"Whoa," Magda said, and then stared at the demonling. "No, I will not fill out the forms to allow you, you of all people, to become a demonic host. We'll have a new hell prince if you host a demon because there are people afraid of you. We can't add demonic possession to it," Magda said, looking at me for only a moment.

"I have never had a desire to be possessed and that is not going to change, ever," I said sternly.

"Then why do you have a demon in a cage in your kitchen?" Magda's expression changed. "And why does it have a body? What on earth are you doing?" Magda asked me, suspicion on her face.

"I'm trying to figure out where it came from. I was told you were the closest thing to a cambion expert in existence." I said to her. "It has a body, because I was hoping to identify its sire based on its appearance. Unfortunately, it has characteristics I associate with multiple hell princes, but none of them are exactly correct. Like Asmodeus' demons have iridescence in their skin, but they are the only ones and they are black, not like people black, but like black hole black. It doesn't have violet eyes like Leviathan's demons or his creations, so we can rule out Leviathan as its sire and as its creator. Belial's demons have red skin. Beelzebub's demons all buzz. This guy doesn't have any of those things. It doesn't have a name or a sire."

"If it were cambion, its demon parent would have named it," Magda Red said.

"Apparently not," I said. "I understood without a name a demon couldn't get power and the same for cambion. I have to wonder if it is cambion; if half its soul is in a leaving, breathing boy somewhere while the other half is in my kitchen. Also, how did it get put into the teenager I took it out of today?"

"If it doesn't have a name, it doesn't have a living breathing, boy counterpart with half a soul in it," Magda Red said. "Furthermore, I don't see how it can be cambion."

"It does seem unlikely there's a demon in physical form here," I agreed. "But not impossible." I almost added that I had checked, but stopped myself.

"Have you been summoning demons and letting them lose?" Uriel asked me.

"Of course not. Demons need the Stygian and it needs them," I said.

"Then it is impossible for there to be a cambion in your kitchen," Uriel said.

"If it's cambion, Soleil should be able to tell by reading its soul," Jerome said. We all looked at him.

"I can't read living souls," I reminded him.

58

"True, but you can read demonic souls and that should give you some idea if it is fractured or not," Jerome replied. He was probably right. I had touched Azazael's soul in the Stygian, and it had left me creeped out. But it was possible that was because it was Azazael and not because he was cambion. Using magic, I reached out to the demonling and probed at its soul. It felt like a normal demonic soul at first and then, I felt something else, life. The spell broke and I pulled back from it. Gingerly, I repeated the push of magic and began looking for the life I'd felt just a moment ago. When I found it, I knew.

"It's cambion," I said, dropping the magic. "But the demon soul doesn't know anything about its parents."

"It's an orphan cambion?" Jerome asked.

"I think so." I said. "Does anyone have ideas on what to do with orphaned cambion? Is there a procedure for this?"

"No," Raphael immediately said.

"I think your idea is a good one," Remiel said. It was now his turn to be looked at.

"What is your idea, Soleil?" Raphael asked me.

"Lucifer. I think he's been in the Stygian already, I think that's how he got involved in my exorcism. I think we talk Lucifer into adopting him for lack of a better term and if he won't, I think Leviathan will."

"You don't think the teen you pulled him from is the parent?" Magda asked.

"No, she's half angel and 12 years old. I don't think it's possible she was the parent."

"Because angels never have sex with demons, especially young ones?" Magda asked scornfully.

59

"No, I'm sure they have the same predilections as other teenage girls. But the stars have to align and a divine edict has to be issued for an angel to become pregnant," I said. Magda cast her eyes downward, but said nothing. "I suspect he was born here and as soon as he was his mother shoved him into the Stygian knowing he was cambion. She may have expected the father to be immediately involved, but demon society being what it is, the father may not even know."

"Why do you think that?" Raphael asked.

"Because he had latched himself onto another demon. That demon was pulled across for a possession and he came with it," Jerome replied. "I agree with Soleil."

"Why does the living parent have to be a woman?" Magda asked.

"Because Lucifer would have been aware of any pregnant female demons in the Stygian and other demons would have noticed one missing," I said.

"Maybe they did and didn't tell you about it," Magda said.

"Soleil has a secret network of demonic spies in the Stygian, she pays them using food. None of us are supposed to know about it, but demons can't keep secrets," Azrael replied.

"Yeah, one of Belial's demons tried to get the Bureau of Exorcism to make a similar arrangement, and we refused," Uriel said.

"I'm guessing since Belial is trying to take possession of Soleil's soul, she refuses to use his demons in her spy network and they are envious and trying to get something going with someone else so they too can enjoy milk shakes and fast-food cheeseburgers," Azrael said.

"Good grief," I muttered.

"You are working with demons?" Magda's eyes were narrowed and her lips were thinned into a tight frown.

"Only certain demons," I admitted. "Hell princes loyal to Lucifer who aren't trying to take possession of my soul and that I trust to be loyal to me. Earth food is a sought-after commodity and I pay using that. It's how Remiel and I recovered those bodies in January."

"Of course," Magda said. She still looked angry, but I wasn't sure what she was angry about. "Technically, that is illegal. I'm going to pretend I don't know about it, because I trust you know what you are doing and it might be useful to have an idea what's going on in the Stygian."

"Would now be a bad time to suggest the AESPCA create a special unit that goes into the Stygian once in a while to recover dead bodies and return missing people?" I asked.

"What?" Magda turned dark eyes on me.

"One of the bodies we recovered was alive when it entered the Stygian. If we had known about it in time, we might have recovered the being alive," I said. "But I can't do everything myself. The missing fairy from last October was sent to the Stygian still breathing, wingless and severely injured. If we had known about it, we might have been able to save her. That's when I decided to start my Stygian spy network. The hell prince Ashtoreth said she lived for nearly a Stygian week and that he cared for her before she died. Which means that if the demons had told me about it the first or second day she was there, I might have been able to go get her and bring her back alive."

"Oh." Magda frowned. "How long is a Stygian week in our time?"

"About five and a half days," Jerome answered. "Time there passes faster than here. You can enter the Stygian and spend a full day there and only be gone about six hours here."

"Well, if you think Lucifer will adopt and care for the cambion you have, I suggest you get to it, because he needs a home and a family," Magda said.

"Yes, but he's still partial demon. Let's say you adopted him and named him, you would have a connection with him and would become recognized as his sire. His powers would be based on your powers," I said.

"Really?" Magda asked.

"Yes." I nodded.

"What would happen if you named him?" Magda asked.

"There'd be a living hell prince," Azrael said.

"That is a theoretical possibility," I said. "Lucifer worries about what will happen to the Stygian if I die. We already know I can manipulate and control the Stygian like he can." I did not mention I had gained power from my demon spy ring, but I had.

"How would that even be possible? A living hell prince, I mean?" Magda asked.

"We aren't sure." Uriel said. "But it isn't something we are ruling out."

"Soleil's Stygian powers are similar to those of Jophiel's. None of us can say with any certainty what she can and cannot do in regard to the Stygian. The fact that any of the hell princes were willing to make an alliance with her that really gains them nothing is testament to how powerful she is. In Leviathan's case, there is some familial loyalty, but not Ashtoreth." Remiel said.

"Furthermore," Raphael said, "This piece of information doesn't leave this room, Magda. But I've seen first-hand when demons are afraid of her, she becomes more powerful, which means to some degree she has demonic powers. Fear can and does make her stronger, but it has to be demonic fear. Fear from the living does nothing, but when demons are afraid of her, she gains from it."

"We suspect it's happened because either Soleil is supposed to prevent hell princes like Beelzebub from coming to the throne of the Stygian or because she will someday replace Lucifer," Uriel said. "Especially since she has absolute command over the Demonation. Even Belial was forced to kneel before her when she commanded it. As did Azazael."

"Demons aren't the only beings that can't keep a secret," I said, looking at my father and uncles.

"True." Raphael smiled sheepishly. I'd forced Belial and Azazael to kneel at my feet when I'd gone into the Stygian to rescue Aurora after she traveled through a demon box meant for my father.

"Okay," Magda said. "Do they know I've employed you?"

"No," I said.

"I have a feeling they might as well know. Your family seems to share all information." I nodded. "There have been two murders, both committed on nights of the new moon, the victims were turned to stone and their hearts were removed, probably not in that order. I've hired Soleil to look into them, because I believe the murders are being committed by a demon in physical form."

"And now we have a cambion," Raphael said.

"Yes," Magda nodded. "Finding someone capable of pulling a demon in physical form through the Stygian has proved difficult. I admit Soleil and Jerome were the first suspects, but one of you arranged for them to be in AESPCA custody the night of the second murder, so I've secretly hired her to look into it."

"If you're right, the next murder will happen in two nights. Unfortunately, all I know is that none of the demons in the Stygian know of any demons in physical form on this plane," I said. "My uncles are right; demons, especially hell princes, are rampant gossips and terrible braggarts. If they knew of a demon intentionally killing people, every being in the Stygian would know about it."

"Aren't they also all liars?" Magda asked.

"No, only Mammon's demons have the ability to lie. It was one of Lucifer's edicts. Having the ability to lie is what raised Mammon to the position of hell prince. Even BEDR has learned Mammon and his demons can lie, which is why they never summon them. At least with Ashtoreth's demons, if they ask a question about the possession, they know they will get the truth."

"If Lucifer or Leviathan takes the cambion, will they kill it?" Magda asked.

"No," I said, a bit surprised.

"Take it to them and then let's discuss how many people would be strong enough to bring over the physical form of a demon," Magda Red said to me. I took hold of the cage and transported myself and the cambion to the Stygian.

Chapter Seven

The Stygian reminds me of pictures of Mars. It has reddish brown rocks, reddish brown dirt, and the water is a vivid green. The working theory on the Stygian is that it is a completely artificial construct. In recent months, I had begun to doubt this. I was beginning to believe it was a planet, because it had all the features of a planet. It had a sun that traversed the sky, several moons, a night sky with stars. The stars are very different than what I see on Earth, but it does have them. I'm pretty sure it isn't Mars only because the sun is bluish and it has eleven moons, whereas I was fairly certain Mars only had two.

I could enter the Stygian anywhere I wanted, so I aimed for the front doorsteps of the castles of the hell princes I wanted to see, because it seemed incredibly rude to suddenly appear inside their houses without warning. I'd transported us to the stone gates of Lucifer's palace. It is a huge stone edifice that reminded me of a medieval castle complete with a moat in front. Trees in the Stygian are sparse, but there is a ton of rock, which explained why most of the buildings here were stone. The cambion became frightened as I walked the ten or so steps up to the gate and knocked. A demon called down to me from the ramparts over the gate. Then the gate opened and I was allowed through. I said a few soothing things to the cambion as we walked toward the doors of the palace, which were gaping open welcoming me.

I have been told Jophiel was the most powerful of the archangels, as well as the tallest at eight feet; dwarfing even my father. Lucifer and Jophiel are the same being, but Lucifer is much larger than Jophiel was. Jophiel exorcised his living soul from his body and placed it in the Stygian to control the demons and the Stygian. By freeing his soul from his physical form, he became larger and more demonic looking, which is why he stopped using the name Jophiel and took the name Lucifer.

Lucifer stood just beyond the opened door of his castle. He was the size of a small skyscraper at more than 40 feet tall and very solidly built, which wasn't surprising since he occasionally had to use physical force to deal with the more rebellious hell princes. He has massive horns that curve up from his head and sweep back several feet. His skin is roughly the same color as mine, maybe a shade darker, but it often looks red due to the dust that blows around the Stygian. Today there was no red tint to his skin.

I marched right into the castle. Demons remember who they were when alive in my presence. It usually makes them sad and quiet. However, Jophiel wasn't dead and had never forgotten who he was. He wore a giant smile as I came into the castle. Not so long ago, I would have been terrified to see Lucifer smile at me like that. Those days, though, were past and I had a decent relationship with my Stygian-ruling uncle now. He led me through the great room and into a smaller library. I'd never seen the room before, but it was everything a bookworm could love. Giant chairs and couches, wall to wall books stretching nearly 60 feet into the air with ladders scattered around for shorter demons to reach the higher books.

Unfortunately, all of these items were Lucifer-sized, even the books. One lay open on a table and I realized it was roughly as long as I was tall. Lucifer took a seat on one of the chairs. I stood, because I could not climb into any of the chairs or onto any of the couches without serious help and I wasn't about to have demons form some kind of demonic ladder for me to climb up. I put the cage with the cambion on the table with difficulty. The table was like the chairs, and I had to hoist the cage over my head and push on it with the tips of my fingers while I stood on tiptoe to get it onto the table. Lucifer eventually took it and helped put it more firmly on the table, away from the edge. The great room did have human-sized chairs, unlike this room, and while I was fascinated by the idea that Lucifer had a library, I was still a bit sad there was nothing my size in the room.

After a few moments of pleasantries where Lucifer asked about all his brothers, I leaned against one of the massive armchairs and was surprised by how soft it was. If I was four stories tall, I would probably like the room a great deal—as it was, I felt like Alice after she'd shrunk. A demon rushed in with a ladder and placed it against the chair. I blinked at it.

"Exorcist, you may climb up or we can find a demon to levitate you if you would prefer," the demon said to me. Most demons called me Exorcist, as if it were a title. Dantalian had started it to annoy me a year or so ago and now most of the Stygian did it.

"I don't think I'll be here long, but thank you," I said to the demon, who left the ladder but scampered away.

"Soleil, why is there a cambion on my reading table?" Lucifer asked once we were alone.

"I was going to ask you a similar question. I pulled him of out a possessed teen girl this morning. He had physically attached himself to another demon. He has no name and doesn't know his sire. But he had to have spent at least a little time here before I found him," I said.

"That's not possible," Lucifer said, his eyes flashing with a red light. If I hadn't been watching him, I would have missed the flash.

"That was my thought too, but obviously it is because here he is," I pointed out. "There have also been some murders that have the hallmarks of being killed by a demon, which means somehow a demon has gotten loose."

"All the demons are accounted for," Lucifer said through clenched teeth.

"Oddly, they are," I agreed. "My demon information network knows of no missing demons either. Yet, I found a cambion and there have been two murders."

"A nameless demon or cambion is powerless and can't grow," Lucifer said in response.

"I know. That's why I brought him here. As cambion, he will do better in the Stygian than on Earth. However, until someone names him and claims to be his sire, he's in limbo. I am hoping you will take on the task, but if you don't, I will ask Leviathan," I said.

"Leviathan?" Lucifer narrowed his eyes.

"I trust you and Leviathan. I may not want to adopt him myself, but I want him to be raised by a friendly hell prince and not someone like Belial."

"If you adopted him, it would be bad," Lucifer said.

"That was my thought, but I can't just release an orphaned cambion into either the Stygian or on Earth. He is too young and powerless to fend for himself, that's why he attached himself to the demon Atraxus," I said. "I suspect he was pushed into the Stygian by his living mother and Atraxus just happened to be the first demon he ran across once here. I further suspect that shortly after attaching himself to Atraxus, Atraxus was pulled through for a demonic possession and he took the cambion with him. Atraxus himself was a demonling when the possession happened, but he's grown a bit as a result of it. However, I don't think he was strong enough to detach the cambion from himself."

"I see." Lucifer sighed. "Living mother?"

"Well, if it had been born here, surely you would have known. As would I. Demons can do many things, but keeping secrets isn't one of them."

"And you pay well." Lucifer nodded in agreement.

"Apparently I do," I agreed.

"This is highly irregular. I am not a hell prince." Lucifer sighed. "I do not get assigned demons like the hell princes do. Taking charge of a cambion could be seen as a power play."

"You are already the most powerful being in the Stygian," I pointed out. "The only being that would have issue with it would be Beelzebub, and I don't think his opinion counts for much. However, there is still the Leviathan option."

"If Leviathan took over the care of a cambion that has been on Earth, it's possible he would become more powerful than Beelzebub," Lucifer said. I had considered that and nodded. "Do you know his pedigree at all? I mean, is he true cambion: half demon, half human?"

I shrugged and shook my head at the same time. I did not get the impression he was half human. We stood silently for a long time. I was berating myself for not having my cousin read his bloodline before bringing him to Lucifer. I could have found out at least a little bit about him if I had. But I hadn't, and while technically I could march out of here with him and have it done, it would probably create disorder. I had no doubt the demons that served in Lucifer's household were already spreading it around that I had brought an orphaned cambion to Lucifer to be raised. If I left with it, there might be an offensive planned for when I returned with it, and I might have to deal with Beelzebub. Beelzebub believed it was he who should be sitting on the Stygian throne and not Lucifer, and he'd planned coups in the past. No, I couldn't give him fodder for another by leaving with the cambion and then coming back, especially this cambion. He'd been found in my plane of existence and several people knew about it; that would feed power into whoever took over as his sire, because there would be fear accompanying that knowledge.

For a couple of seconds, I considered bringing my cousin here, but I decided against it, because the Stygian damaged the living, except for me and Jerome. I wasn't sure how fast the damage happened, but I was sure it was quick.

"What is your theory if you don't think he's half human?" Lucifer asked, breaking into my line of thought.

"I think he's part angel."

"Why?" Lucifer raised an eyebrow.

"I don't know. I just think he is. I could be wrong, but I just have this gut feeling he's demon and angel."

"I see." Lucifer sighed. "That is my gut feeling, too. Unfortunately, I can't read the living like I can the demonic."

"Me either. Will you raise him?"

"Yes," Lucifer smiled. "He's an odd-looking one. None of the demons here look anything like him." I nodded in agreement. To the cambion, he said, "We will name you before Soleil leaves. I want her opinion."

"My opinion?" I asked.

"Yes, one day he might be one of your legion," Lucifer said. "How would Xerxes be, after the king?"

"Xerxes?" I asked.

"He was cambion," Lucifer said.

"That is not one of the names I associate with cambions," I replied.

"Xerxes' mother was half witch and half angel and his father was Ashtoreth," Lucifer said. "His mother was a great sorceress, but enjoyed black magic a little much. She came here and bargained with Ashtoreth for her own soul, and left here pregnant. I didn't realize bargaining for souls could negate the sterility of the hell princes. I have since learned and fixed it."

72

I agreed that Xerxes was probably a fine name for Lucifer's new cambion, and then I took myself out of the Stygian.

I had learned two important things; that there were more cambions than even the oldest living beings on Earth realized, and that if there had once been a loophole allowing hell princes to trade breeding for souls, there might once again be a loophole allowing hell princes to breed with women willing to sell their souls for a child. Lucifer had seemed certain he had sorted out that problem and fixed it, but knowing DemonationDemonation and the Stygian as I did, I felt it was possible it was a new reoccurrence and Lucifer might not yet be aware of it.

I thought over this as I stood in my quiet living room. It seemed my house had emptied out while I'd been gone. I checked the clock in the living room; I'd been gone about a half hour. I went to the dining room and retrieved my cell phone from the table where I'd left it when I picked up the cambion cage. I had one text notification. I opened it and saw it was from Jerome. Remiel had decided that there was a need for banana splits and they'd be right back.

I sat down to think about all the information I had: there was a demon coming to the Earthly plane killing people, and there was a cambion. The two had to be related. Was it possible when a demon was brought across in physical form they were no longer hindered by Lucifer's spell of sterility? Or was it possible there was a killer cambion on Earth who fathered the cambion I'd just taken to Lucifer? The second seemed less likely based on the fact that I had found the cambion parasitically hanging onto another demon who had taken possession of a child. If he'd been sired by an earth-bound cambion, I felt certain the cambion father would have taken custody of him. Hell princes took care of the demonlings assigned to them as if they were their own children, and I had gotten the impression from Leviathan more than once that demons had maternal and paternal instincts. If demons and hell princes had biological drives to rear their young, surely cambions as a subset of the breed would have those same biological instincts. Unless this cambion was already going mad and couldn't give a fuckabout its offspring.

But if there were a cambion on this plane right this second having mini-cambion for thousands of years, it seemed like we would have discovered a few before now. I performed an average of exorcisms a month the previous year, and I was on track to do at least that many again this year. The original Xerxes was dead and he'd never fathered children as far as I knew. Magda's two cambion were also deceased, from what I could tell.

"Xerxes was a lunatic," Remiel said, walking into my house.

"Lucifer told me he was a cambion," I replied.

"That could have been. I've never really thought about it. I just figured Xerxes was a bit too much like his mother. She was also a lunatic." Remiel sat down a banana split in front of me. My stomach growled; my jaunt to the Stygian had used a large amount of magic because of the cambion in the cage. If it was just me traveling there and back, it barely tipped the scales of magic usage for me, but taking someone or something with me that I had to hold onto required a hefty amount of magic.

"For the record, when Remiel says she was a lunatic, he means she fought against the patriarchal society she was born into and became a strong willed, powerful woman without need for a man." Magda said, coming into the room.

"She also burned down the second largest human city at the time using magic, killing everyone simply because her brother lived there," Remiel said.

"No one escaped?" I asked, raising an eyebrow.

"If they did, they were swallowed by the sand pit she conjured up to surround the city. Remember, this was a time when humans were still fortifying cities with walls, and there were only a few access points. Basically, she opened up sinkholes under the sand at all the gates and everyone who went through fell into a sinkhole and was lost forever," Remiel said.

"She must have really hated her brother," Jerome said sadly.

"Her brother arranged her marriage, which wasn't uncommon for the time. He could have chosen better. Cyrus was one of those supernaturals that believed humans should be ruled by those with magic. He and Esfir were half siblings, their father Alborz was a wizard. Cyrus' mother was a witch, whereas Esfir's mother was an angel. At any rate, Alborz was murdered using black magic. Cyrus, as the oldest son, inherited most of his money, lands, and title. Both Esfir and Cyrus were young at the time. There were a couple other half siblings, all girls. Cyrus decided to marry all of them to men with titles, again not uncommon for the time, and there were a number of principalities near his inherited lands."

75

"I might be lost; are we discussing Xerxes the Great?" I asked.

"No, we are talking about Xerxes the Evil. He predated Xerxes I or Xerxes the Great of the Persian Empire by several thousand years. Esfir torched a city known as Darinorus," Remiel answered. "It's in modern day Turkey; the only thing left of it is the ceremonial stones at Gobekli Tepe."

"I've heard of Gobekli Tepe, but not the city," I admitted.

"That's because it didn't exist after 6,000 BCE. Back to the point, Cyrus married Esfir to a ruler in a principality close to his own to solidify his power base and possibly start expanding it. The ruler was human and there were immediate problems within the marriage." Remiel sighed. "Darius, the ruler of the principality, was a cruel man, very cruel. He kept a harem of supernaturals because he enjoyed torturing them, since they quickly healed the damage he inflicted. He had a special dungeon room built that negated magic, chained Esfir up in the room and skinned her alive. He then had the skin tanned and hung it on the wall of their bedroom. Esfir left Darius and fled to her brother's house, which was understandable, and Cyrus refused to shelter her and told her she must return to Darius. She refused and instead took shelter with one of her sisters until it became obvious she was pregnant. When the news reached Darius, he sent people to get the baby. His wife could stay with her sister, but the child would be returned to its father. When Esfir went into labor, the baby was cut from her and returned to Darius. Once she recovered, Esfir went back to Darius for the sake of her child. For a few years, everything seemed fine. Darius had taken three wives by then, one of whom was a fairy. Esfir got along well with the other supernatural wives and together they worked to temper Darius' sadism. Darius had two children by then, his son with Esfir and a daughter with his fairy wife Cadala. Before dawn one morning the entire house was awoken by screams. The wives rushed downstairs to find Darius torturing both children. His son with Esfir was being held in a huge pot full of oil over a crackling fire; the daughter was chained to the wall and Darius was mutilating her wings using an unsharpened knife to shred their membrane. They killed Darius and took both children to Michael for healing. Unfortunately, even Michael working with Esfir's full coven could not save her son. The nobles of the town, loyal to Darius because he allowed their perversions to go unpunished, put out death orders on all three wives. They could not return to their home, and Esfir returned to Cyrus' house for shelter. Instead, he handed her over to the nobles to be executed. The execution didn't work. After that Esfir began practicing black magic."

"Not gonna lie, if someone did that to Jerome, I'd probably kill them so I could enslave their souls." I nodded grimly.

"I called her a lunatic; I didn't say it wasn't justified. I cannot imagine her suffering. She gathered a group of ruffians and roamed between her homelands in Turkey and Egypt selling her services as a black magician. About 50 years after the death of her son, she was suddenly pregnant again. No one knew who the father was, and she wouldn't tell. She named the second son Xerxes and taught him her skills as a black magic practitioner on top of his own innate talents. He was a good-looking boy, not dramatically powerful, but a bit twisted. We all thought it was his mother's grief that twisted him, but if he was cambion, that would explain it. He became a serial killer and rapist. If he hadn't had some angel genes, he probably would have fathered hundreds of children. His mother avoided the cities, but Xerxes craved them for the supply of victims they offered. He would enter a home, kill all the men and male children, then spend hours raping all the women and female children in the house. He stuck to the human cities as much as possible, until he entered the city of Alexandria in Egypt. There his spree ended when he entered the home of Haniel. Haniel was helping the Egyptian Emperor Baakoamon build the library at Alexandria, and probably knew more about black magic than anyone else at the time. Xerxes' black magic death spells, which had never failed him in the past, failed against Haniel. Haniel subdued Xerxes and turned him over to the emperor's guards. He killed a dozen or so and escaped, determined to get revenge on Haniel. By then, though, Haniel wasn't alone with his wife and children; he had been joined by two of his brothers. Raphael and Michael had come to assist him to purify himself of the black magic curses Xerxes had hurled at him. They also were serving on the first Angel Council, the body that governed angelic conduct. Xerxes, being part angel, was put on trial by the council, found guilty, and sent to the Third Plane. He was killed some thousand years later when he tried to break out with the help of his mother. It was after that failed escape that Esfir decided to burn down Darinorus to punish her brother for marrying her to Darius. The few supernaturals in the city attempted to put out the flames by smothering them with sand, but the fire was so hot it simply vitrified the sand, turning it into huge glass sculptures that ended up being just as destructive as the fire when they broke and collapsed. Nearly 100,000 human and supernatural lives were lost that day, Esfir among them."

"How awful," I said.

"Yes," Magda Red said. We sat in silence for a while as I digested that information. I suspected Remiel was quiet because he was remembering it.

"Let me know as soon as you can if you have any ideas on how to catch our killer demon," Magda said after about five minutes of utter silence. Her sudden speech made my heart race, and I jumped a little.

"Will do," I said, trying to calm my nerves after being startled.

Chapter Eight

When I'd gotten my exorcism certificate, my family had gotten together to give me one massive gift. They had gone through their personal book collections and gotten copies made for me of all their books on demons, the Stygian, and the different types of magic. My father and uncles were book hoarders, especially Haniel. It had resulted in two whole bookcases of magically copied ancient books. Gabriel had even been nice enough to create a book that was an index of all the other books in the collection. Over the years, I had found the books unhelpful in that I instinctively knew so much about demons and the Stygian that I hadn't needed them, but now I was going to have to go through the collection, because I could think of only one reason why a demon would kill and it was terribly unlikely that there were three people on Earth that could subjugate demonic will to their own.

I took down the index, looking for anything that referenced demonic murderers. It didn't necessarily require black magic, but it seemed likely that the two would go hand in hand. Jerome came in and sat on the little couch in my office. There were nine references listed in the index. I said the book titles out loud and using magic, Jerome pulled and stacked the books on my desk.

We each took a book. It didn't take long to realize that even with only nine references, it was going to be a long night. The first reference I found was several pages long, dealing with demonic behavior. The first section of the chapter gave an in-depth analysis of why demons acted the way they did. I skimmed through this part because I understood most demonic behavior. The demons and their behavior were broken down into groups and functionality based on their sires. The first example was Leviathan. According to the author, Leviathan's demons were interested solely in creation; everything they did was in pursuit of gaining souls with which they could create new things. I read that example out loud to Jerome, who promptly rolled his eyes. We both knew Leviathan was a creator; however, his demons were incapable of creativity—they simply did not wield that kind of power. Instead, Leviathan's demons negotiated for souls for their sire. Like most demons, they could grant small amounts of power when they took possession of a host, but for the most part, they were considered undesirable. Leviathan was the third most powerful hell prince, but his offspring were weak. By contrast, Mammon's demons were much stronger, despite Mammon being only the ninth most powerful hell prince.

I checked the front of the book to see if I could find any indication of when it was written. I had been led to believe that the rise of Leviathan to the third most powerful of the hell princes had been fairly recent. If this was the case, perhaps at one time his demons had been capable of creating things. Of course, it was always possible that the author was wrong. The front of the book gave no indication of the date of publication. The author's name, Akbar the Powerful, meant nothing to me. It could have been written 2,000 years ago or 10,000 years ago or last year. That was one of the problems with older supernaturals; they didn't have last names. Most of them had titles and had appropriated them as their surname when people started using last names. It never ceased to amaze me how many people failed to have surnames, including my own father and uncles. It was the reason my sister and I had been given our mother's surname.

I suspected Akbar the Powerful was deceased. Not simply because I had never heard of him, but because an internet search revealed no more books written by him. The lack of other books coupled with the topic of this book made me wonder if he had driven himself insane trying to write it. It wouldn't be the first time that had happened; most supernaturals who researched the Stygian eventually went mad. We didn't know if this was because time moved differently once a person was in the Stygian, or if it was some other influence that caused people to lose their marbles after spending time there. However, one thing was certain—those that entered the Stygian alive only stayed that way for a relatively short time. A famous short story writer from the early 1900s had come across Pandora's Box, which was basically a portal between the two planes. He had traveled back and forth fairly often from what I understood, and he had gone crazy. Even his house staff had gone crazy, and eventually someone had killed all of them.

I didn't think this would be my fate. I felt fine in the Stygian. Being there felt no different than being here. My mind and body didn't react to the change in how time flowed or seem to notice that the surroundings were nothing like what was on Earth. It scared me just how comfortable I was over there.

I had nightmares about Lucifer falling from power and me being forced to take his place. The Stygian was somewhere to visit once in a while, but I didn't wanna live there indefinitely.

I turned the page in the book, and that was the entire paragraph dedicated to why demons kill, according to Akbar. There were only two reasons demons would kill; the first was to progress in the demon hierarchy and the second was for a bargained soul. I wasn't sure what that meant exactly, I'd never heard of a demon killing to obtain a soul that had been sold to it. Neither made sense to me. It seemed that if a person was willing to bargain away their soul, they couldn't be that terrified of demons, rendering them useless as a power boost until they were dead. On the flip side, if you bargained your soul away in order to have somebody killed, it was possible that would give the demon a power boost from the victim, both from their terror and their bargaining for their life.

In the world of demons and hell princes, not all souls are created equal; this was the reason Belial wanted to possess mine. The hell prince believed if he could take possession of my soul either through bargaining or my death he would usurp Beelzebub as the most powerful hell prince. Luckily for me, bargaining was the primary method of obtaining souls for hell princes, and I had no intention of offering my soul to Belial under any circumstances. Unfortunately, nothing is foolproof, especially when a hell prince is involved. I suspected if Belial ever took possession of my body he could find a way to possess my soul.

Belial was not the only hell prince with these kinds of ideas. Beelzebub had attempted the previous fall to take possession of Jerome. While the hell prince would have used Jerome's magic to his advantage while alive, ultimately it was his soul he wanted. Jerome and I felt certain that Beelzebub believed if he could obtain Jerome's soul, he would be able to overthrow Lucifer and rule the Stygian. However, like me, Jerome was not going to go willingly or bargain away his soul under any circumstances. Having the ability to mimic my powers, Jerome could call a demon army if he were desperate, and we had both agreed we'd use a demon army to lay waste to the Stygian before we bargained away our souls.

I wasn't sure whether I found Akbar's information useful; it was true he had given two reasons for demons to kill that I hadn't thought of, but he failed to expand enough on the ideas. Also, Akbar had not mentioned black magic, which surprised me; for some reason I was convinced that using a demon to kill someone would require black magic. I knew demons were not inherently evil; they were simply trying to eke out an existence like everyone else. This meant that using a demon to kill, while bad, didn't necessarily require evil to perpetrate.

I opened the second book. My first step was to examine the title page and see if there was a publication date as well as the name of the writer. I wasn't sure this information was necessary or even useful, but I felt like it was something I needed to know. Once again, the author was someone I'd never heard of and there was no publication date. This didn't exactly surprise me, as publication dates were a relatively new invention starting sometime in the 1800s.

I flipped through the book. The first sentence of the section on demon murders made no sense, and I realized I was going to have to go back and read previous pages to get context. As I started reading, Jerome got up and got another book, helping whittle down the stack. Jerome was able to magically assimilate some books without having to read the entire thing, giving him an advantage over me. He could just flip the pages and as he did, the information just entered his brain. It was difficult to explain. Whereas I found myself having to go back to the start of previous chapters to understand what the author was talking about.

Book two used roughly three paragraphs to say the exact same thing as book one: demons kill to hurry the collection of a bargained soul. Once again, it did not elaborate. The rest of the chapter was about the accumulation of power needed for demons to move up in their hierarchies. Apparently, killing to access a bargained soul was not a good way to gain power and could actually result in the loss of power, as bargained souls went straight to hell princes, and if the demon trying to gain power wasn't a hell prince, they got nothing from it.

This brought me full circle back to my original thought; killing served little purpose for demons. It seemed to be more of a hindrance than a help.

However, siring a cambion would do a great deal to boost the position of a demon. As the true father of the cambion, a demon would gain power from the fear instilled by its child on human beings. I just couldn't figure out how a human and a demon had managed to mate. The cambion and the murders had to be connected. Somehow there was a demon in this realm with a physical body capable of committing murder and fathering children. How did no one, human or demon, know about it? I could understand how people missed it, but not other demons. A demon had once given me a full account of all their fellow demons currently in possession of a host. I have learned over the years that demons were braggarts and gossips, which meant every demon was up in every other demon's business.

"Have you learned anything?" I asked Jerome.

"Demons sometimes kill because that is what someone asked for when they sold their soul," Jerome said. "And sometimes it's because they need to collect the souls bargained to them. Beelzebub did this at some point in the distant past in order to become the second strongest hell prince."

"I'm still hung up on the how as well as the why," I admitted. "It seems to me if a demon had crossed over in physical form, all of the Stygian would be buzzing about it."

Jerome nodded and did a spell, causing more books to fly off the shelves and stack themselves on the desk. I looked at the titles, mildly confused. One of them was a *History of Demons,* written by Haniel and Uriel. I tried not to frown. They were not my favorite uncles; I found them both mildly judgmental and snobbish. Uriel mildly disapproves of the mixing of supernatural genes, both amongst different supernaturals and humans. In his mind, angels should only have children with other angels. He was very vocal about Helia and I being designated as archangels over the winter. After all, we were nephilim and the very term denoted that we were not genetically pure angels. However, despite his feelings on our genetic variation, even he had to grudgingly admit that Helia and I could perform magic that other angels couldn't and were magical powerhouses.

Haniel was less interested in genetic purity; he was all about knowledge and power. He'd thawed a bit since I'd earned the archangel designation, but it didn't erase the memories of his superior attitude the entire time I was growing up. However, next year he would be one of Jerome's teachers, so I was trying to learn to like him more. I was unsure if either one of them had the experience with demons to be able to write a comprehensive history of them as a species of beings. I picked up the book and turned it over in my hands a few times before opening it and reading the introductory chapter.

"I think I'm going to summon a demon and ask him some questions," I said to Jerome.

"Like what? You've already asked if there's a demon missing. Which demon?"

"Abaddon," I said, as if it was self-explanatory.

"Abaddon?" Jerome raised an eyebrow. Abaddon had been one of the original hell princes. He'd lost his seat of power some time long ago and was now a subject of Leviathan. I suspected the bit Jerome had told me about Beelzebub collecting bargained souls was done to unseat Abaddon. Abaddon was loyal to Lucifer and Leviathan. Leviathan had prevented his death when Beelzebub challenged him for his territory. Over the last couple of years, I had slowly been given pieces of information like this from Leviathan, Ashtaroth, and Lucifer. I had a gut feeling that if any being could explain to me why a demon would kill and how a cambion had been born recently, it was Abaddon. He had been a demon king before Jophiel and Zadkiel had created the Stygian. Once the Stygian was created, Jophiel had kept Abaddon as a demon king and given him the title hell prince to serve under him. He was the first hell prince and was among the most powerful. Beelzebub was born before the Stygian was created and was biologically the son of Abaddon and a demoness named Aswang who was killed by Beelzebub in his quest for power.

I believed that hell prince or not, Abaddon was still incredibly powerful and could be the solution to the Beelzebub/Belial problem. However, as long as they were just quietly plotting against Lucifer, I couldn't do anything about it. If they outright challenged his authority to rule, those loyal to Lucifer could take action against the challengers. Technically, I was not a hell prince, but in reality, I had powers that would allow me to assist in the defense of my uncle's throne and I abso-fucking-lutely would use them, even if it meant killing an actual hell prince.

I got up and walked to Jerome's game room. I imagined at one time, Abaddon had been bigger in size than Leviathan, but these days he was roughly the same size as my father and could be summoned inside the house. Jerome got up and followed me. He usually watched my summonings, just in case something went wrong. It didn't take much power or even time for me to summon Abaddon. He appeared in physical form in the windowless room.

As I mentioned, he is roughly as tall as my father, but maybe a touch stockier. Abaddon is dark-skinned like a Middle Easterner. Like most demons, he is completely hairless, which gives him a surreal appearance. His irises are an off-white, not quite the same color as the whites around the irises, but still white with big, black pupils. He turned those unnerving, ethereal eyes on me now and I suppressed a shudder.

"This is a surprise," Abaddon said to me. I nodded. I would only summon physical bodies for demons I trusted, which was common knowledge in the Stygian. They were less dangerous in spirit form than physical. "I saw little Xerxes. He is quite interesting and I'm guessing related to the reason you summoned me, although..." he let his sentence trail off.

"I am hoping my instincts about you are correct," I said to Abaddon.

"Which instincts are those?" Abaddon asked.

"There are three really: one, I can trust you; two, you retain more power than most people realize; and the third is that you know more than most demons," I said.

"If I confirm any of these, would you believe me?" Abaddon asked.

"Yes." I nodded. "I know you are bound by Lucifer's spell to speak the truth. I feel it in you. I also suspect the reason Beelzebub overthrew you is because in order for Jophiel and Zadkiel to design the Stygian they would have needed demonic help. I believe that came from you."

"Did either of them tell you it was me?" Abaddon asked.

"No," I admitted. "It is something I figured out on my own. Leviathan was willing to risk his immortal demonic soul to save you, but Leviathan would have been among the least powerful hell princes at the time. Then Lucifer informed me that originally demons remembered their former lives, but it was emotionally painful for them, So he caused them to lose those memories. This got me thinking—Leviathan's loyalty to you had to exist for a reason. Zadkiel sacrificed himself to the Stygian in a slightly different way than Jophiel, so if the young hell prince Leviathan remembered your assistance to create the Stygian, he would be exceptionally loyal to you out of gratitude. I believe you helped the two angels design and build the Stygian, and as a demon king, I believe you originally provided the magic to move demons there."

"My children underestimate you, Exorcist," Abaddon said. "I am willing to help you, but I require something in return."

"I will not bargain with my soul nor the soul of Jerome," I said skeptically.

"I do not want your soul nor the wizard's. No, your soul is too dangerous to collect. However, what I want is equally dangerous." Abaddon said to me. This statement puzzled me. Beelzebub had gone after Jerome's soul and Belial was desperate to claim mine by hook or by crook, so why did Abaddon believe my soul was dangerous to possess?

"I will require knowledge of what it is you want before I agree," I said, frowning at him.

"I would expect nothing less. I have two sons in the Stygian making mischief, but they are smart enough to not directly challenge Lucifer. My request is that you help me reclaim my territory and title. I want your assistance restoring me to my status as ruling demon king, what you would call a hell prince. To do so will require me to challenge Beelzebub first, but I suspect his brother will come to his aid, and I will eventually be forced to challenge Belial as well. Having your support and possibly your magical assistance would be of great use. Leviathan has agreed to assist me, but I suspect the three of us could defeat them without bloodshed, which would be ideal," Abaddon said to me. I frowned harder. Beelzebub and Belial scared the shit out of me. However, it would be useful to have another hell prince loyal to Lucifer. Right now, only three of them were supportive of Lucifer, as most of the hell princes felt he was too restrictive.

The only thing that kept direct challenges away was the lack of power among most of the hell princes. However, Beelzebub was gaining power, as was Belial. The strength of Leviathan and Ashtaroth would only remain a deterrent for so long, and eventually, I worried that Beelzebub, Belial, and the others would be in a position to not just overthrow Lucifer but to overthrow the three hell princes loyal to him, including the sire of the incubi and succubae, the most commonly summoned demons in existence. Ashtaroth's power limitations were mostly self-imposed, since he only allowed a handful of incubi and succubae to be summoned and limited how many could be hosted on this plane at a single time.

"I need to think on it, I worry my agreement is less about harmony and balance in the Stygian and more about my desire to be rid of both Beelzebub and Belial," I admitted.

"Would it matter that it would personally benefit you?" Abaddon asked me.

"I want to say no, but I know myself well enough to know if my intentions are not pure, I will feel guilty for assisting you if one or both dies," I said.

"Why would the death of a demon prick at your conscience? It is only a demon," Abaddon said, and I wasn't sure if he was testing me or if he really meant it.

"I may not want demons running around free on Earth, but in many ways demons are no different than any other being. They want to live, a desire I can relate to. I feel that unjustly killing one of them, even Belial, is murder," I said with a shrug. My feelings on demons had changed a great deal in the last five years, and I was aware of it. I used to believe all demons were inherently evil and should be destroyed, but as I got to know more and more of them, I learned that wasn't the case. Yes, some demons were evil, but I didn't find the rate of evilness in demons to be any higher than in living beings like angels or vampires.

"I can respect that position. While you consider my offer, I will leave you with a bit of wisdom. To understand why the killer is using a demon, you have to understand why he is killing the people he is killing. If you assist me, I will give you the responsible demon's name and you can demand the name of the summoner from him. Understand though, that if you don't grasp the reason for the killings, even getting his name from the demon may not help you catch him. The key lies in who is being killed and why," Abaddon told me. Then I felt Abaddon send himself back across the Stygian Divide.

This confirmed I was correct; Abaddon did have more magic than people realized, as it was rare for a hell prince to cross himself back. Leviathan said it was exhausting for him to do it, which is why he relied on me to do it when I summoned him. I knew Beelzebub was Abaddon's son; I had not known Belial was also his son. I still didn't know why Abaddon thought my soul was dangerous to possess. Beelzebub wasn't after my soul, which made me wonder if Abaddon was implying Jerome's soul was equally as dangerous to possess.

"Why are our souls dangerous to possess?" I asked Jerome.

"I wondered the same thing," he replied. "And if the key is in the victims, then there has to be something that connects them that everyone missed."

"Agreed." I nodded. We went back to my office. I dug out the thumb drive Magda had given us, plugged it into the computer and pulled up the case files again. They were huge; the AESPCA had talked to hundreds of people who had known the victims and had not made any connections, which made me wonder if Jerome and I could.

"I'm going to bed. If you need me, come get me," Jerome said after a few minutes.

"Night, kiddo," I told him. Not that he was much of a kid anymore. He was taller than I was, lean and strong like only athletic teenagers can be, his jaw was starting to square, and soon someone would need to talk to him about shaving. Part of me didn't want Jerome to grow up, and part of me was convinced he was already grown up when I met him and now his body was physically catching up to his mind.

I grabbed the demon index to look for references on hearts. Maybe I could find a clue there. Unfortunately, there weren't many. Apparently, demons weren't that interested in hearts, which I had already known. Since my collection was primarily demon-related, I only found three references, none of them particularly useful. I was going to need to understand magic better than I did to find the significance of removing someone's heart.

Again, the idea of black magic welled up in my mind, but I wasn't sure that was accurate. I didn't know much about black magic beyond it being death magic. Of course, there was black magic and then there was forbidden magic. Love spells were a type of forbidden magic. Love potions wore off much faster than love spells, and the potions weren't illegal. They had special properties that caused whatever they were put into to change colors, ensuring a person was aware there was a love potion inside. Commercially bought love potions turned the medium that hosted it either bright red or hot pink, depending on the maker. The love potion Megan and Walter's son had used to spike the mashed potatoes at their school had turned the potatoes neon pink. Which meant everyone who ate them knew they'd been tainted by a love potion and ate them anyway.

I stared at the index, put it down, and picked up my phone. The digital readout informed me it was after midnight; I put the phone back down and turned to my

94

laptop. I opened my email and started adding all my uncles' and my father's email addresses to the address line. I took a few seconds to consider how to title my email. It was going to surprise them; it kind of surprised me. My senior year in high school my guidance counselor told my parents I was willfully ignorant, in those exact words. I had huffed and protested, but as an adult, I have realized multiple times that guidance counselor was spot on. I *was* willfully ignorant. I titled the email Willfully Ignorant: Need More Books and then moved to the body, where I begged all of them to supply me with copies of all their books relating to magic and anything else. I might need to know about the magical world I lived in and didn't understand. Now it would take decades to get through all their books, but I was silently hoping Jerome could make a magical index like my uncle had, so I could just flip to the relevant sections to start.

The first victim was a personal trainer, and a human. The second was a physical therapist, also human. I briefly wondered if the third victim would be a physical education teacher, since the first two dealt with physical fitness. While I hated physical exertion, it didn't seem like a good enough reason to kill them. There had to be something else that connected them. They were both human, both men, both had brown hair, one had green eyes and one had blue. One was over six feet tall, but the other was short, especially for a male, at five feet seven inches tall. They were single, their driver's licenses listed them as organ donors, and yeah, you couldn't harvest organs from a stone corpse no matter how much magic a doctor had.

I didn't have an email for Magda Red so I grabbed a pad of Post-it Notes and wrote a note to myself: Do the two victims have the same blood type? I recently read an article while at the vet's office about the rare Bombay or HH blood type. They were universal donors who could only receive blood from people who had the same blood type, because they were missing a protein that protects red blood cells from being attacked by the immune system or something, and there were only a couple hundred thousand people in the world with the blood type. If you wanted to kill someone who needed a liver transplant but had the Bombay blood group, killing possible donors and turning them to stone seemed like a good way to do it. Albeit, it was a very complicated way to kill someone on a transplant list. I was pretty sure people in need of organ transplants died all the time of natural causes, a killer would really only need to wait it out. But it was one of the few ideas I'd had; even though it was ridiculous, I kept the note because at least it proved I was trying to come up with ideas. I glared at the Post-it wondering if I had lost my mind and if Magda Red would laugh at me if I suggested it. If someone had suggested it to me, I might have chuckled. Maybe I was just tired. It was a preposterous theory and if they'd both belonged to that specific blood type, someone would have flagged it; it was rarer even than AB negative.

I did not tear up the Post-it. Instead, I shut down all the electronics in my office, grabbed my phone and started toward bed. Immediately after turning out the light in the office, I heard a tap on the glass that nearly made me jump out of my skin. Then the shade rolled up on its own. A ghoulish face shrouded in darkness was pressed up against the glass. I immediately shot a spell at it, a small fireball. It whizzed from my hands and melted through the glass in less than a breath. Remiel began screaming, and I realized the ghoulish dark face was my uncle. He was holding a stack of books, and two of them were smoldering.

"Holy fuck!" Remiel shouted, dropping the books and either ducking down or falling backward. I rushed to the window. I could hear Jerome's feet as well as Angel's feet running toward me. I grabbed a vase of flowers that sat near the window on a decorative table, threw open the window with one hand and then dumped the flowers and water out the window on the books and Remiel.

"What the fuck are you doing!" I shouted at him. My heart was beating even faster now that I knew it was Remiel.

"Soleil, are you okay?" Jerome shouted as he entered the room—I felt his magic swirl in with him, it shuddered and pulsed in the dark behind me.

"Yes, Remiel just scared the shit out of me," I said. "Come help, I think I burned him." Angel shoved her head out the window next to mine. She breathed on Remiel and the smoke stopped emanating from him and the books he'd dropped.

"I think the books protected everything but my hair," Remiel said. "May I come in for a drink at least?"

"I don't know." I sighed and stuck a hand out the window. The archangel took it, shook out his wings, touched his slightly singed hair, and started picking up books and shoving them into my hands. Once he'd passed the dozen or so books into the room, he climbed in the window. I considered commenting on this, but since I had nearly set him on fire, I decided to ignore it.

"You literally sent the email less than five minutes ago. I knew if I hurried, I could catch you up and then I saw your light on in your office."

"You could have texted, 'Hey, on my way with some books,'" I snapped.

"I was so excited I didn't think of that," Remiel admitted and blushed. "I have had copies of these books waiting for you to realize you need more knowledge for more than a decade. I was beginning to think this day would never come. When I got your email, I just grabbed all of them and headed over."

"What if I had already gone to bed? I could have been emailing you from bed," I pointed out.

"You don't have email on your phone," Remiel replied. This was true. I pointed at the laptop. "Meh, maybe, but you weren't and I really wanted to bring you these."

"Obviously," I said. "What do you want to drink?"

"Whiskey, I think," Remiel replied.

"After that, me too." I sighed again. "It has been a long day. Jerome you, can't have whiskey, but I'll let you have a bit of wine if you want," I told the teen, who was still holding a lot of magic at his command to defend me if he needed to.

"What made you think you needed more books?" Remiel asked.

"Abaddon said we needed to understand why he was killing to find out who it was, and my books don't contain much information about removing hearts from victims. It doesn't seem to be something demons normally do."

"What did you agree to in order to get that information?" Remiel asked, trying not to sound suspicious.

"That was freebie information. I get the name of the demon involved if I agree to help him take down Beelzebub," I told him.

"He wants his position as a hell prince back?" Remiel asked, raising an eyebrow.

"Yes." I nodded and we went into the kitchen. I got down the whiskey and then remembered I had a bottle of scotch that I had never opened; now seemed like the perfect time. It was a single malt bottled the month my parents learned they were pregnant with me. Dad had bought two bottles, one for himself and one for me, and he'd given me mine when I'd graduated from exorcist training.

"This is a good scotch," Remiel said, looking at the bottle. "I have a bottle, too. We'll use mine." As he said this, a bottle of Scotch with the wax seal broken appeared on my island counter.

"I didn't know you could do that kind of magic," I said.

"Jerome's been teaching me," Remiel admitted. "You should at least let him taste this scotch."

"He's 15, he's prone to nightmares, and I think letting a 15-year-old drink scotch is considered contributing alcohol to a minor and is a criminal offense."

"Five hundred years ago, he would have been able to drink all the alcohol he wanted," Remiel said to me.

"Yes, but now we know alcohol damages developing brains and kids are more likely to become alcoholics if they start drinking hard liquor at a young age. He can have a glass of wine, if he is at home with me and only on very rare occasions," I said. Alcohol, ancients, and modern society did not agree on much. Alcohol had not been taboo in my house as I was growing up; I'd had the same rules I'd set out for Jerome—a single glass on rare occasions, with parental supervision. Compared to my counterparts with much more modern parents, alcohol hadn't been that interesting to me as a teen or young adult. I hadn't gone through a phase of binge drinking, blackout drunks, or even heavy drinking. I enjoyed a glass of wine now and then with dinner or dessert and occasionally, a stiff drink was called for when I'd been scared out of my skin like tonight. Older supernaturals felt that letting a teen have a glass of wine or beer now and again was no big deal, because for eons everyone drank alcohol with every meal because you really didn't want to drink much water. This practice was frowned on by most humans and younger supernaturals who were parents.

"Fine. Jerome, you are wound really tight tonight, what's up?" Remiel asked. We both turned our gaze on him.

"Honestly?" Jerome asked, and we both nodded. I held out a hand for him to take and he took it, proving Remiel was correct; there was something emotionally wrong with Jerome tonight. "I find it hard not to worry when Soleil gets mixed up with demons and murders. No one has said it out loud yet, but Soleil is investigating a supernatural serial killer who is summoning a demon to do their killing. How am I not supposed to be worried?"

"Well, it isn't like a demon is going to hurt me," I said sternly.

"I know," Jerome sighed. "I know it's silly, but I am still worried. The demon might not be able to hurt you, but the supernatural summoning it can try." I was powerful enough that I'd made even Belial kneel at my feet once to remind him he was not strong enough to take me on. I was strong enough that I could have made all the demons in the Stygian kneel before me that day at the same time. I hadn't, but I could have. If I commanded a demon, it had no choice but to obey, which meant a demon couldn't kill me even if it wanted to.

"It's not silly," I told him. "It is scary, it is just as scary for me as it is for you. Because if he comes after me, he will come after you too. However, I promise not to go out of my way to bring him or his pet demon home with me."

"I know you won't, but sometimes in the heat of the moment, you make bad decisions," Jerome said. I nodded, because Belial had nearly eaten me last fall.

"And there's me," Remiel said. "I like working with my niece, and I'm not going to let her take unnecessary chances, but if you want her to quit this case, I'll talk to Magda Red about it and make it go away."

"Saying yes would be incredibly selfish of me," Jerome said. "I can't ask her to quit the case even if it does worry me, because no one else has the skills to deal with it like Soleil does. If I thought even for a moment that Azrael

101

and Uriel could deal with it on their own, I'd have her hand it over to them, but this is uniquely a case for Soleil's skills." I pursed my lips at that last statement and sighed heavily. The demon had to be Belial or one of his minions.

"Okay, you two had warring thoughts there. Soleil thought it had to be Belial and Jerome thought it couldn't be Belial because possessing Soleil's soul was dangerous," Remiel said, looking back and forth between the two of us. "Since I know Belial does want to possess Soleil, I don't understand your thought on it, Jerome."

"Abaddon said possessing Soleil's soul was dangerous and implied the same was true of mine and that his kids were too stupid to realize it, but I can't read demon thoughts even if I've been around you for a really long time, so I don't know what he meant by it."

"Some souls seem to be destined to be hell princes, souls like Zadkiel's. Leviathan was originally a demonling under a different hell prince. Eventually Leviathan killed him and took over his position as hell prince. I think Abaddon suspects both of your souls are destined to be hell princes, if not replacements for Lucifer. If that's the case, if Belial claimed Soleil's soul…"

"I would rise up once I was strong enough and overthrow my ruling hell prince to replace him, and Jerome would probably do the same," I finished for him.

"You're sort of correct, except there wouldn't be much of a wait time. Some demons are more powerful from the start and immediately have the power to overthrow a hell prince if they desire." Remiel sighed and drained the Scotch from his glass. "When Abaddon was the ruling demon king, he told us the king could always tell when a demon had been born that was more powerful than he was. I believe that's still true. You thought when Beelzebub wanted Jerome it was to use his magic, but I think it was possibly to destroy his soul and prevent him becoming a hell prince. Belial's desire for your soul may be the same."

"Huh," I said, and refilled the Scotch in my glass. "Serious question, why did you open the shade in my office? I wasn't freaked out until you did that. When it happened all I could see was a strange ghostly figure outside the window."

"Oh, well," Remiel blushed again and refilled his own glass. Then he poured Jerome a glass of wine and set it before him. "You're gonna need that to sleep the rest of the night. I wasn't trying to open the blind, I was trying to open the window and I missed."

"You missed?" I asked.

"Yes," Remiel nodded, his ears turning crimson.

"Dude, you missed because you can't open our windows using magic." Jerome looked at Remiel as if the archangel were incredibly stupid for several heartbeats. "My protection spells on the house would be rather useless if an archangel could magically enter the house by opening a window."

"I didn't think of that." Remiel said. "For some reason, I don't always remember that I'm not exempt from your protection magic."

"Why would you be exempt?" I asked raising an eyebrow.

"We spend so much time together," Remiel said with his hands out in front of him, palms up. "I don't think you realize how special you both are to me. I think of you like my daughter, that's why when you needed my help getting your private investigator's license and starting your business I immediately agreed. And Jerome, I think of him like my grandson. I know Gabriel has always been the uncle you were closest to, but I have hoped in recent years that I have become more important to both of you." There it was, the confirmation of what I had thought for a while. My uncle was lonely and felt he was competing with Gabriel.

"Remiel, I can never thank you enough for what you've done for Jerome and me the last couple of years. Not just helping me with my business, but with life and learning to be a parent. Your immediate acceptance of Jerome was heartwarming. Furthermore, you were willing to fight the council and Balthazar Leopold to get him designated as an angel. Gabriel isn't my favorite, not really. During my teen years, Gabriel was willing to fight for me, like you have fought for Jerome. Gabriel didn't believe I should be expected to behave in a certain way or even be forced to learn all the things the schools thought I should learn. Looking back, I suspect it's because he was expecting me to want to take over for Lucifer in the Stygian. But no one in the family has done more for Jerome than you have except my parents, and if I thanked you every day for the rest of time, I would still feel like I wasn't expressing my gratitude enough. You are a huge part of Jerome and my lives, and I hope you always will be. However, it won't get you an exemption from the protection spells around the house." I said the last with a smile and then walked over and hugged Remiel. I felt my uncle stiffen in my arms and realized I couldn't remember having ever hugged him, which was weird because I came from a family of huggers. Jerome almost immediately joined us in the hug.

"I have been lonely," Remiel said after a few moments. "I see my brothers and their kids and I wonder if I missed out."

"I think you are like Raphael. Unlike most of your brothers, Raphael wanted more than just a woman to mother his children, he wanted a life partner and for an angel that's a long time. It's not a decision to be made lightly. I think you are waiting for a woman who knocks your world off its axis before trying for children and an eternity together," Jerome said.

"Because you've been willing to wait, I think when she comes along, you'll be madly in love like my dad," I told my uncle. "Now it's my turn to be selfish; if you were married and had kids of your own, you wouldn't be here at this exact moment with a stack of books for me. You also probably wouldn't be helping me become a private investigator or helping Jerome learn to be an angel." Both of Jerome's family lines had divine births, and Jerome had enough genes from my uncles and father that he had been able to register with our archangel host as well as take some angel courses in high school. However, it was Remiel who had advocated for Jerome to be formally recognized as being of angelic stock.

"All my life, people have been determined to tell me everything happens for a reason, even if we don't understand it. Perhaps it's true and that's why you haven't found Miss Right yet. Soleil's correct about how much we need you and how you wouldn't be here if you had a family of your own right now," Jerome said, and then he hugged Remiel again; I noticed his eyes were sparklier than normal. Jerome was dark-skinned with beautiful blue eyes that sometimes reminded me of my father's, although he had one iris ring fewer than Raphael.

"Do you believe them when they tell you that?" Remiel asked Jerome.

"I used to not. In the last three years, though, I've begun to change my mind. However, before meeting Soleil and Raphael in Chicago it used to make me angry when people said it. I may not understand Fate's plans, but I'm starting to see that all of this is part of something else and without it happening I wouldn't be where I am, and I wouldn't be able to achieve whatever destiny I have. Although, I admit whatever destiny is planned for me, the journey has been kind of shitty."

"Yeah, I guess I was just feeling sorry for myself there for a few minutes." Remiel's cheeks and ears turned red again. It took me a moment to realize Remiel felt bad for his pity party when compared to Jerome's short and rather shitty life up to this point. The kid was an orphan, after all, and Remiel was sad because he hadn't found a woman to marry, but he still had a close family that was very supportive of each other, something Jerome didn't have without making a new one.

"It happens to all of us from time to time," Jerome said. "However, I am grateful for your support, assistance, and love."

"Thanks, Jerome." Remiel smiled at the teen. "I am grateful you and Soleil found each other. You make her a better angel and I love having you in my life to spoil."

"Okay, well this is very sad and mushy, we should all go to our respective houses and go to bed," I said. "Tomorrow's Sunday and I've got a ton of work to do on this case."

"Getting help from Jerome doesn't make you a terrible parent," Remiel said. "Good night kids, see you around eight this morning."

"Oh fuck," I said. My family did Sunday brunch every week and missing it was basically like telling my mom she was unloved and unappreciated. Most of my uncles came with their wives, girlfriends, and kids, my sister and her kids, and unless I was being murdered, my mother would be very annoyed if Jerome and I missed it.

We watched Remiel walk the two and a half blocks home. Then I sent Jerome to bed and decided I would worry about black magic after the sun came up.

Chapter Nine

Brunch was a super noisy affair, as per usual. All seven of my living uncles had shown up, along with a handful of their kids. When my parents decided to start Angelville, my father designed a magical solarium, except he hadn't put plants in, or not many anyway. It did have a handful of beautiful, exotic plants, but most of the space was taken up by a huge table that would fit 50 people, even allowing for wings. It also had a huge buffet cabinet that housed plates, silverware, and had a stone countertop for placing hot pans on.

The buffet top was covered to capacity. The deal was everyone had to bring a dish, whatever they wanted, in exchange for a spot at the table. Even after hundreds of years, no one ever pretended they had forgotten a dish. Jerome and I came bearing three huge containers of waffles. We had gotten up early to make six different types of waffles, because while I was a decent cook, waffles were my specialty. There were chocolate chip, strawberry, blackberry, maple pecan, spicy, cinnamon and apple, and plain.

Everyone at the table knew I wasworking for Magda Red on a special case, and they all brought me books. There were multiple stacks totaling about a hundred books near the door of the solarium. Apparently creating magical copies of a book was a fairly easy task for all the archangels, albeit illegal. However, since none of these books had ever been in mass production and they were going to a family member, it wasn't a huge deal. If they did it for the purpose of profit, the AESPCA had a special division devoted to investigating crimes of that nature, and they came with hefty fines and jail time.

I thanked each of them individually, silently grateful that Remiel had brought his stack to my house the night before, since I was going to need Jerome's magical help getting all of them home. I had glanced quickly at the titles as my uncles stacked them, and I was feeling both a little overwhelmed and maybe a touch defeatist about all of the ancient tomes. Remiel took a seat next to me and whispered he'd be over after brunch to help Jerome and I create an index and help me find what I was looking for, since he'd read most of the books already.

Thankfully, his singed hair and eyebrows had recovered. He also told me he'd fix my window while he was there. I thanked him for his assistance and wondered if I was totally correct about Remiel's attention. Maybe it was about more than just my uncle being lonely. I couldn't pinpoint what exactly was bothering me about it, but there had been something that nagged at me as I'd gone to sleep the night before. I pushed the thought away quickly. I didn't want Remiel to know I was questioning his motives for hanging out with Jerome and I, especially since I didn't know why I felt there was something more to it. Or maybe I was just freaked out by it because I didn't believe someone thousands of years old would want to hang out with someone like me. I mean, I had first cousins that were thousands of years old that I'd never met.

Sunday brunch at my parents' house isn't about food. Yes, there's a lot of it and everyone is expected to bring something, but the food is just the excuse to get a couple dozen angels around a table talking to each other. My father and his brothers have jobs, and in some cases, families. Over the millennia they have moved apart and then back together and then apart again. My mom once told me when she met my father he was the only one of his family in Brittany, France, and they were married for more than 50 years before she met any of the others. Preventing that from happening again was the purpose of these Sunday brunches. Sometimes they go great, sometimes they end with a table flipped over and one or more angels storming out while vowing to never speak to someone else again. If a fight broke out, Mom would cancel the next week's brunch and work as mediator between the annoyed parties. Then in two or three weeks, we'd all be back here again.

Usually, I could tell whether it was going to be a quiet, chatty brunch or one in which a table got flipped within a few minutes of arriving. However, what happened at this brunch had never happened before. I was sitting across from Remiel thinking about lobster when the roof of the sunroom shattered and tiny shards of glass and pulverized glass dust rained down on all of us. Then something very heavy fell from the sky, hit the table with a loud thud, and the table collapsed. Stunned silence followed this commotion as we all tried to get a peek at what had literally crashed our brunch. Unfortunately, Jerome and I were sitting at the furthest end and the angels had stood up and spread their wings. There was a loud snort followed by some squeaky squeals, no doubt issued by the standing angels, and then there was movement that shook the walls and floor. Jerome stepped toward the kerfuffle, and I followed him.

Then it stood up. Large, squarish head, bright red in color, spikes on the top, with big pointy ears. The creature stretched its neck, and it was taller than the sunroom. For a crazy moment, my brain told me there was a red giraffe in my parents' sunroom and then my brain adjusted, and the word dragon screamed through my head. Except there are no dragons on Earth. They are pure carnivores that eat anything smaller than them, which includes archangels, elephants, and humans. They'd been sent to the Stygian by Zadkiel ages ago. I'd only seen a few dragons in my life, and most of the encounters had taken place in the Stygian. Dragons are huge and dangerous, but they are thankfully not particularly magical, which meant someone else had brought the dragon from the Stygian to my parents' house. This gave me two ideas; either a very powerful hell prince like Leviathan or Beelzebub had sent the dragon, or someone very powerful on this side of the Stygian had done it. I frowned. Bringing things across the divide was incredibly difficult. Jerome and I could do it, but traversing the divide was one of my innate powers.

"Soleil?" I heard someone say, and I blinked. Sometimes Leviathan turns souls into dragons, I'd dealt with one of those before. But this was an actual dragon; born to dragon parents, hatched from a large egg, and grew up in the Stygian. If it had been one of Leviathan's dragons, I could have sent it back like I did demons. I wasn't sure it worked the same for real dragons. No, I was positive it didn't. Dragons were flesh and blood creatures like unicorns and I had limits when it came to living, breathing beings and the Stygian. Interestingly, I was also positive the dragon was just as confused by being in my parents' sunroom as we were about its presence. Then Aurora took hold of my hand, it felt warm and I looked down at the little girl. I could almost see the magic vibrating off her and for a wild second I wondered if she had somehow summoned it.

"It doesn't want to be here," Aurora told me.

"Yeah." I nodded. "I don't suppose it knows how it got here?" I asked her. She shook her head.

"It's afraid!" Aurora replied, still shaking her head.

"Soleil!" The voice was adult and more urgent, and I finally recognized it as being Uriel's.

"It's a dragon; I don't know what you want me to do about it," I snapped.

"You exorcised a dragon in Chicago," Uriel replied.

"No, I exorcised a soul from a dragon form," I reminded him. "It wasn't a real dragon like this one. Any ideas, Aurora?" I asked, squeezing the girl's hand. At that point I realized Aurora had a faint glow around her, and her eyes had gone completely white. I went to pick her up, and my dad touched my shoulder.

"It's fine. She's young, big magic can do this to them," Raphael told me. I tried to tear my gaze away from Aurora to look at him, not sure I understood what he meant.

"Uh." I couldn't figure out how to say what I wanted to say. It looked like Aurora was about to explode like an overheated bomb. My experience with children was limited to Ariel and Aurora. Instead, I turned my attention back to the dragon. It was shaking its massive head.

"Aunt Asha, it wants to go home, send it home," Aurora pleaded. When I was a child, I had once torched my yard with Stygian fire, earning me the nickname Asha. While Soleil is a pretty name, it's not child-friendly, so both my nieces referred to me as Aunt Asha more often than not.

"If anyone has one of Zadkiel's books lying around with instructions on how to send living things to the Stygian, I would greatly appreciate reading it," I announced.

"You travel the distance, surely it isn't much different from sending yourself," Haniel said. I sighed. I was fairly sure sending people like myself and Jerome across was a fuck of a lot different than sending dragons across. For starters, part of me was attracted to the Stygian. Ditto for Jerome, since some of our magic came from there to begin with. Sending someone like Aurora or Haniel was a lot harder, because they didn't have a natural attraction to it. "I'll need emergency permission to open a large portal to send it back," I told everyone. Several people began searching around for cell phones. My mother forbids cell phones or any other digital device at the brunch table. She confiscated all of them as we came in, then she put them somewhere until brunch was over, at which point she gave them back to us.

"We'll have to call the AESPCA. How big of a portal?" Uriel asked.

"Big," I replied sarcastically. It was a dragon, not an imp or even a person. The portal would need to be big enough for the entire dragon to fit through, which meant there was the possibility something could come out. That was why portals were illegal, especially big ones. Without AESPCA approval, opening a portal like that could land me in jail for a couple of decades. I'd already been threatened with imprisonment after the Chicago incident. My mom appeared with a large basket and set it on the broken brunch table. People began digging for cell phones. Then the noise became unbearable as multiple people called other beings involved with the AESPCA.

"It's a fucking dragon!" My father's voice was suddenly louder than everyone else. My mother gave him a look that would have turned a mere mortal to stone. My father lowered his voice and the conversation continued with more swearing that I was almost sure my mom couldn't hear.

"I called Magda," Remiel said. I nodded. I had yet to think about the fact that dragons, cambions, and killer demons were all related, but once he said Magda's name it all clicked. Sadly, I didn't think it did much to further my investigation. I had another puzzle piece, but still didn't have a clue what kind of puzzle I was putting together or have any notion of what it might look like when completed. Also, it raised another question: Leviathan could send a hellhound and a unicorn across with Jerome's help, and he'd sent across a storm god and a soul in dragon form once without any help. Was it easier to send stuff across from their side of the divide? I always assumed the answer was no, or hell princes would be sending legions across to conquer the living. But it seemed possible that assumption was wrong, and something else prevented hell princes like Belial and Beelzebub from sending across hordes and legions.

There was another crash, and the wall of the sunroom exploded outward as Leviathan appeared. I gaped at him; had I been so wrapped up in my own thoughts I summoned him without realizing it?

Normally, if I summoned Leviathan or Lucifer, I did it outdoors because they were not structure-friendly. The appearance of a hell prince in this realm meant something had to be moved out of the way—walls, roofs, doors; wherever there was a weakness the structure gave way to make room for the new matter. Well, fuck, this was going to be an issue. Not just because I had taken out a wall of the sunroom, but because the AESPCA was on the way and I now had a dragon and a hell prince. It was going to be impossible to convince them I had not intended to bring either across the divide. Plus, I was certain I hadn't brought the dragon across. I was crunchy and tasted good to dragons. I actively avoided crossing over things that might want to eat me, which is why I would never summon Belial either.

"Soleil?" My father said my name as a question. I shrugged and looked at Jerome. Jerome shrugged back. If it wasn't me, Jerome was the only other person in the room capable of summoning a dragon or Leviathan. However, the teen looked as perplexed as I felt.

"That isn't one of my dragons, so there isn't much I can do about it," Leviathan said.

"I didn't summon you to deal with the dragon. I didn't summon it and I didn't mean to summon you," I said. "Unfortunately, I'm going to need to open a portal to send it back, so now you'll have to wait for me to get the approval to send you back." This was partially true. I could send Leviathan back via portal, but it wasn't a requirement. I could snap my fingers and send him back before the AESPCA arrived if I really wanted to, but I felt like the AESPCA needed to see everything: dragon and hell prince. Although I wasn't sure why I felt this was necessary, especially since I was sure I was going to get blamed for both of them being here.

"You cannot keep the dragon," Magda Red's voice suddenly said near me. "Is there something wrong with it? Normally, dragons are snapping and growling when they see people."

"I think Aurora is responsible for its tranquility," I said. "I assure you, I do not want a dragon. I have my hands full with the unicorn and hellhound."

"Why did you summon a dragon?" Magda asked.

"I didn't," I told her. "I don't think I summoned Leviathan, either. They both sort of appeared while we were having brunch."

"I see." Magda pulled out her phone and made a call. I heard her tell someone we had it under control and then she hung up. "If you didn't summon them, we need to find out who did, and that will be much harder to do if we have ten agents here who all believe you did."

"Magda, I swear I wasn't thinking about dragons. I did think about Leviathan, but I was busy trying to figure out how to get the dragon back across," I told her.

"I believe you." Magda nodded twice. "The dragon came through a portal, but it was opened from the other side. I can authorize you to open a portal to return it, but we need to figure out who or what opened a portal to our side. That isn't a skill most demons possess." She looked at

Leviathan. "What do you know of it, hell prince?" she asked him.

"Only a few of us are strong enough to open portals. Every demon should know about it when one is opened, yet I didn't know there was a dragon here until I arrived," Leviathan answered, looking down at her. "If this is being done by a demon, it means there is about to be a great power shift in the Stygian, because another hell prince is about to rise."

"There's never been more than ten," Raphael said. "It is one of the protections Jophiel and Zadkiel built in."

"Correct, for another to rise one must fall." Leviathan nodded.

"Crazy question: could the new hell prince be on this side?" I asked.

"It is not you or the boy," Leviathan said. "You are both fated to eventually be hell princes, we feel it in your souls, but you are not in that position yet."

"No, I meant if a demon were somehow living on this side, could it become a hell prince?" I asked.

"In theory, yes. In reality, I doubt it. That would require the new hell prince to be a cambion no one has found yet. So, unless someone is raising a cambion in secret somewhere..." Leviathan did a complicated gesture that might have been a shrug or might have been something else I didn't understand.

"Everything I've discovered the last day or so seems impossible, and yet, has to have happened," I said.

"Cambions make humans and supernaturals both physically and emotionally uncomfortable. If a cambion had taken up residence anywhere in the world, people would have noticed by now," Leviathan said.

"People avoided about a ten-mile area around where Azazael lived when he was on Earth," Raphael said.

"But it can be overcome; Magda was partnered with a cambion," I pointed out, and Magda turned dark eyes on me. "I didn't mean that disrespectfully, I just meant it can be done."

"It can, but Leviathan's correct, it would be noticed. The living are repelled by the semi-living, fractured cambion soul," Magda said. "We lived near each other, but not together, and once we had our son, living near each other became a burden. It is part of why he gave up on life, with two cambion living together, everyone avoided them as much as possible. I was their connection to the outside world, and I struggled to be near them. I don't think the average person could do it." I considered this. I didn't feel uncomfortable around either demons or cambion. However, I'd been told a lot of people do feel uncomfortable around demons. I always figured it was a visceral reaction to the idea of it, sort of like a placebo effect. However, if what Magda said was true, maybe it wasn't a mental thing, maybe demons and cambions really could make people feel uncomfortable or even bad, like a virus.

"It is still more likely the demon responsible is traveling from one side to the other somehow." Uriel said. "I assume you always know when you are responsible for summoning a demon?"

"Yes," I nodded while frowning. "It might not be big magic for me, but it's enough that I know it's been done, even if I do it in my sleep." And yet, Leviathan was sitting in the sunroom and I didn't think I had summoned him. "Leviathan, did I summon you here?"

"Yes and no," the hell prince answered. "It was your magic that pulled me at first, but there was something else with it, something demonic." What the fuck? Surely I would know if I was possessed, wouldn't I? I'd always noticed it in the past. Or I thought I had.

"You're not possessed. I would know," Jerome told me.

"Are you sure?" I asked, raising an eyebrow.

"Yes, you can see souls, remember," Jerome retorted.

"I can only see souls of the dead," I replied.

"Yes, but if you were demonically possessed, I would see the demon soul in you and I haven't seen one." I nodded, and then under Magda's watchful eye I opened a portal to send both the dragon and Leviathan back to the Stygian.

Chapter Ten

With the dragon and hell prince gone, Magda asked if she could join Jerome and I this afternoon at my house. We agreed and Remiel followed us out of my parents' house. We'd only gotten a few feet outside when Jerome stopped us, muttering something about a magical lilac bush and how it hadn't been magical when we arrived. Sometimes I worry the amount of magic at Jerome's disposal is going to drive him mad. As he muttered, I had one of those moments. No one had used the word omnipotent to describe Jerome, but I had suspicions that under the right circumstances it was possible there was nothing the teen couldn't do, including making new worlds and creating life if he desired. I'd been brushing up on some family history and learned that part of the reason Zadkiel decided to die was because of the immense power he'd wielded. Jophiel didn't die, but had a similar problem, and that info had made me worry even more about Jerome. On top of that, Leviathan had informed me that most of the truly evil supernaturals that had once lived had been driven crazy by power; not the pursuit of it, but the amount they had. I'd spent several sleepless nights having nightmares about Jerome becoming like Ramses or Darius. Men who had been truly great until they decided to slaughter oodles of people or commit other atrocities.

Leviathan told me part of my responsibility as Jerome's guardian was to help prevent this kind of madness from taking hold. Truth was, I wasn't sure I was up to the task. Eventually, I'd broken down and confessed all to Jerome and he'd told me I was a doing a great job because just being part of his support network was one of the prevention measures. But as the teen muttered about magic bushes, I was assailed by doubts. I watched him walk over to the lilac bush and begin trying to get through the leaves and branches. My mom wasn't magical, but she had a hell of green thumb and her plants were amazing. My lilac bush was a miserable shrub in comparison. Jerome made a noise and then straightened up.

He was holding a large, pinkish, translucent stone. We all gaped at it. Quartz and limestone are natural amplifiers of magic. It was part of the reason so many supernaturals had moved to St. Louis; the area was inundated with natural quartz and limestone formations. You couldn't dig a hole in the region and not turn up a pile of rocks containing quartz. However, refined chunks of pink quartz did not naturally occur under lilac bushes. Somehow, quartz absorbed magic and then doubled it. Magic users could buy quartz amplifiers in pendants and other forms of jewelry to wear to help them use less of their own magic. In my personal experience, though, quartz also made magic go a little haywire. I avoided owning anything with quartz because in high school, when I'd participated in the magic classes that dealt with quartz, any manner of things were likely to go wrong when it was around my magic. My worst, though, had been the accidental summoning of four dozen imps into the classroom when I'd been trying to learn to move a glass. Needless to say, the glass got moved, then broken, then trampled on by the imps and a half dozen classmates suffered bites from the infernal things. Helia kept some refined quartz in her house to help her do everyday magic, which was part of the reason we hung out at my house and not hers.

Someone or something had put the quartz in the lilac bush while my family had been enjoying brunch. Which might explain why I summoned Leviathan by thinking I needed to ask him a question. It didn't explain the dragon exactly, unless maybe Aurora had been thinking about dragons and had the ability to summon as well as talk to animals. Or perhaps the quartz had been used as a homing beacon for the portal opener to send the dragon to my parents' house. Magda had said the AESPCA knew the portal had opened, and it had opened from the other side.

"You realize this means I need someone to cast some negation spells on the sunroom? I opened a portal in there. I'm shocked nothing went wrong when I did, and if the area isn't neutralized there's enough quartz underground to hold the spell," I said, looking at Magda and Remiel. Magda was talking on her phone. Using her free hand, she produced a large bag from thin air and handed it to Jerome. Jerome put the pink quartz in the bag and handed it back to Magda Red.

"A neutralization team is on the way, as well as an investigative team," Magda said after she put her phone back into her pocket.

"I have a super crazy idea," I told her in response. "What if the demon is the head of this thing, and he has someone here helping him?"

"I was thinking the same thing."

"That works only up to a point," Jerome said. "None of the demons we've talked to believe it's a demon involved."

"Maybe they are lying or being kept in the dark," Magda suggested. Jerome snorted out a quick chuckle.

"What?" Magda asked him.

"I just forget most people have spent eons avoiding demons and therefore don't realize what incredible gossips demons are," Jerome replied. "There is no such thing as a demonic secret. It's why the demon spy network is so large, once Soleil started it, she had demons asking her if they could join, because every demon knows about it. Not just in the Stygian, but the ones being hosted on Earth have been informed as well. Possessed people controlled by their demons have shown up at both our house and the office asking if they could join. The flow of Stygian gossip has never crossed the divide until recently, but that's because no one has been willing to listen to it before, not because it didn't exist. Soleil rewards her informants for passing info across the divide. As I understand it, demons are incorrigible gossips, and she rewards them for the copious quantities of information they give her," Jerome told her.

Magda then asked the tricky question of what kind of information I could get from the Stygian gossip network. I sighed and debated what to tell her. Finally, I confessed I knew who was making and selling the "prank" demon boxes that were popping up all over the place. The idea of demon boxes had been lost to history for thousands of years until the previous fall. Now they were somewhat in vogue. However, these were not real demon boxes. The demon boxes that had become popular summoned imps, which were bothersome but not as dangerous as demons.

"Keeping this info from the AESPCA is for job security?" Magda snapped, obviously pissed off at me.

"No, I went and talked to the makers and we reached an agreement. They wouldn't make anything dangerous, and if they got orders for one that was supposed to summon dragons or hell princes, they would let me know. So far, they haven't and I haven't bothered with their schoolboy hijinks." I sighed again.

"It's a group then?" Magda asked.

"Of course it's a group," I replied. "Demon boxes might be illegal, but they are now out in the world again. My solution means we are unlikely to be surprised by one that is super bad and keeps the "prank" boxes in circulation to create only minor havoc."

"That wasn't your decision to make." Magda snapped again.

"I don't trust the AESPCA not to make the situation worse, so I took the matter into my own hands. If the AESPCA raids these guys and shuts it down, which they will, then people who want them will turn to the internet to get plans to make their own. Most people can't do the magic involved and shit is going to go very wrong. It's an inelegant solution to a serious problem, I admit, but we haven't had to deal with Belial crashing through towns."

"Why?" Magda asked.

"Because I could imagine a room full of teenaged boys trying to make one and accidentally releasing a horde of dragons on their town or school or summer camp."

"Or poltergeists," Jerome added.

"Or hell princes," Remiel quipped quietly.

"All of you knew about it and kept mum?" Magda asked.

"Yes, Soleil is correct. It's not a perfect solution, but it does prevent bigger problems. We gave the makers a list of things the boxes could safely summon—imps, demonlings, brakku—things of that nature, and a list of things we wanted to know about immediately if they got a custom order request," Remiel said.

Brakku were algae spirits; when summoned they coated dry land in algae slime, but didn't really do any damage unless they were put into water. In lakes, brakku mutated all the fish and turned the water brackish. Eating the mutated fish or swimming in the water mutated people into merpeople, and they were dangerous. Which was why the brakku were in the Stygian. The Dead Sea still hadn't recovered from the brakku that had lived in it for six weeks sometime before the reign of Ramses III of Egypt. I had seriously questioned Remiel about his putting brakku on the list, and it turned out they couldn't live in flowing water, such as a river. They required a contained body of water like a pond or lake. Even in a pond or lake, too much rain could kill them; flowing water was oxygen rich, and unlike fish, brakku breathed carbon dioxide, meaning they needed stagnant, oxygen-poor water to live. They were also really hideous. I'd made a point to see one in the Stygian; they resembled fish with flat heads, wide faces, and fins that worked like feet. They were brown and orange with tealish colored stripes. They also had massive teeth that reminded me of a dog's. Overall a very strange creature.

We stopped talking as a van full of people pulled up. The blue van had the AESPCA logo on the side. Some strange part of me expected them to be wearing hazmat suits and was slightly disappointed when they weren't. I didn't know any of them, although I recognized one man as an angel that I had crossed paths with before. Then the driver got out and waved. I did know him; he was dating my sister. His name was Kabal. He was an angel and had worked protection for Jerome and I once. He had nieces about the same age as Ariel and Aurora, which is how he'd met Helia.

The arrival of the AESPCA team brought the rest of my family either out of their houses, which they'd returned to, or out of my parents' where they were helping with the devastated sunroom. A woman I didn't recognize did some magic, and red footsteps magically appeared on the ground leading from the sidewalk and road to the lilac bush. Magda informed everyone about the quartz Jerome had found in the lilac bush, and we were all interviewed to see if we'd noticed anything out of the ordinary. When asked this by a witch named Annabeth, I raised my eyebrows at her. She tried to clarify, but the truth was everything about my family is out of the ordinary and a little weird. I mean, ten archangels had only produced a handful of archangel children, and my human mother had birthed two of that handful; then my half-angel sister had birthed two more with a human father, and unlike most families, mine didn't wander away from each other. Ancient families like mine didn't maintain close relationships with siblings or children or cousins or nieces and nephews, and yet, the majority of my family lived in a

20-mile radius. Even my hermit uncle Michael, who lived in a cave, was now within that radius. Don't get me wrong; it is a nice cave, but it's a cave.

Hundreds of years ago, my uncle Michael bought a cliff with a natural cave in it. Then he built a house into the contours of the cave, including a front door with a lock. It's very well insulated and he doesn't require luxuries like air conditioning, but it's obvious that it's a cave. I'd only been there twice in my entire life and I'd felt damp both times when I'd left. Somehow he has running water and other modern conveniences, but I think it's weird even for an archangel.

Jerome, as a minor, was questioned with me present and repeated his statement that the lilac bush hadn't been magical when we arrived for brunch, but had been when we left. I didn't know the man who questioned him at all, but he had a file on Jerome, which made me uncomfortable. I was going to ask Magda Red about it when this was over. Also, the file seemed useless, since Jerome had to repeatedly explain that he could see magic. Then came the real questions, like had Jerome summoned the dragon. He swore he hadn't, but I wasn't sure the guy believed him because he kept pressing him on it. After the guy rephrased the question for the tenth time, Jerome asked him why the hell he'd summon something that might eat him? So, the guy rephrased the question to make it seem like he was sympathetic and Jerome was a teenager who occasionally did silly things by accident. However, Jerome was unshakeable on the fact that he didn't summon the dragon. He wasn't conspiring with anyone to summon dragons. He didn't think dragons were cool or nifty or neat, he thought they were bloody dangerous and unpredictable. Then he said he might have accidentally summoned Leviathan. He didn't look at me as he said this. He told the guy that he was thinking of questions that needed to be asked of Leviathan about the dragon when the hell prince suddenly appeared in the sunroom, and that sometimes when he was around quartz, his magic went a little wonky, even in his protected classrooms. When there was quartz, he cast spells without realizing he was doing it.

"I'm a mimic," Jerome said to the guy.

"And quartz acts like a mimic," the guy said slowly. Jerome nodded.

Jerome knew more about magic than any other person I'd ever met. There is a theoretical record of all of history called the Akashic Record. It has been suggested to me that Jerome might be tapped into it somehow. At times I doubted both the Akashic Record and Jerome being able to get information from it, and at other times, like now, I believed it was probably true. He'd once explained to me that quartz set my magic wild because I didn't have small magic, it was all big magic, and when amplified and repeated by quartz it couldn't be handled. I was still trying to wrap my head around the concept of big magic and little magic. Jerome was trying to teach it to me, but I had been willfully ignorant about magic all my life and learning about it now that I was in my forties was a challenge.

"Are we done?" I asked after a few minutes of silence.

"You opened the portal?" the guy asked me. No one had introduced us, and I didn't have a clue what his name was, but I didn't like him.

"I opened the second portal with Magda Red's supervision," I said.

"We're done for now," the man said. I stood up from where I'd been sitting on the grass. Jerome stood up a moment later. We were allowed to go home. We walked the half mile to our house to find Remiel in the backyard with Angel playing fetch with a soccer ball.

"If anyone asks, I accidentally summoned Leviathan at the brunch," Jerome told me sternly.

"Did you?" I asked.

"No, I'm pretty sure that was your magic coming in contact with the quartz, but that guy thinks you're involved with the killings, so we should all just agree that I did it accidentally." Jerome told me. I frowned. "I know you didn't intend to summon Leviathan, but around people who think you're a killer, it's better they don't know you can randomly and unknowingly summon hell princes."

Chapter Eleven

Once home, I took Jerome and Remiel to Jerome's game room and summoned half a dozen demons to ask about the portal that had released the dragon. I picked three dukes and three counts. The dukes were loyal to the hell princes I trusted, the counts were from hell princes that were semi-neutral, and then I added a minor demon of Belial's stock, leaving just Beelzebub and Mammon unrepresented. However, it was obvious they didn't know any more than I did. I sent all of them back except Dantalian. Him I invited to sit. Remiel stepped out to grab Ashtoreth's duke some cold pizza and a soda, while I asked how someone in the Stygian could be up to nefarious deeds and no one know about it.

Remiel returned with the food and drink and Magda Red. I didn't say anything about this sudden addition to the party, but I had concerns about it. Technically, it wasn't illegal to summon demons, but I figured when confronted with it someone in a position of power, like Magda, might find a way to arrest me for it. Especially since the incubus was in physical form. Magda said nothing and didn't even give me a dirty look. She took a seat on the couch between Remiel and Jerome and just watched as I interrogated Dantalian about how a demon could open a portal without anyone knowing. He ate the pizza and drank the Dr Pepper as we talked. Remiel had been smart enough to bring the entire box of leftover pizza as well as the 12-pack of Dr Pepper. Dantalian ate the entire half a pizza and drank three sodas. Sugar wasn't a thing in the Stygian, and he was a bit of a sugar junkie. I sent the rest of the soda back with him.

The consensus was there was only one way for a demon to use a portal and have no one know about it; it had to be one of the original portals. When Zadkiel and Jophiel had designed the Stygian, they'd had to create a few portals, and those portals had remained open long after the Stygian was finished. I'd been told that they'd attempted to dissolve them without any luck, and so now they were guarded. The hotel I'd stayed at in Chicago had housed one in the basement. There were ten or so original portals, spread all over the world. North America had two; one in Chicago and one in Mexico City. In theory they couldn't move their locations, but there wasn't an original portal in St. Louis. If a demon went missing for a long time to say, kill and have a cambion, other demons would notice. Which ruled out the idea they were coming through the Chicago portal and then making the four-hour trek to St. Louis to cause mayhem and mischief.

But again, that was theory, because time in the Stygian didn't work exactly like time here did. It wasn't even a constant in the Stygian. Time moved slower around the more powerful hell princes and Lucifer, which I understood to mean they had their own gravity to some degree, unless time just worked completely different there. However, having visited several times over the last year or so, I was certain the Stygian was actually a different planet, possibly in a different galaxy, and that time should be at least somewhat similar to ours. It had a sun and multiple moons as well as stars in the sky at night, which was why I thought it was a planet. Oddly, the stars were different than our stars. Or possibly, all the magic involved in the Stygian was why time didn't work exactly the same. It wouldn't really surprise me to learn that Lucifer, Beelzebub, Leviathan, Ashtaroth, and Belial were strong enough that they created their own minor gravitational force.

"Except portals can't be moved," Remiel said, after we had all sat in silence for a long time. "If they could be moved, we would have moved all of them to a more secure location ages ago."

"Do you do that often?" Magda finally spoke to me.

"Not really. Today we needed information in a hurry. While demons gossip, sometimes it takes a while to get through all the kingdoms, which is why I summoned demons from seven of the ten hell princes. However, anything Beelzebub knows, Belial knows. And Mammon's lot can lie, which is why I didn't bother to summon from either Beelzebub or Mammon's demons."

"They seemed absolutely determined to give you information," Magda said.

"That's because while we spoke Jerome sent bags of cookies to each of them in the Stygian. Demons love sugar; cake, cookies, pie, waffles, soda, sweet tea. But sugar isn't available to them in the Stygian. They'd sell out their hell princes for enough sugar," I said.

"Or carbs," Jerome added. "Demons love bread and pizza too. For today, I sent the cookies before Soleil summoned them. If one of them could have told us which demon opened the portal to release the dragon, I would have sent that demon a loaf of bread afterward. They couldn't, so I sent each of them a slice just to be nice."

"Like Wonder Bread?" Magda asked.

"Soleil doesn't buy things like Wonder Bread. She stops at a bakery near her office to get bread loaves. She buys extra for bribing demons," Jerome said. I nodded.

"And food is really all you give them?" Magda asked.

"Yes." I pointed toward the empty pizza box. "Surely you noticed how much Dantalian was enjoying the pizza while we spoke. f I give them food here, around me where they remember their humanity, they enjoy it even more. Dantalian pre-dated the invention of pizza, but he definitely approves."

"They do get something else," Remiel said. "We've noticed the demons that work with Soleil, like Dantalian, are getting more powerful. Four years ago, Dantalian was a count; he's moved up to being a duke in the last year or so and soon he'll be a demi-prince."

"Are you afraid of them?" Magda asked.

"No, and until today, I didn't know most beings were physically uncomfortable around demons. I thought it was all mental. However, my reactions to demons are limited. With Dantalian, I feel the pull of the incubus but it isn't overwhelming, and he doesn't make me uncomfortable unless he's trying to make me uncomfortable, and then it's just my prudishness, not him."

"Ashtoreth and Leviathan suspect it's because Soleil could be a living hell prince if she wanted. To prevent horrible things from happening, once we realized demons were gaining power with their loyalty to Soleil, we made a list of demons we could summon with most of the hell princes, allowing them to pick demons they believe loyal, especially with the demons that were already stronger, like Dantalian. Ashtoreth actually wants Dantalian to become a demi-prince, so if we need to summon from his line, we always try to summon Dantalian."

"How strange," Magda said.

"Agreed. The guy that interviewed Jerome had a file on him. Why?" I blurted out.

"The AESPCA has files on all supernaturals. They are reference guides, mostly. They list powers, affiliations, and that kind of stuff," Magda replied.

"The guy didn't seem very informed about Jerome from his file," I said.

"A great deal of Jerome's file is top secret," Magda said.

"That's weird," Jerome said.

"Not really. We do not know the limits of your powers or if you even have any limits. However, not everyone that works at the AESPCA needs to know that. Just like not everyone at the AESPCA needs to know that Soleil can command an army of demons both in the Stygian and here. That information is in there, but without clearance it can't be read." Magda told him. "There is more stuff in your file that is secret than hers. However, if I decide to put the Demon Information Network in the file I will make it top secret, too."

"If?" Remiel asked.

"I'm not sure it's something those in power above me need to know. I'm sorta surprised you let all your brothers know. I could see Uriel having problems with it," Magda said, looking at Remiel. I wondered about Magda's English. She wouldn't have been born into an English-speaking family. It would have been learned much later; I wasn't even sure English was around when Magda was born. Given her use of slang and colloquialisms, I didn't get the impression she'd learned English from a Brit. I also doubted she'd been speaking it for hundreds of years. The problem was that supernaturals who weren't exceptionally adaptive in all areas of their lives were maladjusted to modern living and ended up living in caves hiding from the world or worse. My father and uncles were prime examples; as technology advanced and the cultures they lived in evolved, they immersed themselves in the new stuff and learned all they could about it. Sometimes I worried about this for me; in a few hundred years would I be speaking an archaic version of American English, unable to use whatever passed for telephones?

"He found out by accident and we expected him to turn her in to the AESPCA for unauthorized demonic dealings or something." Remiel shrugged. "Then he got a list of all demons currently in possession of a host and decided it could be a useful thing."

"We already have that kind of list," Magda said.

"No, you have a list of registered demons and their hosts. This list goes beyond that list, giving Uriel and Azrael an idea of how many accidental and non-intentional possessions are happening right now. The ones that may only last a few days or few weeks and happen because people are people. Not the ones who register and intend to be possessed," Remiel said.

"Oh!" Magda's eyes widened. "Meaning they have a list of all possessed people on Earth right now."

"No, they have a list of demons in possession of hosts," I corrected. "Knowing a demon is here and not there, doesn't tell us who is possessed, it just tells us the names of the demons being hosted. Unfortunately, it has to be updated frequently. At least once a week because accidental possessions are constantly changing."

"Pretend I don't know much about possession of any sort..." Magda said. Here was the problem—I liked Magda but I wasn't sure I trusted her yet.

"These are mostly teen and child possessions from playing with Ouija boards and trying to summon ghosts," I said.

"About 75 percent of all supernatural teenagers will become possessed at some point during their teen years. The majority of them are accidental possessions. Then there are curse possessions, another popular thing with teens," Jerome said. "At my school there is a possession monitor spell set up around the cafeteria that quietly lets Principal Grace know when a student has become possessed. It goes off about once a month."

"If it's quiet how do you know how frequently it goes off?" Magda asked.

"Soleil can see demonic spirits in people. I live with her and I'm a mimic," Jerome said.

"From what we can tell at any given time, there are around 3,000 accidental possessions in progress," I said. "There are hundreds of ways a supernatural teen can become possessed by accident. When the weather is warm

I average ten exorcisms a month. When it's cold, it goes up to about 15 exorcisms a month."

"That's more than I expected," Magda said.

"It was more than I expected when I first started working with Soleil, as well. Now I'm more surprised when I meet a teen that isn't possessed than when one is. Jerome's generation doesn't bully by giving wedgies in the locker room, they bully by causing demonic possession."

"Not me," Jerome said. "But she's correct. There's one kid at my school who is basically untouchable. He threatens kids with possession if they don't do what he wants." Magda made a strange face at this information.

"Leonard Vance's kid," I said, by way of explanation. As a witch, I knew Magda would know Leonard Vance, and I also knew that punishment for Bradley Vance usually meant a loss of pocket money, not that this mattered because then he shook down his classmates for more money. Leonard Vance sat on the Witch Council as well as the board of Jerome's school. The family was rich and magically powerful. Personally, I hated Leonard Vance and kinda wished he'd spontaneously combust. His kid was way worse.

"I wouldn't have thought Principal Grace was intimidated by Leonard Vance," Magda said.

"I don't think she is. I think punishing Bradley Vance is problematic for her; the board can overrule her decisions on disciplinary action and Leonard Vance isn't interested in punishing his son," I said.

"How much of your money has Bradley taken?" Magda asked Jerome.

"None. Try as he might, he can't cause me to become possessed; I'm more powerful than he is. He did have a spell backfire in class that caused one of our teachers to become possessed. However, I was in class when it happened and with Principal Grace's assistance, we performed an exorcism on him right there in her office. She called Soleil as backup in case it failed, but..." Jerome finished his sentence with a shrug.

Chapter Twelve

I awoke with the knowledge that someone was going to die tonight if I didn't figure out which demon was killing people and how. I'd read the books my uncles had given me until after three in the morning, and I was no closer to figuring out what was going on than I had been before I got them. Jerome had helped me and we'd gotten through several books, so I was slightly disappointed that we hadn't had a eureka moment. However, while showering, I did have one, sort of, maybe. It had to be Azazael. Azazael wasn't dead, he was in an unknown state like his father. His soul had been exorcised from his body while alive and put into the Stygian.

Azazael was also the main demon involved in anything that related to death and chaos. All demons found chaos helpful, but most didn't intentionally kill. Azazael did.

"Somehow Azazael is involved," Jerome said as he came into the kitchen.

"Huh, I was about to tell you the same thing," I said.

"His movements aren't tracked like the other demons because he doesn't have a hell prince to answer to and he's basically a hermit there," Jerome said. "He can probably do a number of things that other demons don't know about."

"Like plan rebellions against his father." I nodded.

"The problem is, Azazael doesn't have a physical form anymore," Jerome said.

"Right," I agreed. That had struck me, too. Jophiel's corpse was buried under my house because it refused to decompose. It had been moved from Chicago to under my house in Chesterfield when the Chicago house had burned down. Now, it had moved again to reside under the floor of the house in Angelville. From what I knew about Azazael, his corpse had done the opposite; the moment his soul had been exorcised, it had turned to dust. "Is it possible the rapid decomposition of his corpse resulted in him getting a demon body?"

"No, he's cambion, he had a spiritual form and a physical one and the physical one decomposed," Jerome said. "Well, almost no. I suspect there's a way, but I think it would require Zadkiel's creation knowledge and some outside help."

"Outside help?" I raised an eyebrow.

"I think it would require Zadkiel," Jerome said. "I'm not sure Leviathan could stand in for Zadkiel even though it's the same soul. But this is all extremely theoretical."

"I was wondering if he could take the body of an infant, like Beelzebub did," I said. "Well shit, I need to go to the Stygian today and find Azazael."

"Maybe not the body of a supernatural infant but the body of a cambion infant?" Jerome asked. I nodded. "But he wouldn't be able to kill as an infant." I nodded again. "If you go looking for Azazael, I expect you to take living beings and a few demons with you," he said with a heavy sigh.

I dug out my cell phone and called Magda Red. I explained my new thoughts to her about Azazael and told her Jerome was worried about me going to the Stygian alone to look for Azazael. She agreed with Jerome, and then I did something unexpected even to myself.

"Magda, would you call the witch school and find a way to get Jerome out of classes today? I think as a fellow coven member Kim Grace will acquiesce to your request to excuse Jerome better than she would me."

"Plus, I can make up an excuse better than you about why I need Jerome to assist you today on my case?" Magda said, and I was sure she was smiling.

"Exactly. I will take Jerome and one of my uncles and arrange to work with Leviathan once we are in the Stygian," I told her. She agreed and we hung up.

"Does that work for you?" I asked Jerome as I considered which of my uncles to text. Eventually, I texted Remiel, Gabriel, and my father. Within ten minutes all three of the archangels were at my house. There was some half-hearted debate about my going to the Stygian to look for Azazael, but I could tell all three of them realized it needed to be done. Then I had to call Magda back. I could transport myself to the Stygian with little effort and Jerome could do the same, but the other three archangels would require a portal, because if I took them with me there was a chance something could go wrong and I could lose one of them. Magda translocated into our house, setting off the magical alarms Jerome had installed. I tried not to glare at her.

"Why not just take one?" Magda asked.

141

"Because I'm not an idiot. When people go it alone they get hurt or dead, and I'm not ready to begin my rise to hell prince. There is safety in numbers," I said. "Working for you, even covertly, you can authorize me to open a portal big enough for the five of us." She agreed, but muttered something about me being a pain in the ass. I could see her point of view. I opened a portal and all five of us went through.

The Stygian reminds me of rover pictures of Mars. The earth is a brick red color. Rocks, dirt, nearly everything is brick red, and the soil is very loose compared to the soil I was used to in Missouri. It got everywhere in a hurry and coated everything in a fine dust. The sun is brighter than ours and a little hotter. There are trees with nearly black bark, the leaves are brick red either because they are coated in dust or because they absorb whatever it is in the soil that causes it to be red. There is grass; in the urban areas it is yellow and scrubby like desert grass. When you moved away from the cities, it became thick, tall, and lush, yet remained yellowish.

The portal exit was in Leviathan's courtyard. Leviathan and the other hell princes live in what I would describe as medieval style castles made of brick red stone. Each was circled by a moat and a wall of the same red stone used for the castles. Demons walk ramparts on the walls. Outside the castle wall and moat is a large urban area of apartments built of stone that the hell prince's demons inhabit. Leviathan has the smallest number of demons in his service and so has the smallest urban center. I knew there were stables and farms outside his urban center. Demons do not require food to eat, but Leviathan is all about his creations and most of them, as well as the animals sent from Earth to the Stygian, do require food and the farms are for the animals more than the demons.

The courtyard was filled with hellhounds, some strange birds, and demons. I knew immediately we'd shown up during feeding time for Leviathan's legion of hellhounds. Leviathan's hellhounds are all much larger than Angel. Angel was the runt of a litter, and was specifically set aside for Jerome and I; A gift from Leviathan to protect us. Hellhounds can eat the souls of the living, and in theory, Angel could use that to protect us from someone trying to do us harm. Unfortunately, she'd been too young to do this when my house was firebombed and Valerie mortally injured. I'd never seen a hellhound eat a soul, but I was sure I'd have nightmares about it if I ever did.

Most of the demons waved to me. I waved back. No one commented on this, which was good, because if they had I wouldn't have known what to say to them. Every demon loyal to Leviathan was sorta my friend. I walked a very tight rope between thinking of demons as my friends and trying to remember they were dangerous to me as well as mankind. Sometimes I fell off and began thinking positively of demons, which was bad. They were like tigers in captivity—most of the time they were fine, but once in a while they remembered you were food. It was my responsibility to remember I was food all the time, no matter how friendly the demons were.

The door opened before we got up the stairs leading to it, and Leviathan stepped out.

"You are creating quite the stir, Exorcist," Leviathan said to me. "My demons are wondering if arriving with a party means you are here to cause mayhem."

"No, I need to find Azazael and make sure he's still in the Stygian," I responded.

"Ah, yes." Leviathan nodded. "And you want my assistance while making sure."

"I would like it," I agreed. "Last I heard he was living on the outskirts of Belial's territory."

"You definitely cannot enter Belial's territory alone," Leviathan said. "But Belial has allies and I alone can't protect you."

"What do you recommend?" I asked.

"Going home." Leviathan sighed and sat down on the steps of his castle. "I know you won't, but that is what I would recommend. We can take Asmodeus and pick up Ashtoreth along the way and maybe a few other powerful demons, because Belial and Azazael have formed an alliance. Belial will not agree to let you check on Azazael without persuasion."

"And if I don't want violence?" I asked.

"Go home." Leviathan told me. I had humiliated Belial. And he'd wanted possession of my soul before I'd done that. Leviathan was correct, Belial wouldn't just accept me coming into his territory to check on his favorite pet. Some part of me had known this before I came to the Stygian. Consciously or not, it was why I had texted Gabriel and my father. Remiel was a good man and an archangel, but I had battled demons with Gabriel and Raphael more than Remiel, and I wanted them at my back because I knew Belial would not accept my presence without a fight. I considered leaving Jerome at Leviathan's castle, protected by his demons and hellhounds, but I knew the teen wouldn't agree. I couldn't blame him; if roles were reversed I wouldn't have agreed to be left behind.

We were protected in Leviathan's territory and could walk to Ashtoreth's, but I could open portals in the Stygian and it seemed like the safer and faster mode of transport. I opened a portal to Ashtoreth's territory. Leviathan called his hellhounds and the six of us set off.

Ashtoreth's territory was more urban than Leviathan's. The city beyond his castle walls had skyscrapers full of incubi and succubae. When they aren't in possession of a host, demons sit around and chat the time away. They don't have jobs, but they are sentient beings and have to spend their time doing something—it was one of the reasons for the copious amounts of gossip in the Stygian. They have things like board games and cards, but when you don't have to eat and you don't sleep much, you have to while away the hours somehow, and they do it by hanging out and talking amongst themselves, usually within their own societies, which were made up of demons of the same hell prince. However, Dantalian had assured me that the factions of the hell princes hung out with each other as well, it was just more complicated.

We found Ashtoreth hosting a group of demons and playing something that resembled dominoes in the courtyard of his castle. Among them was Dantalian and another demon I was very familiar with, Nandia. Nandia was a succubae on the rise, who enjoyed pizza almost as much as Dantalian. When I told Ashtoreth why I was there, he agreed to come with us and volunteered Dantalian and Nandia to join as well. Both the demons agreed readily and joined the group. I was about to open another portal when Ashtoreth told me we had one more stop to make; he wanted to stop and collect Belgaphor. I was less excited by this prospect, but Ashtoreth assured me that Belgaphor had issues with Belial and the enemy of my enemy. I agreed simply because if Belial had help from Beelzebub, I wasn't sure I had enough strength on my side without more hell princes. There was a reason Beelzebub was at the top of the hell prince hierarchy. Sure enough, after picking up Belgaphor and a few of his dukes and demi-princes, we arrived at the border of Belial's territory to find that he and Beelzebub were together and waiting for us.

"I just want confirmation that Azazael is in the Stygian," I shouted to Belial.

"Would you take my word for it?" Belial countered.

"Why? You obviously don't trust me enough to take my word that all I want is to see Azazael with my own two eyes," I replied. The hell prince looked at Beelzebub and I didn't know if he wanted clarification or if they were preparing to attack.

"We have no reason to trust you, Exorcist!" He hissed the last word, and I felt the tell-tale buzzing sensation in my skull that made my brain feel foggy and somewhat painful.

"If I wanted to engage in hostilities, Beelzebub, I would have come alone and I wouldn't have started in Leviathan's territory. I simply would have entered the

Stygian outside Azazael's door." The hell princes exchanged another look.

"If all you really want is to see Azazael for yourself, come across and I will take you to him," Belial said. I was shaking my head no before he'd even finished the sentence.

"Belial, you and I both know I employ a network of demons to give me information, and they have told me you placed a bounty on my soul. As such, I cannot trust you or the demons within your territory, including Azazael, to not attempt to take my soul if I cross into your territory. I did not come here for a fight, but I won't back down from one if you force me into it. I will not give you an advantage by separating me from my allies, and I do not trust you to keep any oath regarding my safety. Instead, I ask you to bring Azazael here to the border to let me see him."

"I have no power to command Azazael, Exorcist, and you know it. He is not one of my demons; there is nothing that binds us. He resides here because he is my friend," Belial snipped.

"I believe Azazael is preparing to take over a position as hell prince. The only way he can achieve that is to take it from one of the current hell princes and since he resides in your territory..." I trailed off and shrugged. But I could tell by his stiffened posture that Belial understood what I was implying and had some doubts about Azazael.

"I can command him to come, if you will allow me to use my magic across your territory. If he's here, we'll both get peace of mind," I called out. Beelzebub protested, but to my surprise, Belial agreed. I quietly pushed magic toward Belial's territory, and thought about how the division between Beelzebub and Belial might come in handy at a later date. Beelzebub wanted to replace Lucifer as king of the Stygian. In theory, so did Belial, however, I had been wondering if Belial really wanted to serve Beelzebub. It seemed more likely Belial was interested in protecting his own interests and installing Beelzebub as king probably didn't do that. If a wedge could be driven between them, it could work in the favor of those who supported keeping Lucifer in power, a goal I was working toward. That was one of the problems with being powerful, things were expected of you and one of the expectations of me was that I would one day rule the Stygian. Except I didn't want to, and the only way I could prevent it was to keep Lucifer king for as long as fucking possible. This made Lucifer's battles my battles and any advantage I could glean in the process was a good thing.

My command found Azazael. Part of me was disappointed. If he hadn't been in the Stygian, I could have popped back to Earth and started searching for him. I felt Azazael begin to resist the magic, but I was stronger than he and eventually he began to come to me.

"Belial, I have found Azazael with my magic. I must ask you a question; do you know of any demon that might be using a portal to travel to Earth? This is incredibly important not just to Earth, but to the Stygian."

"Go away, Exorcist," Beelzebub spat.

"You don't understand, Prince Beelzebub; the demon traveling to Earth is gaining the powers of a prince. The Stygian was not designed for more than ten hell princes, which means one will have to fall for another to take over. The Exorcist suspected it was Azazael, if it isn't, that means one of our loyal demons is not loyal and is planning to overthrow one of us. Whether we agree or not, we know nothing about this demon and his accession would mean the death of one of us. It is in our interests to work together to find this demon," Ashtoreth said.

"None of my demons would dare go rogue; it must belong to a weaker prince than me," Beelzebub replied.

"They are killing people to collect their souls," I blurted out. The world grew silent around us. The smug look on Beelzebub's face disappeared.

"That was forbidden even before this forsaken place was created," Asmodeus said quietly. "As demons of the blood, you know this and you understand the repercussions of it."

"You are sure they are killing to collect souls?" Beelzebub asked.

"Yes." I nodded. I wasn't sure why I was sure, but I was. The thought had just randomly occurred to me, but now I felt the truth of it in my soul. I also knew something else–Beelzebub was older than Belial and older than I had thought him to be and remembered life before The Stygian, when demons roamed free.

"That is impossible!" Beelzebub said.

"That was my thought too, but he is strong enough to father a cambion. The one I gave Lucifer to raise was found inside a host, but I know it was born on Earth and sent to the Stygian before it was old enough to fend for itself," I said.

"I don't believe you," Beelzebub said without conviction.

Chapter Thirteen

I caught sight of Azazael striding toward us as I made a mental note to ask either Leviathan or Ashtoreth before I left what it meant that the demon was killing to collect souls, and why it was forbidden. Azazael sneered at me as he stopped near Belial.

"Ok, that's all I wanted," I said, getting ready to leave.

"What did you want?" Azazael asked.

"To lay eyes on you. If you're here, you aren't on Earth," I said.

"Why would I be on Earth?" Azazael asked.

"Because I don't trust you," I replied. "Thank you, Belial."

"Exorcist, if you find this demon and it is one of mine, I would like you to inform me of it," Belial said.

"Me as well," Beelzebub added. I considered their request. I didn't know if hell princes could kill demons, but it seemed likely, and I wasn't sure I wanted the demon killed by Belial or Beelzebub.

"I will agree only if you promise to tell me if you find them," I responded. "Also, I will tell you that if I find them on Earth, I will kill them."

"Understood." Belial nodded.

"Ashtoreth is correct, this isn't just an Earth problem. This has huge ramifications in the Stygian as well. I propose a temporary truce between Lucifer's allies and us," Beelzebub said.

"Perhaps it's because I wasn't told what is going on, but I will not agree to a truce," Azazael said.

"I agree to it," Belial said. "As long as you reside in my territory, you will abide by the terms we set, Cambion." Belial turned large dark eyes on Azazael.

"Exorcist, the cambion you brought to Lucifer, can you describe it for us?" Beelzebub asked. "If we know what it looks like we might have a better chance of tracking down the father."

"I will do one better," I said, and opened a portal and sent magic toward Lucifer. I had no doubt he knew we were here. It took maybe 30 seconds for Lucifer to come through the portal holding the cambion I had brought down. As he held it, my mouth fell open.

"It's yours!" I said to Lucifer in complete amazement. I hadn't noticed the resemblance until I could see it in close proximity to Azazael.

"That's not possible. I cannot return to Earth without your help," Lucifer replied. However, he saw the resemblance to Azazael as well. His face changed, as if he were in great pain. Then I had another realization; the mother of the cambion had to be Lilith. The resemblance was too close to Azazael to have a different mother.

"Oh God," Raphael said. "How?"

"Lilith is dead, isn't she?" I asked.

"Yes," Gabriel replied, and there was quiet for a long time from both demons and angels. They all stared at Lucifer and the cambion he held. Somehow Xerxes was the child of Lilith and Jophiel. But Lilith had been dead for more than a millennium and Jophiel was now the king of the Stygian and sterile like the rest of his demons.

"We should go," Raphael said.

"Wait, we must negotiate the terms of the truce," Beelzebub said.

"Here are my terms; until I know how someone created a cambion of Lucifer's blood and until I figure out what demon is killing to collect souls, I want the bounty on my soul removed, and you will not make an overture toward the throne of the Stygian," I replied.

"I agree to those. My terms: until you find this you will not visit the Stygian without permission from myself and Belial. Also, you will keep the Stygian informed of your investigative progress."

"I agree," I said. "You and Belial will pick one demon I can summon to provide you with updates."

"For me, summon Naghzi," Belial said, and a demon appeared next to him that I didn't know.

"My emissary will be Mishial," Beelzebub said, and a female demon appeared next to him. Belial and Beelzebub explained to the demons that I would be summoning them to Earth from time to time to provide them with information they were to immediately bring back to them. Both demons nodded. Then Belial did some magic and rescinded the bounty for my soul.

Lucifer and Xerxes the cambion returned to Lucifer's territory, and I opened multiple portals to return the other demons to their own territories. Finally, I opened a portal for us. We walked through it and back into my living room where Magda Red was playing on her phone.

"What did you learn?" Magda immediately asked. I looked at my hands; my entire body felt gritty and my hands were red from the dust that blew around the Stygian.

"Someone is making demons," I told her as I walked toward my bathroom. *What the absolute fuck?* I thought as I turned on the shower. I knew everyone wanted to talk to me, but I wanted to shower and clear my head first. Someone was making demons; that was the only solution. But how the fuck did someone make a demon? Demons were reincarnated souls; they were mostly spirit. I was sure they had DNA and it could be cloned, but that wouldn't be a demon. It would be, well, I didn't know what it would be, but something that wasn't a demon. I toweled off, got dressed and realized I still heard water running. I had three bathrooms; mine, Jerome's, and a guest bathroom. I suspected everyone had gone to shower when I did simply because Stygian dust got everywhere. I grabbed my dirty clothes, tossed them onto the floor of the shower, and turned the water back on to rinse them. The water turned red as it went down the drain. How the fuck did someone make demons? The question just kept repeating itself in my head. And why were blood demons forbidden to kill? That didn't make sense to me either.

Demon reproduction was forbidden because it killed supernaturals. When a demon became pregnant, if there wasn't a soul waiting for the demonling, a supernatural had to die to give up its soul. Did the same thing happen when a cambion like Xerxes was created? I didn't know. And why would you forbid demons from killing when it was the only way for them to get souls? So many fucking questions. I was too young to have any answers. Yes, I was connected to the Stygian and demons, but I didn't know the ancient knowledge of demons from before the Stygian, and at the moment it seemed important. I turned off the water and walked into the living room. Jerome and Gabriel were freshly scrubbed, and Gabriel was attempting to wear Jerome's clothing. The boy was tall, but not as tall as Gabriel, and the pants only hit him about mid-calf. My doorbell rang.

"That will be your mother with clothes for us," Raphael said. I nodded. Magda was still sitting in my living room playing on her phone.

"What did you mean?" Magda asked.

"The cambion I pulled from the girl is somehow Jophiel and Lilith's child," I told her. "I don't fucking know how, but it is."

"Belial and Beelzebub were just as concerned about the fact that a demon was on earth killing as we were," Jerome said. "We can rule them out as having a hand in it. Also, Azazael was there, so I think he's out of it as well." As Jerome spoke Raphael and Remiel headed toward the bathrooms. They left reddish footprints on the floor as they walked, and I noticed there were three other sets from where we had gone to take our showers. My mom handed Gabriel clothes. My uncle took them and went toward my bedroom. I didn't protest, he looked silly in Jerome's clothes.

I took about 20 seconds to decide to summon Dantalian. I hadn't asked why it was forbidden for demons to kill people, and I needed to know now, immediately. Dantalian appeared in the living room.

"This is not where we usually meet," he said, looking around.

"It's an emergency, Asmodeus said it was forbidden and as blood demons Beelzebub and Belial knew," I said.

"Uh, you mean forbidden for demons to kill?" Dantalian asked.

"Yes." I nodded.

"Killing to collect souls makes a demon more powerful quickly, but it also drives them insane," Dantalian said. "Even accidentally killing a person can drive a demon insane. Forcefully taking the soul from another is haunting; we acquire their memories. I accidentally killed a host once, and Ashtoreth had to lock me up in the dungeon of his castle for several centuries because all I could think about were the memories I acquired from my host. I recovered only because my host had invited me and died of natural causes, a heart attack while fulfilling the reason I'd been summoned. Eventually, Ashtoreth had to track down the host's family and ask them to forgive me, which they did. Those words had power and I felt free only after they said them."

"What?" I asked. Dantalian looked around. He seemed to make a decision.

"Demons are primarily souls. Killing a person, whether a host or someone else, reminds us of our own deaths. We become haunted by our deaths, our lives, and the lives of those we killed. The Rite of Forgiveness hasn't needed to be performed in ages, but it is an ancient rite and if a demon kills, even by accident, the rite has to be performed by a living relative or descendent of the person we kill in order to help us not go insane," Dantalian said.

"Not getting the rite performed is very bad for the demon involved. Eventually all we can think about is what was and what should have been, and it consumes us until we do something to ensure our own soul is destroyed. It is why you are so feared. It used to be Jophiel and Zadkiel that a demon turned to in order to have their souls destroyed. No one else could be trusted to understand and complete it. Then you came along, and we all knew you could do it as they could. All those little guilts through the eons began to echo back to us–even I felt it. I was never a demon on Earth, but I have heard the stories. If a demon can't get the rite of forgiveness performed, someone like you is the only option to free us."

"What the ever-loving…" I finished the sentence in my head. "I'm not just an exorcist, I'm an executioner, is what you're saying."

"Yes," Dantalian said. "Lucifer forbid any of us from telling you, but if you are correct, you need to know because there is a demon that needs to be executed."

"What happens if he doesn't get the rite performed?" I asked.

"He'll keep killing until he's destroyed," Dantalian said. "The only way to move on from the memories of one victim is to acquire new ones."

"That's fucking horrible," I said.

"It is." Dantalian agreed. "Only the oldest demons have ever had to experience it. Most of the deaths were related to when demons roamed the Earth; now that we are safely tucked away in the Stygian, demon-induced deaths are rare. Since you became an exorcist, it's become even rarer because most demons will seek you out for an exorcism before destroying the souls of their host. There are exceptions, of course, and Beelzebub is among them; eventually he will need to have the rite performed or he'll start killing intentionally and need to be executed."

"From what?" I asked.

"He destroyed the soul of an infant. Not entirely by himself, which is why he hasn't gone insane yet—the mother of the child started the process so Beelzebub could move into its body, but Beelzebub was involved and eventually it will be a problem. Collecting souls instead of killing them slows down the process, but it doesn't stop it."

"Thanks," I told him, and sent him back to whatever he was doing. Sometimes I wondered if I was running the risk of interrupting something important when I summoned a demon.

Chapter Fourteen

Magda Red forced us to come into AESPCA headquarters because of this newfound information. She hauled the investigative team as well as some scientists into a large conference room that reminded me of a college auditorium. My father, uncles, mom, and Jerome took seats in the auditorium behind the investigators while she dragged me up onto the stage with her. Thankfully, she provided me with a chair because I felt my knees quake as I stared out at all the faces in front of me. There was probably close to a hundred people there and I had no idea what Magda Red was about to tell them or what she expected me to tell them.

"I'm about to give you information that you are going to have a number of questions about. I want you to hold those questions for the end," Magda started. "Everyone knows Soleil Burns, correct? She's a gifted exorcist who is able to communicate with demons within the Stygian. After the last demon murder, I asked her to help us investigate the case. Specifically, I asked her to see if she could find the demon responsible by questioning demons in the Stygian. During the course of her regular duties as an exorcist she discovered a cambion on Earth, and today she finished questioning the hell princes about the cambion and the murders, and it revealed some startling information. Now, this information is classified. It doesn't leave this room and I will be casting spells to ensure it stays that way. Is that understood?" There was some murmuring and Magda waited for the group to settle down. Then she called me to the podium.

"This morning, I checked to ensure the cambion Azazael, who is formless, but whose spirit still resides in the Stygian, was still there, because I originally thought if there was a cambion on Earth, it most likely came from him. However, if he is using a portal to travel, he wouldn't have been there if he was going to commit a murder tonight. There wouldn't have been enough time. That got me thinking about time. Even with a watch set to Earth time, it would be really astounding to have even a clue about what time it is on Earth in the Stygian. Time moves so differently, we don't even have a similar calendar year, let alone try to figure out when it's day or night on Earth from the Stygian. I do not believe the lunar calendar for Earth could be followed from the Stygian with any sort of accuracy. Leaving only one solution—the murderous demon has to be here. Which brings up the second obstacle: if a demon or cambion was running around on Earth like a regular person, we'd know about it, because the living are uncomfortable in the presence of the demonic. Leaving only one option; there isn't a demon running around. There is a demon in someone's custody, and they are taking care of it somehow. Furthermore, no hell princes are reporting one of their demons missing. While there, I had the opportunity to observe Azazael and the cambion Xerxes, and they are incredibly similar. This is important because demonic features are inherited from parents, and the new cambion only has two possible parents: Jophiel and Lilith. Except Jophiel has been Lucifer longer than nearly anyone in this room has been alive, and

Lilith has been dead nearly as long. The cambion had no ties to a sire, something I thought impossible until it happened the other day,and it was parasitically attached to another demonling. After talking to the hell princes today, I realized how this could happen: the cambion I found the other day was created on Earth. It was an infant and with no demon parent to teach it about being a demon, it didn't know what to do, so it parasitically attached to another demon. The problem is that all demons have sires. They are assigned a hell prince when the soul reincarnates, and in thousands of years it has never once not happened until this cambion came into being. I have a theory, and it is not going to be popular." There was more murmuring and the entire room seemed to go into motion; people shifted uncomfortably in their seats, they whispered to each other, they shuffled their feet and papers. Magda nodded encouragingly.

"The only way all of this could happen is if the killer demon was created and not born," I said. "I believe someone capable of working with DNA somehow managed to get a sample of DNA, and they created a demon they are attempting to control. The cambion is the child of this laboratory created demon and a human parent. However, I won't rule out the possibility that the cambion was also created in a lab. I learned today the fastest way for a demon to gain power is by collecting souls through killing. Because of this, he is rising to the power of a hell prince. This is incredibly dangerous, not just for us, but for the Stygian. The Stygian was not designed for more than ten hell princes and it certainly wasn't intended to have a hell prince here. Furthermore, I can't imagine a genetically engineered demon is the same as one created naturally."

Dozens of hands shot into the air. The murmur returned, louder this time. Magda came to stand beside me.

"We'll take questions in a few minutes. I want everyone to take a minute to just sit and think about the implications of what Miss Burns just said. A genetically engineered demon isn't just about the demon, it is about humanity. We need consider where and by whom a demon could be engineered. Because this isn't going to be possible in just any home garage science lab. The other thing to consider is how they got genetic material from Jophiel and Lilith. Lucifer did not recognize the cambion Soleil gave him as a clone of Azazael, therefore it is unlikely Azazael's DNA was used, yet somehow, they got DNA from both Jophiel and Lilith, which, like so much of this, seems impossible." The murmur got even louder now.

A woman on the front row stood up. She'd had her hand up since I had finished talking.

"Dr. Lane," Magda said pointing to her.

"My lab has been experimenting with taking genetic snippets out of DNA strands to identify them. We used the technology when analyzing Jerome Dusdain's DNA for the Angel Council. Basically, we isolate certain gene combinations classified as specific to certain types of supernaturals or humans. In Mr. Dusdain's case, we used it to identify all the genetic markers specific to angels. We were even able to pull out gene sequences specific to the archangels. These are sequences that exist in Raphael, Remiel, Gabriel, Uriel, and even some of their children, like

Soleil and Helia Burns, but not the rest of the angel population. In a hypothetical situation, the technology could be used to identify and isolate gene sequences in Azazael's DNA specific to Jophiel and working backward to isolate DNA specific to Lilith," Dr. Lane said. Another person stood up.

"Now that Dr. Lane has brought it up, our DNA lab is the most advanced in St. Louis, and it seems possible that one of the AESPCA labs could genetically engineer a demon. However, while it is possible, it doesn't seem plausible. I can't imagine any of our scientists wanting to create a demon or cambion," the man said. Another man immediately stood up.

"Yes, why would anyone want to genetically engineer a demon? Furthermore, why would anyone want to, then raise its power level by having it kill?" the other man asked.

"That is a question for the ages," I replied.

"The motive for why someone would do this is unclear. If we knew the why, we might figure out the who," Magda Red said.

"Perhaps it started as a purely scientific achievement, proof it could be done, and once done it got out of hand," Dr. Lane suggested. I had considered that as a motive as well, but rejected it because the demon was now killing and not wandering the streets like a regular being.

"That wouldn't explain why the creator was letting it kill or reproduce," the third man who had spoken said.

"Why do you think the demon is male?" someone else asked.

"Because demons have surprisingly strong parental instincts, and I can't believe a female demon would just push her demonling into the Stygian to fend for itself as an infant. Whereas I could see a living being doing it to hide their shame or humiliation tied to giving birth to a cambion," I said. This got more murmurs. "When a demonling is formed in the Stygian, it forms in the territory of a hell prince and that hell prince raises it like it were their child. Hell princes treat all the demons given to them as if they were their own children, that is part of the reason the Stygian functions as well as it does. The hell princes were horrified by my suggestion that a cambion had been born and shoved by a parent into the Stygian without any demon training or attention. I gave the cambion to Lucifer so the balance of power would not be upset by one hell prince gaining a cambion and then gaining another demonling should a supernatural die sometime soon. However, I could have given it to any of the hell princes to raise and they would have treated it like any other demonling; as an infant in need of love, care, and rearing. Every hell prince and demon I have ever spoken to about demonlings have agreed that demons are devoted parents."

"We can attest to that," Raphael said from the back. "When demons were still being born on this plane, demon parents were incredibly protective of their offspring and most demon/supernatural conflicts involved threats to demonlings. Demon kings like Asmodeus would even take in supernatural children that were abandoned and outlawed the possession of supernaturals or humans with young children. Asmodeus once told us that demons were overprotective of their children, because they understood that being a demon was the last step for a supernatural's soul and if something happened to a demon or demonling, that was the end; the soul was just no more."

"You believe him?" another person asked.

"Except for Mammon and his children, demons literally can't lie," I said. "And even Mammon can't lie to me," I added quietly. Someone made a flippant comment and Magda leaned into the microphone.

"Despite what you may think of demons or hell princes, another person is going to die tonight if we can't find out where the killer demon and his handler are," Magda reminded the room. This seemed to refocus the group and quiet it down some. Ideas began to be kicked around again about what would be needed to genetically engineer a demon from two beings who do not have genetic material on Earth. Then another woman toward the back of the room stood up. It appeared Remiel was encouraging her.

"I know we keep saying their DNA isn't on Earth, but that might not be true. I can think of a couple books in our restricted section that were handwritten by Jophiel the archangel. Some of the older demons, especially demon kings and queens, kept grimoires and diaries. We have one of Asmodeus' grimoires there. It seems possible Lilith has one as well. With advancements in technology, it might be possible to get her DNA from a grimoire she authored," the woman said.

"Even after thousands of years?" I asked skeptically.

"Yes, they've been kept in a highly controlled environment for the last thousand years, and before that they were in the possession of some of the oldest among us. They kept them in controlled environments to prevent them from molding and deteriorating." I considered that. Electricity, air conditioning, dehumidifiers, humidifiers, these things had all been created because humans couldn't do magic and therefore couldn't control the environment the way a supernatural could. I took the fact that I didn't need to create my own light and could flush a toilet for granted, but that hadn't always been the case. I chose to ignore the fact that my father and uncles had once held the books in their possession.

"If there is a genetic sequence that specifically encodes to make people uncomfortable around demons and it could be found, it could be removed from a genetically engineered demon," Dr. Lane said, "which would camouflage it."

"That would require a great deal of trial and error to identify and seems highly unlikely as well as a waste of DNA," another man said. "I mean, there aren't copious amounts of demon DNA lying around to be studied." At this point the conversation evolved into one that went scientifically beyond my understanding, as the scientists discussed sequence multiplication and other ways of getting and recreating DNA. The investigators looked bored, too. Raphael, Gabriel, Sophia, and Remiel took them aside and I joined them. They were quiet as they watched me approach.

"Look, I'm not genetically engineering demons and I firmly believe they need to remain in the Stygian. I don't even understand why someone would join Beings for Demon Rights. I can communicate with demons, sense them, see them even when they have a host, but I'm not interested in sharing my plane of existence with them. I certainly wouldn't allow one to kill someone," I said.

"But you told my son demons weren't evil," a man said.

"The person genetically engineering demons and letting them kill is evil. Demons are dangerous to supernaturals and humans, but that isn't the same as being evil. You wouldn't call a rattlesnake evil, but it is dangerous to humans and sometimes supernaturals. Who is your son?"

"His name is Garth Wallis; he's in exorcism training."

"I'm not familiar with the name right off the top of my head, but I do tell trainee exorcists that demons aren't evil. Demons gain power from fear and thinking something is evil generates fear just because of how people think about it. It is better for someone like an exorcist to understand the difference between something being evil and something being dangerous."

Chapter Fifteen

If my life were a book, I'd go home with Jerome and the problem would magically reveal itself to me via a flippant comment Jerome made on the ride home and I wouldn't have to call Jerome's school and get the homework he missed today. Depending on the type of book, the love of my life would be waiting on the porch with flowers, having just quit his job to spend more time with me, and he'd make me breakfast in bed for a week as I chased down the bad guy. Jerome said nothing witty on the way home that clarified the case for me. He said nothing at all. The kid was lost in his own thoughts. There was a person sitting outside my front door, but it was my sister, who didn't count as the love of my life. She looked grim, and as I pulled into the driveway she puked in my lilac bush.

Supernaturals rarely get sick, but there are a couple of illnesses that only affect supernaturals, such as magic pox and hex illness. However, I couldn't imagine my sister casting hexes, and she didn't have magic pox as far as I could tell from looking at her. She might have a severe and extreme case of food poisoning, but that was rare. No, for the most part there were really only two reasons for my sister to be throwing up: nerves and pregnancy. Something in me told me it was the definitely not nerves.

"You'd better magic that away before you leave," I told Helia, parking in the driveway and getting out of the car. "How far along are you?"

"What?" Helia turned red-rimmed eyes on me.

"The only time you puke is when you're pregnant," I told her.

"Or when someone asks me to marry him," she told me.

"What?" I asked.

"Kabal came by this morning with flowers and made the girls and I breakfast. Then he asked me to marry him," Helia said. "No, let me rephrase that, he asked the girls if he could marry me."

"Oh. You aren't sure you want to marry again or you don't know if you want to marry Kabal?"

"Both!" Helia admitted and then sniffled, then threw up in my lilac bush again.

"Every time you throw up on that lilac bush, it gets a little bit of power," Jerome said, joining us. He did some magic that I felt, and the lilac bush shivered.

"What do I do, Soleil?" Helia asked in a semi-whiny voice.

"You tell him the truth about how you feel." I told my sister.

"Well, that's better than the advice mom gave me." Helia sniffled again. "She told me I couldn't go the rest of my life being gunshy just because Mark was an asshole."

"Also, as touching as it is that he asked the girls, Mark's been out of the picture less than a year. I know I would be angry if it were me," Jerome told her.

"I think Ariel was when she left this morning," Helia said. If this were a book, my sister wouldn't be having a crisis on my front porch immediately after I had talked to a room full of people about the possibility of a genetically engineered demon. The messy personal life stuff never interferes with the mystery in a book unless it is central to the plot, like a woman suspected of killing her husband and then finding out she has a lover. No, in books the sister of the heroine doesn't come over mid-plot to discuss whether she should get married again after leaving an abusive relationship if there is also a mystery afoot. And at the moment, I was wishing I had one of those storybook lives because I was pretty sure if someone died tonight I was going to feel guilty. In a book, I would understand it was outside my control and not hold myself responsible, unless the author needed an excuse for me to have a drinking problem.

"Dating for a single mom is a lot different than dating when you don't have kids, and as someone who is childless, I think you need to point that out to Kabal. He's been watching too many Lifetime movies where the man sweeps the woman and her kids off their feet and then asks the kids if he can marry their wonderful mother and make all their lives better," Jerome said.

"Oh God, he does watch a lot of Lifetime and Hallmark movies," Helia sighed, and then she threw up again.

"Are you sure you aren't pregnant?" I asked.

"I'm not!" Helia said with vehemence, and I sorta wondered if she was trying to convince me or herself.

"Do you want some coffee or maybe some whiskey?" I offered.

"Selfishly, I want to restart the day and call Kabal as soon as I get up and tell him the girls and I are going away for a few days," Helia told me.

"Well, I don't have a time machine. Coffee and whiskey are the best I can offer," I said. "Let's go in and you can hear my problem. It might put your life in perspective."

We went in and Jerome cast a binding spell that would prevent Helia from repeating the information I was about to tell her, while I got both of us big mugs of coffee. I added a touch of Irish cream to both, because I figured a stiff coffee was better than breaking out the scotch or whiskey at ten in the morning. Then I told my sister about the demon and how if it killed tonight, I was going to feel responsible tomorrow for not preventing it. Helia listened to me, and Jerome threw in informational bits I left out. When I finished, I poured both of us another coffee and added more Irish cream to each and handed it back to Helia.

"Your morning has sucked more than mine.," Helia said, as she sipped on her second cup. "I have a thought and if you think it's stupid I will totally understand. Do you want to hear it?"

"I am open to hearing all theories this morning." I nodded encouragingly.

"The only reason to engineer a demon using those specific genetics is to get a demon with the powers of an archangel. I mean, Azazael wasn't just a demon, he was an archangel. I imagine finding ways to combine archangel DNA and demon DNA isn't easy, but there was already proof it could be done because Azazael exists. You assumed it was Jophiel's DNA because the new cambion reminds you of Azazael, but what sorts of demons would be produced using, say, Dad's DNA? Or Uncle Remiel's?

171

You and I look different from our cousins because we are nephilim, but demon and angel DNA may always produce something with enough familial resemblance to the Winter Demon to pass as Azazael's cousin."

"And you use archangel DNA because archangels have special powers," I said when she finished.

"Right, someone wants something specific of this demon," Helia said.

"I buy that, but what?" I asked.

"That I don't know. I think if you could discover what archangel DNA was used you'd have your answer." Helia said. "Like, if they used your DNA, I would suspect the new demon was meant to take over the Stygian. If they used Remiel's DNA, well, I don't know why they would use Remiel's DNA, actually. Michael's DNA, I would suspect they were looking to heal someone."

"Helia, you are brilliant, you really are," I said. "Don't marry Kabal just because. Explain your feelings and concerns and ask him for more time if you want to continue seeing him. If you don't want to continue seeing him, be mean or rude even about how you feel, and chuck him." I was texting Magda Red as I said this to my sister. I wanted to know if there was any foreign DNA on the stone corpses, and if so, if we could test it to find out the genealogy of the DNA. Dr. Lane had said they used archangel DNA for comparison to Jerome, so if there was foreign DNA we could figure out which archangel was the parent.

"Soleil, I don't know if your connection with the demonic would work on a genetically engineered demon, I suspect not. But regardless, if someone dies tonight it isn't your fault. It isn't even your responsibility to stop it. You are not an investigator with the AESPCA. You are doing them a favor and nothing more. Any related deaths are solely the fault of the person that created the demon and the responsibility of the AESPCA," Helia said to me before standing up. "I have to text Kabal and figure out when I can talk with him."

"Good plan and don't puke in my lilac bush anymore; I don't need my bushes becoming magical," I said with a smile to my sister. She left and Jerome took a seat at the island and looked at her empty coffee cup.

"She is pregnant," Jerome suddenly said. I blinked at him. "Very early stages, but she is. Your sister is a fertility angel like Gabriel. I think Gabriel knows, and that's why he offered her up to run the council. If the council gets run by a fertility angel, it might increase fertility rates among angels. Something Balthazar Leopold hasn't managed to do, even with his clinic and black magic."

"Huh," I said and went to get one of the books I'd received yesterday from my uncles. It was a description of the archangels written by Aldous the Witch around the time humanity had come into existence. I wanted to re-read the sections on Jophiel and Zadkiel, because something Jerome had said about my sister triggered a thought. I brought the book back into the kitchen with me. Aldous had believed that the archangels had evolved in some fashion from magical beings he called The Before. I'd dismissed the book as the ramblings of a madman, but maybe he hadn't been. Maybe there had been a small group of sentient beings that came before angels.

173

However, once Jophiel came into existence, other beings began to evolve too. I found the passage: 'Jophiel took in a small lion cub and from it came weres.' It was just the one sentence.

"Could Jophiel be a fertility angel?" I asked Jerome.

"Like Gabriel and Helia?" he asked.

"Sorta similar but not exactly like," I countered.

"Maybe, although he and Zadkiel get referred to as creator angels, not fertility angels. It was how they created the Stygian."

"I wonder what happened to the lion cub, or if the story is even true," I said.

I called my dad. He answered on the first ring. I asked if Jophiel were a fertility angel like Gabriel, and if the story about the lion cub that became a werelion were true. He told me it wasn't a lion and it wasn't an abandoned lion, it was one Jophiel created from the dirt. Jophiel and Zadkiel both had the ability to create life from the magic in the dirt. Jophiel and Zadkiel had created the life, and Gabriel had ensured it had flourished. Then I asked what he thought of the theory of the Before beings. He told me he was raised by something, but he didn't remember what exactly it had been. He didn't believe it had been an angel and he couldn't describe it to me; it was more of a spirit than a being. So, I asked the important question: could it have been a demon? He assured me it wasn't, but he couldn't explain what it was, and then he told me the first demon didn't appear until after Jophiel's cat died. Then he wanted to know why I asked. I explained Helia's theory of parentage and archangel powers in demons, and how a demon of his DNA might resemble Azazael, because both would technically be sired by archangels.

If it was Jophiel's DNA, perhaps they wanted a creator demon like Leviathan. Zadkiel hadn't reproduced, but if he and Jophiel were both creator demons, someone might believe one would be a decent substitute for the other. The problem was, I didn't know why someone would want a creator demon like Leviathan. Magda texted me back. *We did find foreign DNA, but we ran it for a match in our system, not for genealogy. Have asked Dr. Lane to handle that immediately. Should have some information this afternoon.*

I read the text to Jerome. He nodded as our doorbell rang. I looked at the clock. Then I called Janet while Jerome went to the door. Janet was my business partner, and obviously I wasn't going to be in today. And possibly neither was Helia or Remiel. Janet answered on the first ring. I immediately began apologizing and then I told her Jerome and I were headed into the office to talk to her and we'd bring lunch. Principal Kim Grace came into the kitchen following behind Jerome. Definitely not a storybook life.

"Magda Red called my office this morning and told me she had you and Jerome working on a special assignment for the Witches' Council and to gather about a week of Jerome's homework because she didn't know how long she'd need both of you," Principal Grace began. "I gathered all of this week's homework and spoke to Jerome's teachers. There are only four weeks of school left. If something happens and Magda Red needs him longer than one week, we think we should go ahead and schedule his final exams and let him start summer break early. He's a very competent and capable student and most of the work for the next couple of weeks is review for the finals."

"I see. Did she make it seem like she was going to need him more than a week?" I asked.

"That was the implication I got. I know you and Jerome are working to figure out who is sabotaging the council, and it could take a while," Principal Grace said. My mouth fell open. I knew nothing about the cover story Magda Red was using, and this one bothered me. Especially if it was so believable that Principal Grace thought it would take longer than a week.

"Can you tell me anything about the sabotage?" I asked, trying to make it seem like it was just routine questioning of everyone involved with the council.

"I can really only tell you my thoughts. I mean, when we found the quartz during our meeting in January, I thought it was a fluke. We were using an auditorium at the AESPCA and maybe one of the scientists experimenting with quartz had just misplaced it. It was about a two-pound chunk, which is bigger than most people have access to. But then in February, after we moved the meeting to Magda's house, to find a second one hidden in her flowerbed outside the room we were meeting in, well Magda isn't irresponsible like that. Someone had to put it there. Now she says one was found outside your parents' house during brunch. I don't know. The thing is, none of these gatherings seem like top secret meetings, which means I have to think the quartz is being placed there to gather magic. The 14 members of the council are the strongest witches on the planet, and then outside a gathering of archangels, it must be someone wanting power beyond what they normally have. Right?" I nodded and made a mental note to ask Magda Red about it.

"That would explain the size, then. The chunk at Raphael and Sophia's was a little over two pounds. It could store a huge amount of magic in its crystalline structure," Jerome said.

Chapter Sixteen

After Principal Grace left, I took Jerome to the office, picking up Thai food along the way. Janet was the only one in the office. She said Remiel had called in saying he was exhausted, and Helia had called in crying about Kabal proposing to her unexpectedly. She had also just inferred from those calls that I would probably not come in today because it sounded like my family was in crisis. Jerome and I explained about the trip to the Stygian as we ate and my conclusion the demon must be engineered, since he wasn't missing from the Stygian.

"Wow," Janet said when we finished. "I wonder how much magic it would take to control a demon?" She reached for her bag and pulled out a chunk of quartz about two pounds in weight. It was wrapped in foil and a plastic grocery bag.

"Uh, I don't do well around quartz," I said, staring at it.

"Yeah, well I found this outside the window to your office this morning when I got to work. It wasn't very cleverly disguised, either. I wrapped it in foil when you said you and Jerome were coming in to talk to me. In theory, it will help prevent interactions. The plastic bag was just to make it easier to move."

Jerome took the quartz and put it in Remiel's chair for him to deal with tomorrow. We didn't stick around to chat very long, and Janet assured us she could manage the office alone for a couple of days if need be. I thought about the locations as I drove us toward home; two witch council meetings, my parents' house, and now my office outside my window. I saw no immediate benefit of attempting to collect magic via quartz. It could be done, but it wasn't like using magic out of a bottle, which could also be done and was a little less sketchy to access. I asked Jerome for information about accessing magic using either method. The teen frowned. He agreed it could be done, but said both had drawbacks and the risks didn't seem worth the reward. I stopped at a magic shop on the way home and bought a bottle of Magic Boost to take home and experiment with. Jerome's frown grew deeper and heavier and he stuck the bottle under his seat for the car ride home.

Jerome went to take a nap when we got home while I booted up my computer and gave myself a crash course in understanding modern genetics. Then I went back to the car and got the bottle of Magic Boost. The first ingredient was extra virgin olive oil, the second ingredient was artificial flavorings, the third was something I couldn't pronounce, and the fourth was blood. I sat the bottle on my desk and then pushed it a little further away from me. The experiment was over; there was no way I was drinking olive oil and blood—I didn't care what it was supposed to taste like.

After a few more minutes reading about supernatural DNA and modern genetics, I picked the bottle back up to read the instructions and the "how it's supposed to work" section on the label. The instructions said to drink the entire one-ounce bottle in one sitting, and within 20 minutes the consumer should feel an increase in their own personal power. There was a further warning that using more than once a day could lead to serious side effects. I felt the one-ounce bottle contained too much blood for me to drink it even once, let alone more than once a day. I composed a text and sent it to Janet asking if she had ever used a magic-boosting potion like Magic Boost. Then I copied the text and sent it to every person in my phone individually. I quickly started getting replies asking why I would need recommendations on a magic-boosting potion, and my father was kind enough to remind me that if I would practice with magic more often, I'd be better with it and definitely wouldn't need a potion to help. I sent him a thank-you reply after composing a lengthy response in my head about how I didn't really want to practice with magic more often, and that I wasn't thinking of using it myself, I was just trying to understand why someone would prefer using quartz over a potion.

Janet's reply was more what I was expecting: *Those things use supernatural blood to provide the magic boost, which I personally think is disgusting. Don't do it. If you need a magic boost, Jerome can help you without forcing you to drink his blood (which is gross) and without you being forced to drink someone's blood that you don't know. If you're desperate and Jerome can't help you (which is unlikely) I will make a potion for you to use instead of one of those nasty-ass things containing blood from an anonymous person. Also, I don't know which company it was, but one company got in trouble a few years ago for using non-humanesque blood for their magic-boosting potions and another got in trouble for paying homeless humans to donate blood for their potions. This means you could be drinking blood from a homeless person that isn't even supernatural and therefore more prone to diseases of the blood and body, not to mention the rampant drug use among the homeless. If you bought a magic-boosting potion from a witch you trusted and watched them make it, that would be better, but most witches won't make one.*

A couple of seconds after this long text came in, I noticed the three dots were again up on Janet's side of the text message and I decided to ease her mind and assured her I wasn't going to be drinking any magic-boosting potions. I was just wondering why someone would consider quartz a better option than a potion. Her reply was instant: *There's no blood consumption if you capture magic in quartz.*

That was true. Somehow between text messages I had ended up on a scientific journal article written by a doctor of genetics who was writing about splicing genes together to customize children. This linked to a clinic that promised your child could have the eye color and hair color you wanted for them regardless of your genes if you visited their clinic, and then it had a list of eye colors and hair colors available. Their website also said they could customize the texture of your child's hair as well as the color. What the fuck? I didn't think genetically engineered children were a great idea.

I texted Helia: *If you could genetically engineer a child to have the eye color, hair color, or hair texture you wanted, would you?*

"*What the fuck?*" was Helia's near-immediate response. I repeated the question and she immediately texted me back *NO! Ariel and Aurora are gorgeous and amazing little girls exactly as they are, I would not want to mess with that and risk having kids who were monsters just to ensure they had blue eyes.* Aurora did have blue eyes; Ariel's eyes were a greyish-purple color. Aurora was blond like her mom, but Ariel's hair was starting to darken and had surpassed dishwater blond to light brown some time ago. Also, both girls were gorgeous and were going to grow up to be stunning women. Ariel would be headstrong and stubborn like her aunt and grandmother. Aurora would probably be a bit of a pushover like her mom, and I had little doubt she was going to become a veterinarian with her ability to talk to animals. Or perhaps an animal trainer. Or maybe a zookeeper. Whatever she did, she would probably work with animals.

I clicked the link for the clinic to find out if there was a branch in my area. There was, and there was a contact phone number. However, that's where my brilliant idea ended. I couldn't call them up and ask if they could genetically engineer my child to have demon genes, and since that wasn't one of their advertised services it would seem like an extremely bizarre request. Instead, I put all the information and links in an email and emailed it to Magda. In my mind, genetically engineering a child to have a certain eye color, hair color, or hair texture wasn't that much different than genetically engineering a demon.

Oddly, as I waited, I got a text from Helia with a link in it. I opened the link, and it was about dog cloning services. For the rock bottom price of $10,000, I could clone Angel if I wanted. Well, in theory I could, since Angel was a hellhound and not a poodle, I wasn't sure the price would be the same or that I would end up with another hellhound. As I looked at the dog cloning services I had a thought: just because it could be done didn't mean it should be done. Yes, a dog could physically be cloned, but that didn't mean they would have the same personality as the original dog. As a matter of fact, I felt sure that it wouldn't have the same personality. Dog personalities were formed the same way people's personalities were formed; it was a cumulation of their experiences and general temperament. Those things couldn't be cloned. Also, I didn't know how much cloned dogs and genetically engineered demons had in common. Here was the problem; I understood DNA in layman's terms. In my mind, crime scene techs could take DNA from a perpetrator and use it to identify a killer, the killer's family, clone a replica of the killer, or use genes from it to genetically engineer children. Except this didn't happen, which meant you probably couldn't do those things from crime scene DNA, and I didn't understand why.

I found magic and genetics even more confounding. I knew magic had something to do with genetics, but I didn't understand the exact nature of how it worked, which made me wonder: if I cloned Angel would the clone have all the same powers Angel had or would they be slightly different? Or if Jerome was cloned, would the clone be as powerful as Jerome was? If so, what was to stop someone from cloning Jerome specifically to get an evil doppelganger?

Chapter Seventeen

My next search was on genetically modified organisms. This included plants and animals; specifically crops and livestock, which brought up several very interesting articles. Specifically, one about how people were genetically modifying animals and crops long before genetics were discovered in the 1700s. Or before laboratories became mainstream in the 1600s. Before the discovery of DNA, people were selectively breeding livestock for the best traits, which was a primitive form of genetic modification. In the late 1700s, after DNA was discovered by two supernatural scientists, laboratory genetic modification began. In the late 1800s, those same scientists cloned a pig named Holly. A few decades later they again cloned Holly, but this time, they altered her DNA by inserting DNA from a different pig named Max. They choose Max's DNA because Max was the largest hog ever raised in captivity. They named that pig, also a female, Molly, and Molly became the largest female pig ever raised in captivity. Then they went off the rails and found DNA from a dinohyus, an ancient type of pig that went extinct long ago. Oddly, the colloquial term for it is the hell pig, and it was significantly bigger than any modern pig species. They grew a dinohyus in a test tube and once it was large enough, they implanted it in Molly to birth. Things went wrong and Molly died during the birth. The hell pig turned out to be much larger than expected and ran amuck; killing Max, Holly, and a number of other pigs being kept for research. It also turned out to be cannibalistic, something I already attributed to pigs, who didn't seem to be picky eaters. It also killed a couple of human lab techs responsible for its care and did serious damage to a few supernatural caretakers.

This seemed to be the end of their genetic experiments, which probably wasn't a bad thing. Resurrecting extinct creatures became outlawed, as did most genetic modification of animals. You could attempt to prevent livestock from falling ill to certain diseases, but otherwise, genetically engineered animals were banned. Bizarrely, this ban only sort of applied to genetically modifying people. People prone to certain genetic disorders could apply for a special dispensation to allow their embryos to be genetically modified to prevent them passing on something like hemophilia or Tay-Sachs. As long as someone was walked through the risks of genetically modifying their child to have a certain eye color, hair color, or hair texture, they could genetically modify their embryos to have specific, special traits.

I suspected, being supernatural, I was biased against genetically modifying children before birth. Supernaturals didn't have diseases or disorders like hemophilia or Tay-Sachs. Reading about them, I could see why human parents would be freaked out about passing them along to their children. Human children with either disease rarely lived to adulthood or even through childhood. At which point I realized people had been genetically modifying children for eons now, not cosmetically by selecting eye color or hair color from a list, but I had once heard Abigail's husband mention there was a disease in his family that having a child with a supernatural would ensure wasn't passed along. After he and Abigail had gotten married a thousand years ago or whatever, he'd introduced his sisters to other supernaturals, hoping they would find love and not pass on the disease. I believed both had married supernaturals. Unfortunately, I couldn't remember the disease name, or if he'd even told me what it was. But as vampires, his children didn't have it. He did, however, and despite his attachment to Abigail he was wheelchair bound and had been for a long time.

I also knew the black death had nearly wiped out the human population and that it was the reason for the supernatural science revolution in the 1500s and 1600s. Most estimates put the drop in human population at 85 percent in Europe, Asia, and Africa.

My father bound his lifeforce to my mother's because of the black death and only after she recovered had she agreed to marry him. In the early days of scientific research, my mother and father ran a laboratory together. I didn't know if they made any major discoveries or breakthroughs because they had never mentioned it. Now, I used the internet to find out, because it seemed probable that they had done something to contribute to science all those years together, unless they were very bad scientists. Except I didn't think they had been, neither of my parents are dumb. I was aware my mom had worked off and on through the centuries to keep herself busy. She was also a prolific reader of non-fiction. I could remember her reading a book on genetics when I was a kid; I remembered because I'd asked her what it was and she'd tried to explain it. Perhaps my mom could explain how someone would genetically engineer a demon to me. I was about to call her when I got a text message from Magda. *The demon's DNA results are back, and it contains Raphael's DNA.*

I put my phone down and just stared at the computer for a minute. Here was the thing; Raphael was possibly the most powerful archangel alive right now. It depended on whether you included Jerome or not. He was by definition human and witch, but had enough archangel DNA to earn an angel designation and join a host. But Raphael's specialized power to was to read intentions, which was a long way off from Michael or Gabriel, who had more useful archangel powers. It was in the same class as Remiel's, mildly helpful once in a while. Having said that, my father was a magical jack of all trades. He could do exorcisms, although they exhausted him; he could destroy demonic souls, and he could perform tons of little magic all the time. I had been expecting the stolen DNA to be from an archangel that could do lots of big flashy magic, like Gabriel or Michael. However, no one did big flashy magic close to what Zadkiel and Jophiel had done, so it being Raphael's left me at a loss.

I texted my father to tell him someone had used his DNA to create the demon and ask for suggestions. I was guessing Magda had also texted him about it, because immediately the three little notification dots showed up on my phone. I got a one-line text back: *I may not do big magic, but I created two daughters who have big magic. Perhaps the point was to create a demon akin to my children.* Except, human or not, my sister and I also had our mom's DNA in us and the only way to get the same combination would surely be to require some of my mom's DNA. Also, wasn't it more likely they would get a demon akin to my brother and not me or Helia? I had a ton of questions. I texted Magda and asked if I could talk to Dr. Lane because I was confused as fuck, and this new information didn't help.

Magda told me it hadn't been what she expected either, and she was preparing to meet with Dr. Lane this afternoon in order to get some insight. I was welcome to join them at three when they were meeting at the AESPCA headquarters in Dr. Lane's office. I had less than an hour to get there, and it was all the way across town from Angelville, on the outskirts of Webster Groves. I left Jerome a note and headed out. If traffic was flowing well, it would take me 40 minutes to get there. If it wasn't, well it could take hours. I let Magda know I was on my way and to wait for me. She actually hmphed me in a reply text. Then my car announced I had a call from Magda Red. I hit the accept button, and her voice filled my car.

"Why are you driving, why don't you magically travel so you aren't late?" Magda asked instead of saying hello.

"I can't magically travel," I replied. "I can either drive a car there or I can take the bus. The car seemed faster."

"What do you mean you can't magically travel here?"

"I mean I can't teleport or travel through portals to the AESPCA headquarters."

"Sure you can. You just open a portal and go through," she said.

"No, Magda, I can't. I can't use magic like that. I know it's shocking, but I was a terrible student in school and apparently slept through all classes that did not involve demons and don't know how to do most things people with magic can do." I said.

"As powerful as you are and being Raphael's daughter, you can't do minor magic?" Magda said, sounding horrified.

"Correct." I nodded in agreement even though she couldn't see me.

"Are you mentally deficient and your family has just kept it secret? If you can open a portal to the Stygian, you should be able to open one across Earth; it's just a matter of ending geography."

"I don't think I'm mentally deficient. When I travel to the Stygian, I have to visualize the place I want the portal to end at, I know the layout of the Stygian in my head. I don't have that kind of mental map of Earth," I replied.

"I've heard Raphael say you don't do small magic, but I didn't realize he was being literal." Magda sighed. I got the impression she was going to say more and changed her mind.

"Yes, they refer to me as being willfully ignorant because I was unwilling to learn about magic growing up. I could do exorcisms and knew I wanted to be an exorcist, so I never bothered to learn other forms of it," I admitted.

"I hope for your sake you are working to correct that."

"I have been working with a magic tutor for close to a year now, but it turns out it is easier to learn magic as a child. It's been a struggle," I told her.

"Okay, get here as quick as you can, I'll tell Dr. Lane our meeting start time is now flexible," Magda said, and disconnected. If the demon creator was hoping to get a powerful demon ala Raphael's children, I hoped they had worked with Helia's genes and not mine, because yes, I was powerful, but I was also a bit of an idiot. What type of person decides they know everything they need to know by age ten and stubbornly sticks to it for the next 30 years? Me. Proving I'm an idiot. While I was working to correct the deficiencies of my skills, it was very slow because learning magic as an adult is much harder. But, then again, I always was a fan of doing things the hard way.

I arrived at the AESPCA with five minutes to spare. I stood outside the doors and called Magda Red. The AESPCA has a possession alarm system, and I knew from experience if it was turned on, I'd set it off. This would lead to a doctor showing up with a medical demonic possession tester kit and it would take me forever to get through the examination and I'd both pass and fail. I'd react to some of the exams as if I were possessed, but when they gave me the special possession potion, I wouldn't react and then there would be debate about whether I was possessed or not. There was also a black magic alarm, but I'd never seen or heard it go off.

Magda came down to collect me. There was much discussion with Magda standing in the doorway of the building debating with security and the supervisor of security about letting me in. Most of the departments had been closed by the time I'd given my talk yesterday and it hadn't been an issue to turn off the alarms. Apparently, a building full of open offices was a different story and there was debate about turning the alarms off. Magda eventually swore heavily and told me to come through, alarms be damned. I stepped through and sure enough, the entire building began to go into lock down as alarms blared and people panicked. Finally, someone said, "Why didn't you bring her through the door BEDR members use?" Which made me raise an eyebrow. Beings for Demonic Rights were usually intentionally possessed and they had to register their demons with the AESPCA. I didn't know they had their own door. I would definitely ask where that was and how I got permission to use it.

Balthazar Leopold came down and joined the commotion. He frowned at me. Balthazar Leopold is a winged angel of the choir of seraphims and he hates archangels, although I didn't know why. He was also old, not old like my father, but older than me by at least several centuries. He hated everyone in my family, but especially me, although I didn't know why he specifically hated me. I had a suspicion it had to do with power, but I couldn't prove that. Balthazar Leopold was one of those angels that didn't believe angels should have children with beings other than angels. He was a very determined proponent of keeping the angel choir structure, which I thought was ridiculous. So, maybe Balthazar Leopold hated me for a lot of reasons now that I thought about it, I was nephilim, half angel, half human; I didn't believe in the choir orders which were supposedly done to rank power structures of angelic families, and I was an archangel in the only choir order more powerful than his, so my being a nephilim probably hurt his feelings. Long before my birth, nephilim was a choir order below cherubs. I read some literature about how the half breed angels were supposed to be magically weak, only slightly more magical than humans. Aside from nephilim, nearly all other angel half breeds were listed as cherubim regardless of their original choir designation. Meaning if an angel and a vampire had a child, even if the angel were seraphim, the child was categorized as cherubim. Also, in middle school all half breeds were expected to choose a magical path. Jerome had registered in middle school as a witch, but now he was registered as both witch and angel for high school, a designation that had required us to really campaign for. Which was another thing I thought stupid, Jerome had both witch and angel magic, he shouldn't be excluded from angel classes because he was a registered witch. If it hadn't been for witches like Principal Kim Grace petitioning the Angel Council it wouldn't have happened.

If Helia were elected to the council, I was going to beg her to remove the angel choirs as well as the registration process that had nearly excluded Jerome from taking angelic magic classes simply because he was a registered witch.

"I don't know why you're angry, but maybe you could send the demon away. You are making everyone uncomfortable," Magda whispered to me. I blinked at her. Beside me stood the demon Urizak. I sent him back across the divide. I didn't tell Magda what was wrong, instead I looked away from Balthazar Leopold. However, I wondered if I could gain Helia support from half breed angels by offering the removal of the cherubim and nephilim status from the choirs and the registration process that demoted them to lesser magical beings. As nephilim, some magic classes for angels would have been closed to us, if we hadn't been nephilim with an archangel father. Other nephilim and cherubim were probably annoyed by that as well, especially if they didn't have parents that could pull strings for them as we had.

After a certified exorcist declared I wasn't possessed, I was allowed into the building. I rolled my eyes, but dutifully followed Magda, who immediately asked me about the demon when we were alone in the elevator. I explained while she nodded.

"What do you mean some classes are closed to some angels because they are supposedly not powerful enough?" she interrupted me. I explained how angel school had attempted to exclude me from demonology classes because as nephilim, I was assumed not magically powerful enough to become an exorcist, and how I'd been forced to perform a magical test to prove I could do the work in the class, but only because my father and uncles had pressured the school board to let me try. As we walked down the long hallway to Dr. Lane's office in the underground lab area, I explained how Balthazar Leopold was all about preserving the status quo and how I thought it was defeatist setting specific types of angels up to fail. Magda listened intently and then asked me why it was allowed. I shrugged and pointed out Balthazar Leopold had controlled the Angel Council for a very long time now and that it was his to enforce, and how going against Leopold was ill-advised for all but the toughest angels, because he ran a fertility clinic that specialized in angel fertility. Granted the clinic didn't have stellar success rate, but then again angels as a whole didn't have a stellar success rate with reproduction. If by some miracle an angel did get pregnant, miscarriage rates were high. My mother's three births were considered astronomically high, especially given the relatively short time between them. Uriel had just three children and he and his partner had started nearly 10,000 years before my mother was even born.

Magda knocked on Dr. Lane's door, and she told us to come in. Dr. Lane's office was much bigger than I expected. A large antique wooden desk sat near one wall, five antique bookshelves lined another wall, and a wooden table with six chairs sat near the middle of the room. There were some papers on it, but otherwise the office was immaculate and much neater than most offices I'd been inside. There was also a very large wall safe on one wall that was currently standing open. Dr. Lane was pulling paperwork out.

"My first question is how hard would it be to genetically engineer a demon?" I said, taking a seat at the table without an invitation.

"Well, that would depend on how they got the demon DNA," Dr. Lane said as she came over with a stack of papers. She put them on the table and then sat down herself. Magda sat down next to me, so Dr. Lane was across from us at the table. "The real difficulty with engineering a demon is getting demon DNA. Demons haven't been on Earth in close to 200,000 years, according to pre-history. While their grimoires and things still exist, it's really difficult to get a full DNA profile from a book, no matter how carefully it's been stored. The majority of demonic visitations since then have been spiritual, and you can't get DNA from a demonic spirit, it's just not possible. Portals big enough to travel through are noticeable, so I have no clue how they got the DNA to genetically engineer a demon." Dr. Lane pushed a sheet of paper to me. She then handed one to Magda. "This is the DNA sequence that we suspect to be demonic, but we can't verify that, since we don't have a database of demon DNA. Also, it is male and that raises another issue. How to combine two male DNA samples into an organism: it can be done, but it is much easier to genetically engineer something at the time of conception or immediately after when it's an embryo. Which brings us to the rest of the DNA sample. I think it started as a viable embryo, either human or supernatural, I can't say for sure yet, and then the angel and demon parts were put into the already existing embryo DNA. This is difficult and very advanced engineering. Magda, I am sure you remember the tests that involved Max and Holly?"

"I still have a scar from the dinohyus." Magda nodded. "Soleil, you're young enough you might not know that my partner and I once resurrected an extinct species of pig."

"I read about it earlier today, I didn't connect that Dr. Lane to you, though," I said.

"It was me. Roderick Felder retired after the dinohyus incident. I continued to work in the field of genetics, however, and eventually I and my new team figured out how to help prevent human diseases and genetic disorders through genetic engineering. At first it was great; we nearly eliminated several genetic disorders like hemophilia, but then people started requesting stupid shit, like pink-eyed human children that had the triple irises of a full supernatural. At that point, I changed fields of expertise and began studying genetic forensics, because there's a huge difference between preventing a child from having muscular dystrophy and preventing one from having brown eyes. However, there is a lot of money in preventing a child from having brown eyes, so I can see why the technology for it has expanded in the last half century."

"Until this week, I didn't know you even could genetically engineer your children," I admitted.

"Doesn't your sister have two kids?" Dr. Lane said.

"Yes, she was appalled by the idea when I sent her a link I found for it."

"Huh, it's more popular among supernaturals to engineer children, they have the money for it, where a lot of human families don't," Dr. Lane told me.

"Why would supernaturals engineer their children?" I asked.

"Beyond the cosmetic?" Dr. Lane countered.

"Yes," I nodded, intrigued and sickened.

"Well, there are options, you can attempt to make your child more magically powerful, cosmetically stand out among peers, and make them smarter. In the pre-genetic engineering days this was done by sperm banks. A woman could select supernatural sperm or human sperm based on things like athletic ability, intelligence, cosmetic stand-out features, and magic potence. Now, parents can do that based on specific gene selections. For example, two fairy parents could select to have some witch genetics replace some of their fairy genes to make their offspring more powerful and give them magic beyond glamour," Dr. Lane said.

"But why?" I asked, raising an eyebrow. "I don't understand why a parent would do that. Two fairy parents expecting a child know they are going to have a fairy child, why force that child to learn magic even they don't know?"

"Beats me, I have four wonderful non-genetically modified were-children." Dr. Lane shrugged.

"Moving on. You think our demon started as a regular embryo and the demonic and archangel genes were inserted as the embryo grew?" I asked.

"Yes, that is the easiest way to do it, that is if you could get your hands on demon DNA. It might interest you to know some of the genes we identified as non-angelic were witch. These are unlikely to belong to either the demon or the angel, which makes me think they are from the original embryo. One of my assistants suggested you might be able to track down the lab by finding out what witch recently underwent fertility treatments and had leftover embryos that were meant to be destroyed," Dr. Lane said. "Personally, I think that's a long shot, but you might get lucky. Especially since cryogenic storage of embryos can keep them viable for close to 100 years. To me, it seems just as likely a witch who had treatment in 1920 could be the source of those embryos as someone who recently underwent treatment."

"And you're sure the witch and angel genes couldn't have come from Jerome?" I asked. It seemed to me if Jerome's genome was filled with Raphael's genes, it would be easier to use Jerome's genome than that of a witch and Raphael as separate entities.

"Positive. I don't know how much you understand about DNA and genes, but I'll give you a crash course in the simplified version. DNA is a double strand of amino acids, the ladder configuration you're probably familiar with. Groups of these ladder rungs create genes or traits. A great deal of the human DNA strand is filled with white noise; these are genes that may or may not control some critical part of the species formation or behaviors. They exist in supernaturals as well as humans. The DNA structure for supernaturals is slightly different, as these junk genes don't exist in large quantities like they do in humans. Now, in some supernaturals there is another structure in existence. Master vampires, alphas in were packs, fairy queens and kings, and the archangels all have a partial third helix affixed to some of their chromosomes; we call it the alpha helix. In Raphael, this partial third helix exists on his 20th chromosome, and you and Helia both have it, as does Jerome. The difference is that Jerome carries the third helix from all eight of the living archangels; it exists on chromosomes 2, 5, 8, 9, 11, 12, 14, 15, 17, and 20, and he carries a third partial helix on number 13, which is known as the alpha witch gene. It is specific to witches and wizards strong enough to lead a coven. We know the alpha helix of the living archangels, we are guessing numbers 9 and 17 belong to the two that are deceased. Until Jerome's DNA was sequenced we had never seen that third helix on those chromosomes before. Then Remiel told us Zadkiel and Jophiel had donated to Jerome's father's lineage ages ago, so we suspect one is Jophiel's and one is Zadkiel's, but we can't confirm it. Perhaps stranger is that you carry it at number 9, number 16, as well as number 20. Helia also has an extra third helix on number 7 as do both her children, so temporarily we are referring to one on 7 as the Helia gene and the one on number 16 as the Soleil gene. Both of them are definitely alpha helixes, but we don't understand what they do or why they exist. So, if Jerome's DNA had been used, we would expect more alpha helixes to exist in the demonic DNA, but it only has one on the 20 and 21. I don't have demon DNA to compare it to, but I suspect 21 is the demon alpha helix, simply because I've never seen it before."

"Theoretically, do you just need a physical demon here to take a sample from to find out if 21 is the demon alpha helix?" I asked.

"Uh, I think I would need a hell prince." Dr. Lane said softly. "The alpha helixes don't exist in every supernatural."

"Theoretically, if you had a hell prince here you could test it for the alpha demon helix?" I asked.

"Don't you dare summon a hell prince into this building," Magda hissed at me.

"There isn't a hell prince in the Stygian that would fit in this office," I told her. "I was definitely thinking of the parking lot."

"What??" Dr. Lane's mouth hung open.

"If I summoned a hell prince to the parking lot, could you get a DNA test and find out if it's an alpha demon helix?"

"Uh, I don't know. That depends on whether demon helixes are like other supernaturals or like the archangel helixes. If each hell prince has the helix at a different spot, then maybe not." Dr. Lane said.

"Okay then, what would be the best way to catalogue hell prince DNA? Saliva? Blood?" I asked.

"You are not summoning all the hell princes to the parking lot for DNA tests!" Magda informed me.

"No, I was thinking about going to them."

"I have sterile swabs you could use to collect saliva DNA," Dr. Lane said.

"See, I can take a handful of swabs to the Stygian and be done in less than an hour," I told Magda.

"It's not quite that easy; you have to know how to handle them to keep them sterile." Dr. Lane told me.

"Well, hell. I guess if Magda authorized it, I could take swabs and a technician to the Stygian via a portal."

"I'd volunteer," Dr. Lane said, looking a bit pale. "Mapping the demon genome could be huge for my research. Not to mention assisting your case. If we could narrow down what demon family it belongs to, that might help you find the person that created it."

"And we might know for sure if there is an eleventh hell prince." I said to Magda. Magda sighed heavily, and I knew she was about to agree but not like it. "So, in theory, could the third helix at 9 be related to the Stygian?"

"I suppose so," Dr. Lane said. "Although, I don't know how it would be related to the Stygian."

"Me either, but Jerome and I both set off the possession alarms because we carry Stygian magic with us all the time. However, my father doesn't. But Jerome and I both have the third helix on 9." Next time I had to move Jophiel's body, I would need to remember to take a DNA sample to give to Dr. Lane.

"I suspect it's one of the helixes associated with either Jophiel or Zadkiel. Michael's son Amiel carries a partial helix at 3, but neither of his two kids have it and neither does Jerome."

"Okay, well." I sighed. "Doctor, you've quadrupled my DNA knowledge in less than an hour. I only sorta understand most of it. But if you want demon DNA swabs to compare, I can help you do that. Especially if it prevents more people from dying. I just need AESPCA approval. Oddly, while I can help you get demon DNA, I've never helped anyone else and can't imagine how they would have gotten it." I sighed. Then I had an idea. "Well, that might not be entirely true, I might have a few ideas, but we'd need to get DNA from Belial."

"What are you talking about?" Magda asked.

"The doctor said she needed a cheek swab from a hell prince to check for their DNA. She's going to use a sterile swab, but last October the hell prince Belial tried to eat me. My body rubbed against the inside of his cheeks, his gums, his tongue, it was awful. Then I was rushed to the ER, where my clothing was cut away and disposed of."

"The demon boxes," Magda said, with a sigh at the end of the sentence. "Shit, I don't suppose you remember exactly which demons came through in physical form through the demon boxes?"

"I have a list at home, the majority came through in spirit not physical form, but Belial and Leviathan both came through as spirit forms and then gained physical ones because of either my proximity or Jerome's," I said. "The kid's a mimic, sometimes I can't tell whether it's me or him when there's a snafu."

"Take Dr. Lane to get as many hell princes swabbed as possible, I can justify it if need be because of the demon boxes." Magda stood up. "And Soleil, no one else made that connection, good work. Don't open the portal in the building."

Dr. Lane grabbed some equipment from her lab and put it in a small bag. I stood around waiting for her.

"I don't suppose there are any "fearlessness potions" in the building, are there?" I asked her as she walked out of the lab.

"Uh, I don't know, why?" she asked.

"They sorta work with demons." I said. "No matter, I'll call my business partner; she's a witch. She'll have one and she can bring you a possession protection pendent as well." I called Janet and told her what I needed. She said she had actually been cooking up a new batch, so she'd be there in just a few minutes. Sometimes I used them during exorcisms of larger demons. The parents could chug them, weakening the demon's power source significantly. Sadly, we'd found they didn't work when chugged by the possessed. Janet would meet us in the parking lot of the AESPCA about ten minutes after I called her, she used magic all the time, including teleporting instead of driving most of the time.

"Grab your gear and we'll go to the parking lot," I told Dr. Lane.

Chapter Eighteen

"Where's Jerome?" Janet asked by way of greeting.

"He was napping when I left," I answered.

"Okay, well we have a problem then." She looked at Dr. Lane. "What I'm about to say is not meant to be offensive, but if you are offended I'll understand. You cannot go galivanting around the Stygian with a were scientist and nothing else."

"There's a truce in effect," I replied.

"Uh huh, I repeat, as nice as this scientist seems to be, you cannot go into the Stygian with just her," Janet said sternly. "You need at least a witch, preferably a witch and an archangel and prior arrangements with a hell prince to provide protection."

"Oh, shit, I'm glad you said that. As part of the truce, I must ask permission to enter the Stygian."

"What the…" Janet made a face.

"There isn't much Beelzebub and Belial can demand of me that I would agree to, so this is what they wanted; me to ask permission," I said.

"What the…" Janet made another face. "How are you supposed to ask permission? It's not like Belial and Beelzebub have cell phones or take Zoom meetings."

"I guess it's a good thing I'm me," I replied and then I conjured up an imp. This imp was a deep purple. It stood perfectly still, frozen by my magic. I conjured a second one, this one was a deep green. "I need to inform Prince Belial and Prince Beelzebub that I and a group of people need to come through to DNA test them to find the demon and its handler," I told both imps. They chittered a bit and then they both disappeared. We stood there for about 30 seconds and both imps reappeared.

"You have permission from both, Exorcist," the purple imp said to me. I nodded and told it to pass along my thanks and then asked it if it would assemble all the hell princes at Lucifer's so they could be tested. The imps looked less sure about this request, but scurried back across the divide to do as I asked.

"That was flipping weird," Dr. Lane said.

"Great, you still cannot go without an escort," Janet told me.

"Are you terribly busy at this exact moment?" I asked Janet.

"I didn't bring two potions."

"You've dealt with demons before."

"Yes, demons—not hell princes and Lucifer," she snipped.

"Well, you are all I got."

"I'll go," Magda Red said from behind me.

"Okay, do you think you'll need a fearlessness potion or can you hold your own around hell princes?" I asked her.

"I have an amulet of bravery; I should be fine." She gave me a look afterwardsand I knew how she'd dealt with having a cambion partner.

"Mistress Magda, thank you for going in my place." Janet was suddenly falling all over herself to thank Magda Red. I tried not to roll my eyes.

"Is Magda Red enough supervision or do I need to call an uncle?" I asked Janet.

"Bring an uncle or your father," Magda said. "We can wait a few more minutes." I glared at Janet as I called Raphael. I explained what we were doing and asked him to come along and to meet us in the parking lot of the AESPCA. He was there in less than five minutes. Angels can fly really fast when they want to, however, in this case, my father stepped out of a portal. I'd never seen him travel by portal on Earth and it surprised me. Once my party was assembled, I opened a portal to the Stygian. Before we stepped through, I could hear people shouting at me and I was sure they would be interrogating Janet when we returned.

"Why are we DNA testing the hell princes?" Raphael asked, as we stepped onto the red dirt of the Stygian.

"We've been trying to figure out when someone could have acquired demon DNA ,and it dawned on me that I was covered in Belial's saliva when he tried to eat me. A nurse, doctor, orderly, or practically anybody could have picked up a piece of my clothing at the hospital. Not to mention Leviathan was also in physical form at the school, providing yet another opportunity to acquire demon DNA," I told him.

"I'm impressed," Raphael said, smiling widely. "I hadn't connected last fall's events with this one."

"No one had," Magda Red said.

"Depending on how long it takes a demon to gestate, six months might be long enough to get a demon via birth," Dr. Lane said. She chugged the potion.

"Demon physical forms are underdeveloped at birth; it takes about three months from conception to birth and they are instantly capable of beginning possession and they grow based on fear responses. Six months could get you a fully developed demon from birth to demonling to demon," Raphael informed us.

"Interesting," I said.

"It is part of the reason Lucifer stopped demons from breeding. Demons can breed very fast, and some lines are prone to multiple births. However, since demons are more powerful as spirits, they don't need long gestation periods for their physical forms to develop; it develops as they gain power from their spiritual forms," Raphael said.

I felt the ground shake beneath us and turned to look beyond the walls of Lucifer's castle. I could faintly make out the tops of a few heads; Leviathan and Beelzebub were coming to give their samples. The purple imp streaked past me toward Lucifer's castle. The door opened via magic for it before it had finished going up the stairs, and I heard Lucifer speak to it. Lucifer spoke quietly, his words not carrying out to us. The imp spoke in a shrill, high-pitched tone that was incredibly fast. The words poured from him like floodwaters over a levee. Lucifer responded in the same even, quiet tone, possibly done intentionally to soothe the imp, who had appeared harried when he'd gone past us. Perhaps I should have given him more time to gather what I needed and get permissions. Then the imp streaked back past us, headed the other way, and Lucifer stepped outside his castle doors.

"This is quite unusual, Soleil, rarely do the hell princes come here," Lucifer said to me.

"It was the most neutral place I could think of to have them gather," I told him.

"I know you wouldn't have suggested it if it weren't important. What is this the imp said about sticking things in my mouth?"

"Well, we'd like a DNA sample. This is Dr. Lane. She is going to swab the inside of your cheek to collect the sample," I said, trying not to giggle. Dr. Lane was probably five feet, six inches tall, and Lucifer was close to four stories tall. In my head I saw him sitting on the ground so Dr. Lane could swab his mouth, and the image was comical.

"Belial and Beelzebub have agreed to this without eating her?" Lucifer asked.

"I believe they will agree. If I am correct, Lucifer, the demon on Earth is manmade and it is powerful enough to be another hell prince," I said.

"That would be very bad, Soleil."

"I agree. I am somewhat hopeful that your Stygian physical form is genetically similar to the DNA of Jophiel's form, because Jerome and I both have a chromosome we can't explain.".

"An extra archangel gene," Lucifer said. "You suspect it's mine." For a moment, I wondered what Lucifer knew about DNA and genetics and the archangel genes. I also considered asking him, but the gates of the castle wall were opened. If there was an akashic record, Jerome might not be the only being I knew that could access it. Leviathan and Lucifer both talked of things they couldn't possibly know.

"What is this, Exorcist?" Beelzebub bellowed as he walked into the courtyard.

"It is a way to track the demon on Earth," I told him. "I need the help of the hell princes in order to do it. I need your DNA; it resides in your body. Dr. Lane here is going to swab the inside of your cheek to collect it. Since we have a truce at the moment, I expect she can do it safely, Prince Beelzebub."

"She can," Beelzebub said and then looked down at Dr. Lane. "Although I don't know how she's supposed to do it. She's a bit short. Ah, hence why you brought someone with wings, yes?"

"Not exactly," I admitted. "Dr. Lane needs to be the one to collect it; she's the only one trained to do it properly. I was hoping you, Leviathan, Lucifer, and some of the other larger princes would bend down to her level."

"Even sitting down, I don't think she can reach my mouth," Leviathan said. Dr. Lane started to say something and I had a suspicion I knew what it was, so I touched her arm to stop her. I did not want Beelzebub and Belial to have an excuse to spit on us, because I believed they would take full advantage of that.

"I admit I would like your cooperation and assistance with it. If you do not wish to lift her up, I can draw blood near your foot and let her get a sample that way," I said, trying to imply I would ensure it hurt if they choose that option.

"Fine!" Beelzebub said with emphasis. In the spirit of good leadership, Lucifer sat down on the ground and put his large palm face up on the ground. Dr. Lane looked at it blankly.

"There are no elevators in the Stygian," I whispered to her. Magda stepped up close to her.

"Soleil, why don't you step on and help her into my hand," Lucifer suggested. I did as instructed, stepping onto the large palm and then taking hold of Dr. Lane's hand and helping her into it. Lucifer gently and slowly raised his palm up, opened his mouth, positioned his hand to his mouth as if he were eating, and Dr. Lane leaned in withwhat seemed like a very tiny swab and took a sample from inside his mouth. I heard a sound and looked down to see my father holding his sides and laughing. I tried to shoot him a dirty look, but this high up, I wasn't sure he could see it. However, nearly four stories up, I could see over the red stone walls that encircled Lucifer's courtyard and castle. The first thing I saw was the rest of the hell princes walking our direction, even Belial. The hell princes towered over the other demons, even the demi-princes. There were other demons headed our direction as well—dukes, demi-princes, counts, demonlings—they were all coming to watch. I had never seen so many demons congregating in one place. It was awe-inspiring. It was one thing to know there were approximately 50,000 demons in the Stygian, it was another to see all of them. Usually, I only dealt with a few dozen at one time, a hundred at the absolute most if I was in a city.

"Hey, Magda, here comes proof that there's no such thing as a secret in the Stygian," I shouted down to the witch. She and my father turned to look at the gates of Lucifer's castle walls. "Doc, how many swabs did you bring, because you can start your demon DNA database today." Writing appeared on the tube that contained the swab she'd just used in Lucifer's mouth.

"I only brought a box of 50," she said, turning carefully to see what I was looking at. "Holy cow!" she said, sucking in air.

"They are all curious about what you are doing," Lucifer spoke very quietly and I realized it was because this close to his mouth his voice would probably rupture our ear drums. "Are you done?" he asked, continuing in that quiet way. Dr. Lane said she was, and Lucifer began to lower us back to the ground. The first of the demons reached the gates and came pouring through. They gathered in front of us; watching, staring, intent, attempting to figure out what we were doing.

"I really need to do the hell princes first and any leftover swabs can be used on the other demons," Dr. Lane said. She was a touch pale. "They won't attack because I can't take all of their DNA, will they?"

"No, demons are sentient beings and incurably curious," I told her, and found my voice sturdier than I'd expected. "Now, they will probably laugh at us like Raphael did. But for the most part they just want to watch and try to understand what we are doing. A few are probably here to protect their princes, if necessary, but they are mostly here out of curiosity."

"Exorcist, bring your scientist. I am not going to pick you up, as Lucifer did, but I will attempt to bend to you," Beelzebub said, and he sat down hard on the ground. For a moment, it felt like we were standing on a mattress and I stumble-stepped to keep from falling down.

"We could walk up onto the ramparts of the wall," I told Beelzebub.

"Come here, niece," Leviathan said. He did what Lucifer had done, placing his hand on the ground palm up. I took Dr. Lane by the arm and walked her over to Leviathan. We stepped into his hand and he lifted us up to the ramparts. "It is a long walk, this is much faster."

This led to the most bizarre thing I'd ever seen. Beelzebub scooted across the ground to us, leaning into Dr. Lane on the ramparts. I would not have believed a hell prince could scoot, and seeing Beelzebub do it made me feel like I was in an alternate reality or something. Dr. Lane took a swab from the box and leaned into Beelzebub. I watched very carefully to ensure Beelzebub didn't do something awful like pull her off the ramparts and let her fall to her death or eat her. He was a perfect gentleman for a demon and did neither of these things. He even stopped breathing for her. She finished in about 30 seconds, pulled the swab back down into the plastic container, and then labeled it using magic. She tucked it into her bag and pulled out another swab. Beelzebub ungracefully got off the ground and stood back up.

"If you want samples from any of my demons, you are welcome to them as well," Beelzebub said to me and Dr. Lane.

"It is possible, Prince, please don't leave yet," I answered. If Beelzebub could be civilized and not eat us, I could use his proper title and be civil back. In my head, I added that I hoped his brother was just as accommodating, since I was positive it was Belial's DNA in the demon. Leviathan offered himself to Dr. Lane next. He didn't sit on the ground, instead he knelt and leaned forward, getting as close to her as possible. He also didn't breathe on her as she swabbed the inside of his mouth. Behind Leviathan, the hell princes had formed a line, including Belial. Belial gave us no problems either, and was perfectly civil as we swabbed for his DNA. When we finished, Belial offered to help us down. I wasn't sure about that, but eventually I stepped off the rampart and into his hand. Belial was not as large as Beelzebub, Leviathan, or Lucifer, and his hand wasn't big enough to accommodate both me and Dr. Lane. Belial placed me on the ground and then he returned his hand for Dr. Lane. Dr. Lane stepped into it and for a moment I was terrified he was going to crush her, then he was lowering her to the ground and she was safe and sound next to me.

"Does everyone feel okay still?" I asked my group. Too much exposure to the Stygian could make the living go crazy. Everyone said they were okay. "How many swabs are left?" I asked Dr. Lane.

"Thirty-nine," she replied.

"If possible, I would like a sample from either a demi-prince or a duke from each of the princes, and also a demonling," I told the assembled crowd. "I believe who we swab is up to the princes and I hope they will organize it. Any swabs left after this and we will swab those that volunteer. If you want to be swabbed, but your prince doesn't pick you, please line up behind Raphael. If you are selected by your prince, please line up behind Magda Red." I spoke loudly so everyone could hear me. However, Lucifer repeated my instructions. Dantalian was the first in line behind Magda Red, which didn't surprise me.

I touched Belial's leg and he bent down toward me a little. "I would like to swab Azazael; as his friend, I am hoping you can convince him to volunteer," I said to the hell prince. I wasn't sure if Azazael had DNA, his physical body had been destroyed by Magda Red on Earth hundreds of years ago. However, his spirit form seemed solid enough in the Stygian. The problem lay in the fact that all demons in the Stygian had physical forms tied to their spirits, exactly like supernaturals and humans on Earth did. Azazael was a paradox, a spirit form in the Stygian without a physical form, and that was incompatible for life. It put him on the same level of being as a ghost, yet he was far more substantial than a ghost. Which made me think his Stygian form was physical, even if it wasn't exactly like his form had been on Earth. Belial stood up and began to walk to where Azazael was milling around. He and Azazael spoke briefly, then Belial picked him up, tightly holding him in his fist. He carried Azazael over and held him upside down for Dr. Lane to swab. I gave her his name and her eyes widened. Azazael was swearing and trying to curse Belial. Then he spit in my face. Belial threw the smaller demon about 50 feet from us. He landed with a sickening crunching noise.

"Please, Exorcist, do not hold that against me," Belial said.

"I don't, Prince. I know you cannot command him," I said. "Did you kill him with that throw?" I reached up to wipe my face, and Dr. Lane stopped me. Belial shrugged.

"I have your DNA on file, I can get his from this sample," she said, and swabbed the gob of spit on my forehead.

"If I did not kill him, he will wish I had," Belial told me and I believed him. Azazael was basically an adopted demon of Belial's kingdom; his violation of the truce could have serious repercussions for Belial. A demon's oath was magically binding because it was how they bargained for souls. By causing violence to me, even in the form of spit, Belial's oath was in danger of being broken, and if it did break, he would lose his ability to make deals for souls and his status as a hell prince. " If you request I kill him, to resecure the truce, which is your right, I will."

"Thank you, that is not necessary," I assured him. By the time I turned my attention back to Dr. Lane, she had already swabbed half a dozen demons that were in line behind Magda Red. She was incredibly efficient. She pulled out a swab, spent about 30 seconds swabbing the inside of the demon's mouth, then closed the swab, magically wrote on it, and stuck it back in her bag and pulled out a new one. The entire process took less than a minute. By the time she was swabbing the last of the demi-princes and demonlings I'd requested, Azazael was back on his feet, albeit with a limp, and he was limping toward me and Belial. I considered using magic to stop him, but was curious about how far Beelzebub and Belial would go to protect the truce with me. Belial turned on Azazael, but it was Beelzebub he walked closest to, and Beelzebub snatched the cambion from his feet, gripping him so tightly his face turned purple.

"Azazael, I am only giving you this one warning. There is a truce in place. You will not violate it again. You are not just messing with Belial; I felt the magic of the truce as well," Beelzebub said very slowly and very quietly. "He may not kill you, but I will." Beelzebub finished and released Azazael, letting him fall close to 20 feet to the ground. I was enthralled watching Azazael fall. He landed and immediately I felt blood flow down my cheek as the magic slammed into me. The response was immediate. Demons threw themselves in front of me, and Beelzebub brought down his giant fist swift and hard. Azazael crumpled under it and didn't move. One of the demons that had thrown himself in front of me also fell to the ground. Blood thick and dark leaked from his chest. I grabbed him and leaned over him. I'd healed a demon before,, and I felt myself forcing magic into this one trying to heal him.

"What's his name!" I shouted to anyone.

"That's Dogon," Dantalian whispered to me. "You can't save him, Soleil." I felt the incubus touch my shoulder and shrugged him off. Then I really looked at the demon I was holding. The magic had split him from one arm to the other across his chest and I could see his heart slowly beating.

"He will not die for me," I told Dantalian with grim determination. I put my hands on the wound and saw the heart was slowing down. I pushed more magic and felt the demon respond. I suddenly knew he was one of Belial's demi-princes. Then I saw him in a field of tall grasses, as a man, two children near him. Then I saw smoke in the background, lots of smoke. Too much smoke. The man grabbed the children and ran away. I could feel his terror. His name came to me, Brachus, the children weren't his, he had rescued them from the fire in the village, but now the village fire was spreading to the field of grass, consuming

216

it. No, it wasn't a village fire, it was much worse. I could feel the heat at Brachus' back. I could feel it getting closer, despite the speed at which Brachus was running. It was a volcano and the smoke wasn't smoke; it was a pyroclastic cloud, and it was about to engulf them. Brachus performed magic and a hole appeared in the ground before him. He shoved the children in and was about to climb in himself, but it was on him, he had to seal the hole. He did so and then the heat engulfed him, choked him, burned him, rocks and other debris slammed into him, pelting his body. Then there was nothing. I felt the demon's heartbeat rise, becoming stronger, steadier, faster. I sighed, but didn't pull back the magic I was pushing.

"Soleil." The voice was soft and belonged to Belial. I turned to look at him. "He will live," Belial told me. I blinked and realized there were tears in my eyes. Belial had never said my name before and it confused me that he said it now. He leaned down and helped Dogon to his feet. Dogon looked at me.

"You healed me," he said. "I owe you my second life."

"No, Dogon, I was just returning the favor. You saved me first," I told him. The demon hugged me. I stood motionless as he did so, too shocked to move. "Did those kids live?" Dogon asked me after a moment, pulling away, but not letting go of me.

"I don't know," I said. "But I will try to find out for you."

"Thank you, Exorcist. If you ever need anything from me, just say the word," Dogon whispered. Dr. Lane had gotten distracted by the fireworks and healing, she stood, unused swab in hand, staring at me. However, everyone was staring at me; living beings, demons, hell princes, imps, Lucifer, all of them were staring wordlessly at me.

"Should we kill him now?" Beelzebub asked. "To preserve the truce?"

"I do not believe it is necessary, Prince." I sighed. I couldn't give them permission to kill Azazael no matter how much I wanted to. Dr. Lane went back to swabbing demons that had lined up behind Raphael. Magda came to stand next to me.

"Are you okay?" she asked. I nodded. "You were crying," Magda whispered.

"I see their lives, not just their demon forms," I told her. "Dogon was a man named Brachus and he died saving some children from a volcanic eruption. It seemed unusually cruel to let him die for me, too."

"You have an extremely complicated life," Magda said. I quietly agreed. It was possible Beelzebub and Belial would kill Azazael once I left the Stygian. I hadn't forbid it; I had simply told them it wasn't necessary, and I'd be lying if it weren't done in self-interest. By telling them no, I wouldn't be responsible for Azazael's death if they killed him. Yes, my life was complicated, and another complication walked over to me and took my hand.

"Are you sure you are all right, Exorcist?" Dantalian asked, examining my hand and then moving to the cut on my face.

"Yes," I told him. "Why are you fussing over me?"

"Because you keep our universe interesting, we want to keep you alive, healthy, and coming back," Dantalian said.

"If you want to fuss over someone, go fuss over Dogon, he was injured much worse than I was." Except my stunted wings were starting to tingle. Wings require copious amounts of blood, and mine had been poisoned when Belial had tried to eat me. They'd eventually grown back, but were only about two feet long and were rather useless. Which was fine, I found wings to be a giant pain in the ass. Physically speaking they were in an awkward place, attached to my ribs and spine, below and behind my ribs. All angel wings stuck out from the sides of our bodies. It meant our arms had to dangle in front of them, which was not a cool look, or we could rest our arms on the tops of them. Thankfully, the spines contained dozens of tiny hinges that allowed us to fold them forward, backward, or into our body at our sides. Mine were small enough that I kept them folded into my body most of the time. Dantalian was about to walk away when one of my feathers fell to the ground. The red and black feather clashed with the brick red dirt. I stared at it. "Okay, I may have been poisoned." I admitted.

"Princes!" Dantalian shouted and everyone turned to look at the demon. "She thinks Azazael may have poisoned her."

"There's no need to fuss, I have enough Stygian magic in my veins that Stygian poison is unlikely to kill me," I told Dantalian. Probably I'd lose all my feathers and my wing spines would shrivel up and die and fall off and I'd need some magic salve to stop the bleeding. But I didn't

219

have any here, Jerome made it for me and it was at home with him. Suddenly a massive hand touched my back; a single finger felt as wide as my body. I looked up into the face of Leviathan. He nodded and pressed on my back and I felt his magic enter my body. Imagine that, Stygian poison was yet another creation of Leviathan's. Who the fuck would have guessed that? Oh wait, me.

"You're correct, you've been poisoned," Leviathan said.

"Fucking Azazael," I murmured and felt my knees weaken. "I'm going to pass out," I said to anyone as I started to fall. I felt Dantalian catch me.

Chapter Nineteen

I awoke staring into a really bright light. It was not red-tinted. I could feel someone holding my right hand and blinked at the figure, which looked weirdly dark. Where am I? This didn't feel like the Stygian. It smelled of antiseptic. The dark figure leaned into me, and I realized it was Raphael. My head was pounding in time to my heart, but at least my heart was still beating. I felt nauseous. I tried to reach up and move the light out of my eyes, but my arm didn't respond to my command. I felt heavy, sleepy, and awful. Then I remembered Azazael hitting me with magic and the tingling in my wings and cut on my face and Dogon.

"Is Dogon poisoned too?" I tried to ask, but my lips didn't move and no sound came out. Fuck, was I paralyzed? My heart was beating too strongly in my skull for me to be dying. I'd felt dying in various forms through demons' memories, and this didn't feel like dying. What the fuck had Azazael done to me? And had he attempted to do it twice and Dogon was in danger? My father was talking to me, but I didn't understand him, either because I couldn't hear him over the pounding in my head or because I was deaf. I wasn't sure which. Could Stygian poison make a person deaf? I didn't know, but it didn't seem impossible.

"Where are we?" I tried to ask, and this time I made noise, a squeak that didn't seem to be words.

"Just rest," I heard a female voice say, but I didn't recognize it. Great, I was in a hospital. How had I gotten here? How had we gotten out of the Stygian? Why could I understand and hear the woman, but not my father? I tried to look at him, but his face was gone from my line of vision.

"We are running all the antidote solutions Leviathan gave us. I think they are starting to work," the woman said, and again I understood her. Where was Raphael? Where was my dad when I needed him? I felt a tear slide down my cheek. The important part was, I wasn't dead and I wasn't in the Stygian anymore.

"She told you to rest," a different voice said. "Stop trying to ask questions." It was a man's voice. No, a teen's voice. Jerome. I wanted to reach up and hug him. How had he gotten here? "Everything will be explained when you are feeling better," he told me. "Your idea for an imp communication network was brilliant." I tried to talk. What? What! How did imps figure into this?

"Soleil, just rest," Remiel said to me, and I knew he and Jerome were reading my mind. "Stop thinking, just relax and let the antidotes work." My father came back into my line of sight. Raphael touched my face. And then someone else appeared next to him. The face was brownish red, the hair a dark color, but also tinted red. Dantalian. He was covered in dust from the Stygian. How had the demon gotten here?

"They needed help with you, and Dantalian volunteered. Now, stop. I know you have millions of questions, but you need to rest," Jerome scolded me. *There's a demon in my hospital room, you bet I have millions of questions. Not to mention he's in physical form!* I shouted at Jerome and Remiel in my head.

"Soliel, just relax. You are safe and you are healing and you aren't in the hospital. Is there any way you can give her a sedative?" Remiel asked someone that I couldn't see.

"I think giving her a sedative after she's been poisoned is dangerous," the woman said. It was Doctor Lane, geneticist at the AESPCA and travel companion to the Stygian. She'd survived. She had samples of demon DNA. Had they survived? How had we gotten back?

"If you don't do something, she's just going to lay here and try to ask questions," Jerome said.

"I'll get Dr. Richter." I heard a door open, then close. Raphael kissed my forehead.

"Soliel, I know you are confused, but you have got to rest and let the medicine work," my father told me. I tried to stop thinking. I tried to lay there and sleep, but nothing happened. I didn't have a chance to check and make sure Magda hadn't been possessed when we came back. Did someone else check? She hadn't been wearing a protection amulet and the Stygian was a really good place to become possessed. Holy fuck. I had to get up. Someone was going to die tonight if I didn't. My legs didn't move when I told them to and neither did my arms. I tried to move my head to look for restraints and couldn't even do that. I could move my eyes and nothing else.

"The poison caused temporary paralysis," Remiel said. "That's why they needed the demons to help bring you back." *Just tell me how we got back and if Magda was checked for possession*, I begged Jerome and Remiel.

"Beelzebub sent imps to find me," Jerome said. "Your decision to allow Jinx and Chronos to pass through mini-portals for communication with the hell princes allowed them to come find me. I opened a portal to bring all of you back. I checked everyone as they came back to ensure no one was possessed. You were in the Stygian long enough that Raphael couldn't carry you alone. He required help. Dantalian and Dogon volunteered to bring you back through. Dogon immediately went back, but Dantalian begged to stay to watch. Leviathan then used Chronos to send the formulas for the antidotes through." Chronos was the deep purple imp that worked for Beelzebub.

"Magda Red is currently with the upper echelon of the AESPCA and Gabriel arguing the necessity of Jerome opening a portal, allowing two demons through, and the use of imps as messengers," Remiel added. "Next time you decide to use an imp messenger service, if you could explain the particulars to someone else, that would be great. We had no idea how it worked until Jerome explained that the imps weren't free to come and go as they pleased, they could only be summoned by you or Jerome or sent to you or Jerome via the orders of a hell prince." I tried to nod and nothing happened. I closed my eyes. Things could be worse.

Send Dantalian back across, his presence here will make Magda and Gabriel's jobs much harder, I mentally told Jerome.

"Come on Dantalian, time to go back. Thank you from me and Soleil," Jerome told him. "We couldn't have done it without you, but Soleil's right, your presence here makes it harder to pretend we don't have a working relationship with demons in the Stygian."

"Soleil, I hope you get to feeling better soon," Dantalian said. The demon reached down and squeezed my hand. "Now, if something happens and she needs more help, let me know," he said to the others in the room before Jerome sent him back across the divide.

"I think that demon might have a crush on you," Remiel said. *Yeah, no.* I answered in my head. I was very tired now that I knew how we'd all gotten back across the Stygian Divide. I also felt better knowing Jerome had checked everyone for possession as we came through. I felt a little bad about Magda and Gabriel dealing with the AESPCA command, but I'd think about that after I took a nap. Dr. Lane returned with someone else.

"I don't think we can give her a sedative, but if this is painful, we might be able to give her a mild pain killer which would also help her sleep., a new male voice said.

"Does it hurt?" Remiel asked me, leaning in close for some reason.

A little,But I am plenty sleepy, I thought.

"She says it hurts a great deal," Remiel told the doctor. I protested, but nothing came out of my mouth. Then I felt the medicine kick in and I was asleep.

Chapter Twenty

I dreamed a demon, not Dantalian, was dragging his butt across my carpet like a dog. And I kept scolding him for it, just like I would a dog. Then I called the vet that tends to my unicorn to see if I needed to deworm the demon or something. Thankfully, I awoke before the vet gave me deworming medication for the demon. I was covered in a thin sheen of sweat and immediately tried to get up. I swung my legs over the bed and realized I was on a table and I wasn't in my room.

"She's moving!" Jerome said cheerfully.

"Bah humbug," I replied. "My head still hurts."

"It might for a day or two," Raphael said. I wiggled my dangling feet and swung my legs, remembering that some time ago I'd been paralyzed. My entire body ached and I was fairly sure it was from sleeping on a table, because this definitely wasn't a hospital bed.

"Why am I here and not in a hospital or at home?" I asked, grateful to hear my own voice.

"Because this lab could synthesize multiple antidotes and the hospital couldn't," Jerome said.

"May I go home now? Did anyone die while I was out?" I asked.

"Yes and yes," Jerome said. "Magda and her team are working the crime scene. If you feel up to it, Raphael is supposed to take you."

"You are more than welcome to not feel up to it," Raphael told me.

"Did Azazael poison Dogon, too?" I asked.

"Yes," Jerome said. "Leviathan is tending to him, and he should be fine. Belial sent Jinx to tell me at Dogon's insistence that you know that he will recover."

"Good. The dead person? Is it someone we know? Does it give us any new clues as to who is trying to control the demon?" I asked.

"No and no," Jerome said.

"It is Belial's DNA, right down to the alpha helix," Dr. Lane said from somewhere far away. At least the damn light had been turned off while I'd slept.

"Magda Red was running down everyone who worked at the hospital when you arrived after your October encounter with Belial when she got the call that someone else had been turned to stone," Raphael told me.

"That must have been hundreds of people," I said.

"Probably," Jerome agreed. "But it would have to be someone with the knowledge to engineer a demon as well as the lab to do it, which narrows the list considerably."

"Also, the hospital only cut off your shirt, you had trouble getting out of your pants when you got home and they were only interested in looking at your wings. According to hospital records, the shirt was destroyed. We suspect it was someone that came in specifically to swab the DNA from your shirt, which means they might have stepped in for only a few moments and then left again."

"Great, it could be practically anyone," I said. "Dr. Lane spent less than a minute swabbing each demon for DNA."

"For which I want to thank you. I have been trying to understand the magical genome, and the demon DNA will help tremendously with that," Dr. Lane said. I gave Jerome a look, hoping he still had enough of Remiel's power to search Dr. Lane's mind. She had the know-how to engineer a demon and I'd just given her a bunch of demon DNA. Jerome shook his head. He leaned in very close to my ear.

"Not her, but I know who she suspects," he whispered to me. In my head I asked, *Her old research partner?* Jerome nodded. Under normal circumstances I didn't condone mind reading, but this was a desperate situation. I had been starting to suspect him as well, I used Google to find the article about Max, Holly, and the dionhyus experiment so I could get his name, Roderick Felder. I googled the name and got antique articles from his work in the 1700s and 1800s; nothing more recent than 1888 showed up.

"I think I feel well enough to go meet Magda," I told my father, Jerome, and Dr. Lane. Dr. Lane gave me a travel cup of sludge. It smelled surprisingly good, though, like chocolate.

"It's more of the antidote that worked. Dr. Richter helped me flavor it so it should taste mostly like chocolate and strawberries, but it might still be vile," she warned. "Take it if you start feeling weak, dizzy, sick, or anything." She forced the cup into my hand. I assured her that I would and the three of us set off. We stopped at my house to drop Jerome off. Helia and my mom were both there, which meant Jerome probably needed to talk about what happened. Except I was still fuzzy on what had happened, exactly. I knew Azazael had managed to poison me, but I wasn't sure how. The furies excreted poison, but it seemed like a rare skill for anything not created by Leviathan, but Azazael was definitely not a creation of Leviathan's. Somehow he had managed to magically poison me, which I admitted seemed impossible, which I was tired of saying and thinking. Obviously, many things were possible that I had never dreamed of, like genetically engineered demons who killed people and had cambion children. Shit, I should have tested the new cambion's DNA and I didn't even think to suggest getting a sample of it. What a dismal failure on my part. I'd had two great ideas and then flaked out before having a third apparently.

"Since we have some time to talk, what do you think of Kabal proposing to Helia?" I asked my father when it was just he and I in the car.

"I think his heart was in the right place, but the execution was a disaster," Dad said. "He does love her, but the timing was bad, and asking the girls first instead of her was a bad idea. They aren't ready for their mom to marry again."

"Between you and me, Jerome thinks she's pregnant," I blurted out. Raphael smiled widely.

"That would be fantastic," he said after a few deep breaths. "Well, kinda. I would love another grandchild, but I don't want Helia to feel forced to marry Kabal just because she's pregnant. Do you think Jerome is right?"

"I don't know. We've barely scratched the surface of Jerome's powers. I think it is very possible he is right, but I had food cravings when Helia was pregnant the first two times. Even though I wasn't around her, I craved lobster the entire time she was pregnant with Ariel and Aurora and I'm not doing that now."

"You always were incredibly empathetic to your sister."

"If she is pregnant, it will help her chances of winning the Angel Council election," I said. "Three pregnancies in ten years is astounding when most angels don't pull that off in a millennia, let alone a decade."

"This is true," Raphael said. "Magda is going to come talk to you about an AESPCA position when this is all over. She and Gabriel argued a little too effectively with the higher-ups and now they want to start a Stygian division with you in charge."

"Uh, no," I said immediately.

"It could be good for you and the Stygian."

"I like my job and I am less than a year from getting my PI license. I don't want to deal with the AESPCA politics. Plus, realistically, no one is going to want to work for me, and frankly, the higher-ups are going to ignore me most of the time. My demon information network could be handed off and imps could be used as messengers even without me involved."

"I'm going to make a suggestion. Don't laugh and don't immediately dismiss it," Raphael said. "If you don't want to do it, maybe try to talk your mom into it."

"Mom is human," I pointed out.

"True, but it's about time for her to go back to work. She hasn't worked for 40-plus years and she's starting to be bored at home. I think Jerome could make a charm or something that would allow her to summon imps for information and allow them to find her if sent by a hell prince."

"Huh, me too. Actually, that is something I have wanted to talk to you about my entire life. Mom isn't totally human, is she?"

"Yes and no," Raphael said cagily. "Your mom was born to two human parents."

"But it's like Ariel and Aurora and Jerome. It's a very diluted line. At one time some of mom's ancestors were supernaturals and they interbred with humans so often, they basically became human." I shrugged.

"Yes," Dad replied. "Your mom has a small amount of magic that only relates to you, Helia, Ariel, Aurora, and me. It's starting to connect with Jerome."

"Mom has hearth magic?" I asked.

"Your mom has a very tiny amount of hearth magic and not enough supernatural in her to be immortal on her own," my dad said. I was only partly surprised by this; my mom knew whenever one of us was in trouble. She just got a feeling and knew.

"Why didn't you tell us?" I asked, genuinely curious.

"Your mom was worried it would prevent you girls from following through if you fell in love with a human. As nephilim, your kids run the risk of being like her if you have children with a human."

"Nephilim or not, my sister gave birth to two powerful daughters," I said.

"Your mother's line was descended from Hecate," Raphael said.

"THE Hecate? The great witch?" I asked.

"Yes, the great witch that fell in love with a human and was cursed to have human children. The curse involved a part about parents watching all their children die, but Hecate took her own life after watching two different generations of children die and that part went away. Until your mom and I got together, no one in her family had been able to have children with a supernatural, only humans. When Nicholas died, we worried the curse had come back, but Nicholas died as a result of himself and Azazael, not the curse."

"Himself and Azazael?" I asked.

"Your brother worshipped Azazael. Thought he was the greatest being ever to walk the Earth, which Azazael couldn't get enough of; hero worship is as good as fear to a demon. Azazael needed an angel soul for some magical experiment that he called Movement in the Shadows, and your brother volunteered his," Raphael said.

"I don't know why Azazael would need a soul for an experiment," I said.

"He considered himself a magical scientist. I don't know what the spell was supposed to achieve or anything. I just know he took your brother's soul and kept it so long your brother died," My father said. "I also can't tell you why your brother agreed to let him use his soul."

"Was Azazael's grimoire destroyed after his soul was taken from his body and placed in the Stygian?" I asked.

"I think it's in the restricted grimoire section of the AESPCA," Raphael replied coldly. "Why?"

"I want to see what my brother died for," I told him.

"I doubt it was anything important," he said. I nodded and went silent, encouraging the conversation to drop. My parents didn't talk about my brother very often and I could tell it was still painful. Besides, while I wasn't surprised my mom had a little bit of magic, I was shocked to find out she was descended from Hecate the Great Witch. That meant I was descended from Hecate the Great Witch, even if I didn't have witch magic, and that was something to think about.

"Could Mom's magic be getting stronger instead of dying out?" I suddenly asked my dad.

"No."

"Are you sure?" I insisted. "Perhaps that's why you have two archangel daughters and Helia has two archangel daughters. Hecate's power was always much stronger in the female line."

"Except by that your mom should have magic and she doesn't."

"Maybe she doesn't because she doesn't think she should. Maybe, like me, she is willfully ignorant of her magic," I suggested.

"Your mother has a little bit of hearth magic, it isn't strong," Dad said. "You know that as well as I do."

"I do now, maybe. None of your brothers have archangel grandchildren. Most of their children aren't even archangels, but you got two of each and all four of us are girls. I feel like if mom really is descended from Hecate, that explains it."

"Oh boy," My father said as he pulled up in front of a house in a nice-looking neighborhood. There was crime scene tape around the entire thing and Magda Red was standing on the lawn. "You don't have to go in there."

"Yes, I do. A demon is killing people, I need as much information as possible."

Chapter Twenty-one

I texted Helia as I got out of the car. *Did you know mom is descended from Hecate the Great Witch!!??* After I hit send, I turned the volume off on my phone and stuck it in my pocket.

"You look unwell," Magda said, walking over to me.

"I did get poisoned; I think it was yesterday. I've lost track of time recently," I replied.

"Fair point," Magda said, and took me inside the house.

The house should have felt evil or violated. However, when I stepped over the threshold it felt like a normal house. The person that lived here liked pink. There was a large sectional couch in the living room and each section was covered with a bright pink cover. The curtains were bright pink and hung over grey blinds. The walls were also light grey and there was a bright pink round rug under the coffee table and edges of the sectional couch. A handful of paintings on the wall where the predominant color was pink rounded it out. There was a big old transistor radio but no TV. There was an old-fashioned basket full of yarn and spinning wheel set up in front of the couch. It hit me as I stared at the spinning wheel, this one was a supernatural who for whatever reason hadn't stepped out of the early 20th century yet. I'd heard of it happening, but I hadn't actually seen it before. My parents and uncles all smoothly transitioned to new technology, including TVs and computers. My mom, raised as a noblewoman in the 1300s, had a spinning wheel and could spin wool into yarn, but I had never seen her do it. I had just seen the spinning wheel in the attic. While I'd been growing up, she had crocheted, knitted, embroidered, and sewn some clothes for us. But she'd always gone to the store to get the supplies. She'd even made Helia's wedding dress, a mix of knitting and sewing, and it had been gorgeous.

There wasn't a stone corpse in the living room. Someone I didn't know handed me surgical gloves. I put them on and began to meander from the living room to the kitchen. The kitchen was done in muted pink tones, including a dusty pink fridge. The stove was a huge old-fashioned cast iron stove with feet that kept it off the ground about six inches. The corpse was sitting at the dining room table, which was small, very small by the standards of my family, a two-seater with just one chair. The other chair had been replaced with a large wooden box that had a lid. It had a strong, pungent odor, so I moved the lid to look inside. It was filled with raw wool.

The stone corpse's mouth was open, eyes staring straight ahead fixed on something in front of it, features frozen. It was unnerving to look at. There was a hole in the clothing, which hadn't turned to stone, and I was sure under it there was a hole in the stone where the heart had been removed. I leaned in and gently moved the clothing away from where I expected to see the hole in the chest and instead found flaps. It reminded me of a surgical wound that hadn't been stitched closed.

"A demon did that? How was she discovered? She seems to be a loner," I said to Magda.

"She is a loner. But she's also a regular fixture around the neighborhood. She has a massive garden out back, she runs a boutique called The Handmade Thread that sells homespun yarns and some handmade clothing, and she has seven employees. When her shop manager showed up this morning and she didn't, she tried calling and couldn't get an answer, so she called the Creve Coeur police department to do a wellness check. They found the door unlocked, came in and found this. Her name is Valencia Batik. Did you know her?"

"The name isn't familiar." I said. "Why would I know her?"

"She's a cherub."

"Ah, I don't know many angels outside my family. As members of the archangel choir, we aren't welcome at Council functions. Leopold announced Jerome's inclusion in the family in the newsletter, but there was no party or anything."

"I didn't realize you were completely serious when you said Leopold didn't like your family. None of the others have mentioned it., Magda replied.

"Did all the wounds look like this?" I asked.

"Yes." Magda nodded. I nodded once. I'd never seen a demon kill, never even heard of it, so I knew nothing about it, but the precision of the wound bothered me.

"Will I get in trouble if I summon a demon to look at it?" I asked Magda.

"Uh, no. Why would you do that?" Magda asked.

237

"I was expecting the wound to be ragged, like a tear, not precise like a cut. It seems surgical to me; I want a demon's opinion on it," I said. Magda ushered out the crime scene technician, leaving just her and I in the room. I racked my brain for the oldest, least offensive, smallest demon I could think of to summon. Urziuk appeared beside me.

"You summoned, Exorcist?" Urziuk said.

"Have you ever seen a demon intentionally kill?" I asked.

"Unfortunately," Urziuk replied.

"Does this look like a demon kill?" I asked.

"Yes, when a demon rips out the soul of an unwilling living being, it causes a cellular crisis that petrifies the victim." I pointed out the hole in the chest. "A demon didn't remove the heart. Someone living did that," he said

"How can you tell?" I asked.

"Because if a demon did it, the heart would have turned to stone, but there was bleeding. The body was turned to stone afterward," Urziak told us. "However, there is demon magic here. I think the demon paralyzes your victim, the person cuts out the heart, and then the demon rips out the soul as the victim dies in order to cover the human's involvement."

"Thank you, Urziak, this counts as a consult; I will send you whatever food you want as payment," I said.

"I need to tell my sire," Urziak said. "Allow me to do that and we will be even."

"You are always allowed to tell your sire about our meetings," I told the demon. "So, what would you like?"

"No, Exorcist. You don't understand, this is as much our problem as yours. It is not a consult for which you need to pay," Urziak told me. I sent him back instead of standing there arguing with him.

"Why are the demons so concerned?" Magda asked me once he was gone.

"Beyond the possibility of a hell prince on Earth?" I raised an eyebrow.

"Yes, there is something there, they eagerly volunteered for the DNA swabs and invited Dr. Lane back," Magda said.

"When a demon kills, it feels immense guilt. That guilt will eventually drive a demon mad and it will have to be killed," I told her. "They are concerned about the demon coming into the Stygian crazy and super powerful. Also, I find demons are concerned about what they call the final death of the soul, which is what happens when you kill a demon. You destroy the soul for eternity."

"Oh," Magda said. "I didn't..."

"I didn't realize it until recently either, so I suspect it's not a well-known fact for anyone. Dantalian says I make it worse, because I restore their living memories as well as remind them of their first death. He says concerns about the final death of the soul have become more pronounced in the last couple of years. Demons want to live, it is unfortunate they have to create fear to do it, but that is why the majority of the hell princes are fine with the current status quo. Also, I don't dispel most rumors because I want the living to remember demons are dangerous and that bit of information makes them too human for everyone's good."

"I actually understand that completely." Magda said.

I asked to see the rest of the house and Magda began following me around from room to room. I didn't know what I was looking for, if anything. It was a two-bedroom and the second bedroom had a daybed in it, but that was it. The rest of the room was taken up with yarn and a large dye vat. At times during my life, handmade clothing had been rather uncool. But in the last decade or so it had made a huge comeback. The room also held a large weaving loom. After seeing the victim's bedroom, I realized the dye room was actually the master bedroom. She had taken the smaller room for her bedroom. The master bedroom had a half bathroom off it, but it had been converted to a hanging room. Ten poles had been stuck in the walls at a height of about five feet and the toilet drain had been capped off and the room refloored to allow it to be the lowest spot in the room. The floor sloped toward it. There was also a large fan near the ceiling. When I flipped the switch on the wall, the fan came on along with an infrared heat lamp.

After looking in every room, I hadn't found anything useful. However, I was feeling crafty and I had this urge to stop at either a JoAnn's or Michael's on my way home to buy a craft to learn. Helia could paint and she was damn good at it, but I had not taken to any crafts and suddenly felt a bit like a failure. My mom and sister could make stuff, but I couldn't. I could have had a lady's education if I had wanted; after all, my mom had one. I could have learned to sew, embroider, crochet, knit, weave, macrame, something, but I hadn't. I'd learned to cook instead.

"Would it be possible for me to access Azazael's grimoire?" I asked Magda before walking to my father's car.

"Why?" Magda asked. I shrugged and explained about my brother and wanting to see the spell he'd died for. She nodded after a few moments and then told me to meet her at the left side of the AESPCA building in the morning at a door marked Authorized Access Only, it was the only one not alarmed with possession detection.

Chapter Twenty-two

Jerome and I spent the entire day going through my uncles' books examining all mentions of black magic and heart removal. Perhaps most bizarrely, I learned a supernatural could in fact live without their heart. I had never considered that before, but according to most of the books, if we lost a heart a new one would grow, as long as we could find a way to circulate our blood while it regrew. Then I found a machine designed in the year 800 PH that could circulate blood for a supernatural if they suffered extreme heart damage.

Supernaturals had a dating system of pre-history (PH) which was before mankind evolved and history which was after mankind arrived on Earth. I usually forgot to add pre-history to history when doing dates and found the entire system confusing, but I had been a terrible student. History covered the last 175,000 years and pre-history covered about 275,000 years before that. I felt myself frowning at the book. If I had to add pre-history and history together to find out my father's age. Well, it was too much math and it was an unfathomable concept for me. I gave up just as quickly as I'd tried.

"Yes, Raphael is close to 450,000 years old," Jerome told me. "The Stygian is about 150,000 years old in comparison. It started after history starts by about 25,000 years or so."

"You need to spend less time with Remiel. You're keeping his magic longer," I told him. "Did you know my mom had hearth magic?"

"Yes, but since your parents have always said your mom is human, I ignored it," Jerome replied.

"She technically isn't," I said.

"Technically, she is," Jerome replied. "Does angel school teach about Hecate?"

"Yes and I read a book about her," I told him.

"Good, so you know she was hexed into watching her children die of old age, as well as losing all her powers to the hex," Jerome said.

"Yes, but she wasn't cursed with mortality."

"True, but after millennia of breeding solely with humans, she might as well have been," Jerome replied. "At witch school, Hecate is used as an example of what not to do. I had an entire six-week course on Hecate and the hexing of her and her lineage. I didn't realize your mom was a descendent of her until you told me, though. Your parents did a great job of keeping that secret."

"Dad says Mom is super bored at home and needs a job," I told him.

"Your mom is an intelligent and capable woman. I can see that. Most ancient supernaturals work to keep from getting bored, not because they need the paycheck. I would include your mom in that."

"Yeah, I wonder if I will be bored in 700 years," I said.

"I imagine you will have many careers between now and then and find ways to keep yourself busy," Jerome said. "But I get it, on this side of 100 years old, looking toward the future, it is daunting. It's hard to imagine what you will be doing in 200 years when you are 244 years old." Supernaturals usually celebrate the first 100 birthdays and then stop as infinity stretches out in front of them. I was nearly 45, and I couldn't imagine living as long as my mom, let alone my father. Especially since sometimes I thought I was already suffering from ennui.

"You know Hecate was cursed by Jophiel?" I asked Jerome.

"Yes. I told you we did a six-week course on her. Do you know why?"

"She introduced him to Lilith and didn't mention she was a demon until after Azazael was born."

"Sorta," Jerome shrugged. "It was Hecate that executed Lilith after Lilith began killing babies."

"I wonder if demons can experience post-partum psychosis," I said a bit absently. "Killing can make a demon go crazy, I wonder if giving birth can also do it."

"That is a good question and might explain Lilith." Jerome said, putting another book down. After giving birth to Azazael, Lilith had decided to expand the pool of souls available to Demonation and had begun killing infant supernaturals, for which she was executed. That's what made Jophiel decide the Stygian needed to come into existence. He and Zadkiel got to work on it immediately following Lilith's execution by Hecate, the Great Witch. I went back to reading my book, but it only lasted a few minutes before someone was beating on my front door. I got up to answer it, Jerome following behind me.

My parents and Helia stood on my porch. I opened the door to allow them all in. Jerome tugged on my shirt sleeve very determinedly. I turned to look at him, and his eyes were large and his lips set in a hard line. I had no idea why.

"We need to have a family meeting about your mom being a descendent of Hecate," My father announced.

"Uh, well," Jerome said, and then stopped. "Actually." He began again and then stopped again.

"What is it, Jerome?" I asked him.

"Helia, the other day when you came over, had you just left your mom?" Jerome asked.

"Yes," Helia replied. Jerome frowned.

"We really should wait and do a family meeting later," Jerome said.

"Are you not feeling well?" My mom asked Jerome.

"Uh, how you are feeling is the better question," Jerome replied. "Why don't you sit down and I'll get you something to put your feet up on."

"What?" my mom said. She touched her wrist to Jerome's forehead.

"Are you okay?" I asked Jerome.

"Fine," Jerome said and his voice cracked. He got a pillow and put it in a chair and then took my mom by the hand and guided her to it. Then it clicked. It wasn't Helia that was pregnant.

"Oh my god, it's my mom??" I asked Jerome.

"Uh, well," Jerome looked like he was about to get hit by a truck.

"What's Mom?" my mom asked.

"You're pregnant!" I blurted out and everyone looked at me except Jerome, who looked at the floor.

"Don't be ridiculous," Mom replied.

"I'm not. Jerome thought it was Helia the other day, but since he just tried to give you a pillow for your back and he seems a bit tongue-tied, it's not Helia, it's you."

"How would Jerome know before me that I was…" My mom stopped. "Jerome, do you think I'm pregnant?" she asked him, seriously taking his hand.

"I didn't notice it at Sunday brunch, but when Helia came over on Monday, I thought it was her, but today I am sure it's you," Jerome admitted.

"That's why Gabriel came over and left this morning," Mom said.

"What?" I asked.

"Gabriel usually comes by for coffee a few times a week in the morning. He stopped by this morning, I got coffee out and ready and he suddenly left. We weren't trying."

"No," Dad said. "Jerome, how do you know?"

"I just know." Jerome shrugged. My dad was digging out his cell phone.

"My grandson thinks my wife is pregnant. Is this true?" Raphael said into the phone. There was a long period of silence. Then my dad hung up and fell into a seat on the couch. He looked at Sophia.

"Gabriel says it's true; you are less than a week along. He didn't know Jerome would find out if he avoided him," Dad said. "He says he only discovered it this morning."

"Wow, we weren't even trying," my mom said. "It's a miracle." She suddenly burst into tears. Helia walked over and hugged her.

"Is it good news?" I asked.

"Yes, it's great news. I think. I always said I wouldn't be one of those immortals that had children centuries apart." My mom wiped at her face.

"Well, 45 years isn't a century," I said with a shrug. "I know this is rude, but I'm not sure how I feel about you being pregnant. I'm sure I'll be happy eventually, but at this moment I'm just overwhelmed. And confused."

"Me too!" Mom said. "Angels have to try so hard to get pregnant and we weren't trying. To conceive you, I was spending six or seven hours a day, six days a week with Gabriel, and it still took more than a year."

"How?" Dad asked. He seemed utterly shocked. I could definitely relate to that.

"Helia," I said after a few silent minutes in which my family tried to absorb the fact that my mom was pregnant.

"What about Helia?" Dad said.

"She's never had a problem getting pregnant. She wanted kids close in age to begin with and she got two girls 27 months apart. It seems unlikely she was spending that much time with Gabriel to accomplish it." I nodded, getting into it now. "She's an archangel and there is a precedent for fertility archangels, also Hecate's specialty was fertility spells and potions. What if Helia is a fertility angel like Gabriel? Possibly stronger than Gabriel."

"We have been seeing each other a lot lately," Helia said slowly.

"But we didn't feel that in her magic," Dad said.

"I did," Jerome said. "I was expecting Duke and Soleil to end up pregnant after he and Helia started Thursday night movie nights, but then they broke up."

"Yuck," I said to Jerome. "Not the baby with Duke thing, but the fact that you were expecting it."

"You'd be a good mom," Jerome replied.

"No offense, but I hope it isn't anytime soon. I have enough on my plate with you and the rest of life."

"Hecate's other power was a connection to demons," Mom said. "We have long suspected your connection to the Stygian was the result of my connection to Hecate as well as your father being an archangel."

"Well, this family meeting was awesome, but I have to capture someone who has genetically engineered a demon and is possibly driving it mad by having it kill," I said to my parents. "Any suggestions you have about why the handler is taking hearts would be appreciated, but otherwise I am going to need to get together with Magda to go interview a suspect."

"Hearts?" My mom raised an eyebrow. "One of Hecate's spells for a fertility potion for angels involved using bits of heart, but she used the hearts of rabbits."

"Was this potion specifically for angel use or could anyone use it?" I asked.

"I'll give you her grimoire," Mom said and started toward the door.

"You have Hecate's grimoire?" I asked.

"Yes, it's a family heirloom."

"Uh, okay."

"She wasn't evil or crazy, so my family was allowed to retain it. When I married Raphael, my aunt gave it to me," Mom said.

"Interesting, yes I would like to see it."

"Well, I was going to have your father make two copies of it, one for you and one for Helia when we reached that point, now I guess we'll need to make three copies." Sophia said. "If we have another girl."

"If you have another girl?" I raised an eyebrow.

"Hecate's magic only passes to the females in the lineage," Dad said.

"So, Helia and I might be archangels not solely because of dad, but because of Hecate's lineage. As might the two granddaughters."

"Unlikely, but possible," Mom said. "I had no involvement with Jerome's lineage and he's an archangel."

"Jerome doesn't count," I pointed out. "So, let's go get this grimoire." I hurried my family out the door.

Since Helia and I were together, Helia got the original grimoire and Mom and I got copies. Which was fine with me. The copies were more modern and easier to preserve. I told my mom maybe she should try performing some of the easier magic in Hecate's grimoire and then I left, taking Jerome with me to the AESPCA. I knew Magda had said tomorrow we could look at Azazael's grimoire, but I had an overwhelming feeling we needed to see it now, even though I couldn't explain why. Well, I could, but not to my father or mother. Azazael had taken Nicholas' soul for this spell experiment and our new demon was also taking souls. Soul was an incredibly rare spell or potion ingredient. I called Magda and informed her I needed to see the book now. It took a few minutes for her to come down and get Jerome and I, but she did, and I explained why I needed to see it now, not tomorrow. She agreed and into the building we went.

The archive looks like a giant library, except all the shelves have glass fronts and needed a magical key to be opened. Which led to a disagreement between the archivist and Magda Red. Magda informed her we needed to see Azazael's grimoire, and the archivist apparently didn't trust me with a cambion's grimoire because she began to argue as to why I couldn't see it. Her arguments against it were rather personal in my opinion. In her mind, angels that cavorted with demons must be evil, and the grimoire was in the archive for a reason, to keep it out of the hands of evil people. I did not point out I wasn't evil. I also didn't point out demons weren't evil. I kept my mouth tightly closed while they debated it, which I thought was a serious achievement. Eventually, Magda won the argument and I was told to not move from where I was while the book was retrieved. Jerome and I stood completely still, a petty consolation to being treated like naughty children. The archivist placed the book on a table about ten feet from us.

"Well, did you change your mind?" the archivist snapped at me.

"No, I was waiting for permission to move," I replied, earning me a stern look from the archivist and a mischievous grin from Magda Red. After another moment, the archivist told me not to be an asshole and to get over there if I wanted to see the book. The woman actually stood behind me as I looked for the spell. The problem with grimoires is that no one ever thinks to put an index or table of contents in them. I flipped page after bleeding page looking for the one particular spell and ignored the majority of the book.

"What are you looking for?" the archivist snapped at me again.

"A spell called Movement in the Shadows," I told her. "My father told me it was the spell Azazael was experimenting with when he took my brother's soul and ended up killing him. I think it relates to these recent murders that involve taking souls."

"It's the last spell in the book," the archivist told me. I turned to the end of the book. The page wasn't there and it was obvious it had been torn from the book. I showed it to Magda.

"Do you know what the spell was?" Magda asked the archivist.

"It was a fertility spell," the archivist said, and I gave her a strange look.

"The archivists are magically connected to the archive and can recite the contents of it as well as provide information on all its contents," Magda told me. I nodded once slowly.

"Can you tell me who looked at it last?" I asked.

"Before you?" She kinda huffed at me as she said it.

"Yes," I agreed. "You watched me and know I didn't tear out the page."

"That could have been done by anyone," she said.

"Who looked at it last?" Magda asked.

"What kind of fertility spell?" Jerome asked. "Did it involve souls and hearts?"

"How did you know that?" the archivist asked.

"Azazael was building on Hecate's spell, which he probably got from Hecate's grimoire. I imagine at some point Nicholas showed it to him." I opened Hecate's grimoire and sure enough, the copy in my hands had a blank page in the middle of the book. I called Helia and she confirmed there was a page torn out of Hecate's original grimoire.

"Was it Balthazar Leopold that looked at the book last?" I snapped at the archivist. It had not escaped my notice that she had angel wings and was probably a seraphim dedicated to the cause of the council. She didn't answer me, she just stood there glaring at me. "Good enough." I told her. I pushed the useless grimoire away from me and stormed out of the archive. As I entered the hallway, the alarms at the AESPCA went off. Sure enough, I had summoned a demon, this was getting out of hand. I stared a Urziak.

"Tell Leviathan someone has stolen a spell for angel fertility from Hecate's grimoire. Then go to Lucifer's, and if Azazael isn't dead, have Lucifer find him," I told Urziak. Jerome looked at me and I sent the demon back across the divide.

"Did you forget Urziak is Beelzebub's?" Jerome asked me. I shook my head no. I knew Urziak would deliver all my messages to their intended recipients as well as Beelzebub. But I was fairly certain I was going to need some Stygian help in this matter. Magda stood next to me. The alarms continued to blare.

"Well?" Magda looked at me.

"Well, I think Balthazar Leopold is doing it to increase angel fertility rates. Hasn't he been trying for decades without success to get his wife pregnant? Also, it's really hard on his fertility clinic that he isn't more successful with angel fertility," I told her.

"Considering who he is, I hope you have proof beyond a missing spell book page."

"I don't at the moment," I admitted.

"Also, that doesn't explain why he would engineer a demon."

"Actually, it does. He wasn't trying to engineer a demon. He was trying to engineer a hell prince. There is this ridiculous theory that when Lucifer stopped demons from breeding in the Stygian, it caused angels to start having fertility issues. According to my father and uncles, it has always been difficult for angels to breed, though, and the problem predates the creation of the Stygian. I was taught the theory as fact in angel school. As was Helia. If a demon could be engineered to replace Lucifer, then maybe the ban on demon breeding could be lifted and angelic fertility rates would go up as well."

"Wow," Magda said.

"Except there are two fertility angels much stronger than Gabriel, and Lucifer did not impact angel fertility by preventing demonic breeding," Jerome said.

"Two?" I asked.

"Ariel and Helia," Jerome replied. "Sometimes your family is kinda dense when it comes to other members. I suspect Aurora is as well, but for animals, not sentient beings like angels or humans."

"My ten-year-old niece is a fertility angel?" I asked.

"Yes," Jerome replied in a tone that said duh.

"Good to know." I nodded.

"She's a lot more powerful than Gabriel or Helia. I suspect her powers will kick in once she reaches puberty, that's how fertility stuff usually works."

"That's terrifying," I said.

"I agree." Jerome nodded sagely.

"Why now?" Magda asked.

"How long have you been thinking things needed to change on the Angel Council?" I asked her.

"About a century," Magda said.

"Who did you tell?" I asked.

"Mostly the Witches' Council. All of them agree that things need to change. Our last holdout was Simon Vance, but I think Kim Grace finally convinced him when she was assisting with Jerome getting an angel designation. He is the one that eventually took the case to Balthazar Leopold."

"Why would that convince Vance?" I asked.

"Simon Vance's wife is a master vampire," Jerome said. "Leonard's powers are stronger in witchcraft, but he has some effective vampire glamour as well."

"By getting you accepted as both angel and witch, there is hope Leonard might get accepted as both vampire and witch," I said, figuring it out.

"Yes," Jerome nodded. Magda agreed.

"Maybe Simon told Balthazar the Witches' Council was going to endorse someone else, especially since there are only two angel schools left in operation because we are a dying race," I said.

"Why the souls and hearts?" Magda asked.

"Maybe to ensure the pregnant person could carry the demon to term? Maybe since it has angelic DNA,

Balthazar needed to ensure it could reproduce," I said. "What good is it to install a new king of the Stygian if that king is sterile?"

"Why would sterility matter?" Magda asked.

"That's how Lucifer prevents breeding. When Jophiel created his Stygian form, he intentionally made it sterile. It has no sexual organs of any kind. It is male only because Jophiel was male." I said.

"And that worked?" Magda asked, looking confused.

"Yes. Here's your demon pre-history lesson for today. Demon fertility is determined by the demon king. Jophiel and Zadkiel built the Stygian with the help of the demon king Asmodeus. Because a supernatural has to die for a demon to be born, after Lilith's incident with babies, Asmodeus decided it would be better if demons couldn't naturally reproduce because it would mean that eventually the world would only have demons in it, because demons reproduce faster than the other supernaturals. That decision would come back to bite him, because Beelzebub wanted children and his father prevented it, so once they were all comfortable in the Stygian, Beelzebub and Belial overthrew their father and another hell prince to take their places and eventually they will try to overthrow Lucifer. That's why a truce had to be declared," I said.

"Why then would Balthazar believe overthrowing Lucifer would make angel reproduction easier?" Magda asked.

"Because Jophiel was an angel. Some angels cannot divorce the idea of Lucifer and Jophiel. They don't realize Lucifer is an artificial construct; a body made from the red dirt of the Stygian and not Jophiel. It is hard to imagine changing bodies because most people can't do it. It was Jophiel's archangel power, though, he could move his soul to a different body, he just required Zadkiel to create it. And Zadkiel did, he made Lucifer, not Jophiel ,and Jophiel tore his soul from his own body and moved it to Lucifer the Demon King."

"Wow." Magda said. "Okay, I get it."

"Great, now Jerome and I need to go to the Stygian and find out about Azazael's Movement in the Shadows spell and learn what the fuck it actually does. Because I know Azazael didn't give a rat's ass about angelic fertility," I told her.

"Just the two of you?" Magda asked, concern passing over her face. "You had a group last time and still ended up poisoned."

"We will have the demons to help us this time. Lucifer is supposed to be getting Azazael if he's still alive."

"Why wouldn't he be?" Magda asked.

"He violated a demonic truce. In order to keep their power, it's possible either Beelzebub or Belial had to kill him."

"We'll just go from here, we've already set off the alarms," Jerome said to her. I nodded and pushed magic.

I opened my eyes to find I was in Lucifer's courtyard and Jerome was with me. There was a huge commotion in progress and none of the demons seemed to notice us. But then Beelzebub was shouting at Lucifer, so I could see why we were being ignored. Judging from the argument, Azazael was alive but was slated to be executed. Beelzebub didn't care why Lucifer wanted him, he wasn't going to turn him over. Then it dawned on me, Beelzebub thought Lucifer was trying to prevent the death of his son.

"Uh, excuse me Prince Beelzebub. I need to see Azazael," I said. Beelzebub glared at me. "The killings are related to a spell he concocted while on earth. Someone is using it, but no one knows what it is. I need to know and I can only find out from Azazael."

"What are you babbling about, Exorcist?" Beelzebub said, finally giving me his full attention.

"Azazael designed a spell that requires souls and hearts and a demon to kill. It's some kind of fertility spell. The demon on Earth was genetically engineered to perform the spell. I believe the person who created it believes it will improve angel fertility. But this is Azazael we are talking about, and he might have said it would help angels reproduce faster, but I don't believe him and neither would you. So, I need to know what the spell really does. I believe the purpose of it is to overthrow Lucifer and the hell princes in order for Azazael to take over all of the Stygian, because that sounds like something Azazael would do, but he would need a demon army to accomplish it."

"Ah, you think it's a demon fertility spell to allow Azazael to build an army and you want confirmation from the cambion," Beelzebub said.

"Yes," I agreed.

"And you believe he will tell you?" he asked.

"No, but he's half angel and Jerome can read the minds of the living, and Azazael is semi-alive, he has to be, because he isn't a ghost. I think he will lie to me, but while

257

he's doing it, Jerome can read his mind and tell me the truth afterward," I said.

"That's devious," Beelzebub said.

"After I finish my business with Azazael, I would like to come back and speak with you privately about performing a Rite of Forgiveness on you," I said.

"What?" Beelzebub said.

"It has come to my attention, that you have accidentally killed a few hosts, as a demon of your power, this doesn't surprise me; both the supernatural and human forms are too fragile to hold you. However, I recently inherited Hecate the Great Witch's grimoire and she has a spell for performing the Rite of Forgiveness in it for demons when the family of the deceased cannot."

"What makes you think you are strong enough, Exorcist?" Beelzebub asked.

"My mother is descended from Hecate," I replied.

"How do you know I want forgiveness?" he countered.

"I can feel it."

"What do you want in return?" Beelzebub sneered.

"Nothing, Prince Beelzebub," I said. His face went blank.

"I will bring you Azazael," he told me, and the conversation dropped.

"Leave it to your father to have children with a daughter of Hecate," Lucifer said with a smile. "That and Zadkiel's influence explains your power, little one."

"Zadkiel's influence?" I asked.

"The daughters of Hecate always worked as demon executioners. We have been without one since I..." He trailed off. "Zadkiel knew one was needed and since he has the power to dream walk, he knew Sophia was pregnant with a girl and that you could do the job."

"I don't understand why a demon executioner needs to exist," I told him. "My father has killed demons before."

"The final death, yes. But the final death is not within the grasp of a demon executioner. It is only another death for a demon when it is performed by you. Think of it as a reset—if you kill a demon, the soul is reborn into a different demon," Lucifer told me. I tried to close my mouth and discovered I couldn't. "A demon executioner is meant to prevent the destruction of the soul. If you were to kill Azazael today, tomorrow his soul would be reborn to an existing hell prince. The same is true if you executed Beelzebub, his soul would return as a demonling to a different hell prince and one of his demi-princes would take over his territory."

"Really?" I asked.

"Yes, I didn't know what I had done to Hecate and Demonation until much later. I have always regretted it. Once the Stygian was formed and complete, I found the soul I had committed a grave sin for," Lucifer said, pointing to a female demon in the courtyard. I walked over toward her, getting close enough to touch her. When I did, I was flooded with memories of a handsome archangel and I knew it was Jophiel. She turned to look at me, and I saw the tears in her eyes and knew the soul in her was Lilith's.

"Hecate freed me," the demon said. "The death of a supernatural to provide a soul for a developing demon is a hard guilt to bear. I could not and I did not want other demons to experience it. I killed to prevent it, and Hecate killed me to stop me. I was born again to Asmodeus, my memories as Lilith hadn't left, though, so I begged my father to help Jophiel and Zadkiel build a place to protect the world from us and to stop our female demons from feeling what I felt to have Azazael, such joy mixed with such guilt," the demon said to me. I realized I was crying and could feel both her joy and her sadness. They were both soul-crushing. "There has been little need for a demon executioner since the Stygian was created, but I am glad one exists again in case we do need one" she told me as tears rolled down both our faces.

"Thank you," I whispered, turning away from her as Beelzebub returned with Azazael. The cambion was clamped in strange-looking chains that glowed with a dull red light.

"You've been speaking with my idiot mother, I see," Azazael hissed at me. If I hadn't wanted him dead before, I did now. I only had to decide whether I wanted him to experience final death or a second death. Although I had a feeling that for Azazael, second death wouldn't be a reset of his sanity.

"Your Movement in the Shadow Spell, is it a demon fertility spell?" I asked.

"No," Azazael replied flatly. I looked at Jerome, who nodded to me.

"Did you tell someone about it recently?" I asked.

"No," Azazael answered in that same flat tone. Jerome looked at the ground this time when I looked at him.

"Okay, do what you will with him, Beelzebub," I said waving him away with a hand.

"Exorcist, have you been informed of the difference between final death and second death?" Beelzebub asked.

"Yes," I nodded.

"Do you believe his soul is capable of redemption?" Beelzebub asked.

"I would like to believe all souls are capable of redemption," I told him.

"Demons do not forget their first life as a demon, it is important to know if he can change his ways," Beelzebub said.

"The problem is identifying what way he needs to change? Do you want him to stop plotting against Demonation or Lucifer or beings on Earth?" I asked.

"Fair point," Beelzebub said. "My power has already begun to wane since he broke our truce. I have to have him killed in order to regain it. If you do it, he can be reborn. If I do it, he can't."

"You want me to execute him?" I asked.

"I can and will do it," Beelzebub replied quickly. "But if you would prefer to give him a chance through rebirth, I think you should have the option."

"And he will remember it?" I asked. Everyone said yes. I wanted to ask if his new form would retain the alpha helix he currently had, but I wasn't sure anyone here could answer that question. "I will , if it will return your power."

"My truce was with you, so it would," Beelzebub said.

"Fine," I said. "How do I do it?"

261

"Hecate used a spell," Jerome said producing the grimoire out of thin air. He opened to the page. I read it quickly. Hecate just separated the demon soul from the body and then she killed the body with magic. Okay, I could do this, I wouldn't actually be killing him, I'd just force him to be a demonling all over again, which technically Azazael had never been because he was cambion. He'd come back as a full demon and not a cambion. I sighed and re-read the spell. I kept chanting in my head that I wasn't really killing him, I was just forcing him to be reborn and experience childhood over again, he'd probably be the same asshole he was now. I re-read it a third time, nodded to myself twice and turned to face Azazael, still chanting that it wasn't permanent death, he'd be reborn in a short time and he'd still be Azazael. I could do this. I yanked Azazael's soul from his body and tossed it away, then I filled the physical form with magic and stopped everything the body did. When I pulled my magic away, the body collapsed and Azazael's soul disappeared.

"It is done," Lucifer said. "I can already feel him waiting to return."

I could tell myself I hadn't just killed someone, but it felt like I had, despite Lucifer telling me otherwise. I sat down hard on the ground and wiped roughly at the tears. Snot ran from my nose. I hoped I never had to do it again.

"Hecate cried every time, too," the female demon said, coming over to me. "I know it feels like a curse to you, but to us it is a blessing. We remember, but we have no emotions tied to those memories. They don't haunt us."

"It might haunt me," I said.

"It might until you are able to make peace with it," she agreed, handing me something that looked like a handkerchief. "What you have done is quell his rage at the world."

"Shouldn't you be angry that I just killed your son?" I asked her.

"If you had killed him, I might be, but you didn't and I know you didn't," she replied softly, stroking my hair. "I know that what you have done will give him a chance to be happy instead of angry."

Chapter Twenty-three

I returned us to the parking lot of the AESPCA. My phone took a few moments to reconnect to service and update the time, and when it did it said we'd been gone 17 minutes. I went back to the side door. I texted Magda we were back and tried to look at my face in the darkened screen of my phone. Crying always made me blotchy and red, even a small number of tears.

"Who did Azazael tell?" I asked Jerome as we walked.

"Azazael didn't have a name, but he was a dream walker like Zadkiel," Jerome replied.

"Okay, if he can only walk through angel dreams like Leviathan." I shrugged.

"I'm not sure that's the case," Jerome said.

"A girl can hope, right? Do you have any clue who it was?" I asked.

"I know where the person works." Jerome shrugged.

"A fertility clinic?" I asked.

"Mission Fertility," Jerome agreed.

"That's the place that will genetically engineer your child to have the eye color, hair color, or hair texture you desire," I said, pursing my lips. It was not the clinic owned by Balthazar Leopold and I was disappointed. Perhaps I despised Balthazar Leopold as much as he despised me.

The door opened and Magda looked at us expectantly, then her face paled a little.

"Are you okay?" she asked, reaching out to me. I burst into tears.

"I just killed Azazael." I blubbered. "And my mom is pregnant." I wasn't sure which one of these things was making me cry harder. Yes, I knew my mom at 700-plus years old could have another child, but I had never dreamed of them actually doing it. I was used to life with Helia, me, Ariel, Aurora, and Jerome. I wasn't sure I wanted another sibling, especially one younger than my nieces and son.

"Congrats on both those things. I know right now it feels like the world has exploded, but all supernaturals feel that way when they learn their parents are going to have another child after a huge gap in time. And Azazael deserved it."

"Well, she left out the part about the fact that Azazael's soul will be reborn as a demonling—that's what a demon executioner does, allows demon souls to be reborn." Jerome said. "So yes she killed him, but he isn't dead dead."

"As cambion wouldn't his soul have been reborn anyway?" Magda asked.

"Uh, good question." Jerome nodded. "The demons seemed to think it was a huge honor to be executed by someone with the power of a demon executioner, even for a cambion, so I'm guessing no."

"And this was your first execution as a demon executioner? When did you get that power?" Magda asked.

"Apparently, I've always had it. And no, not really, but sorta," I admitted. "I've destroyed a demon soul once before, but I felt really horrible about it and vowed to never do it again. Now I've learned that soul was probably reborn as another demon, complete with demon memories from its previous demon life. I know it's ridiculous, but I feel even worse about killing that demon now and Lilith fucking thanked me for freeing her son from his rage, which made me feel even worse." I blubbered.

"Lilith the demon princess?" Magda asked.

"Yes, Hecate was a demon executioner. When she executed Lilith, Lilith was just reborn, and she and Jophiel are an item in the Stygian, too. She's the one that wanted demons to be sterile. She says giving birth to a demon is brutal on the demon's guilt because a supernatural has to die to give their child a soul, and that's why she went on her killing spree, to have souls available so demon mothers wouldn't feel guilty about giving birth to a child."

"Oh, poor Lilith," Magda said, and I started to cry even harder. "Why don't we go get a coffee or something to give you time to process this information and calm down a little bit," Magda said, closing the AESPCA door and stepping outside. Magda opened a portal and half pushed me through it. We ended up in my front yard, which was better than my house, where Jerome's alarms would go off. "You have excellent coffee." I said nothing, only started to cry harder. The problem was, I didn't know why I was crying. Yes, I felt bad for killing Azazael and I felt guilty over not wanting my parents to have another child, but honestly there was nothing really awful in my life right now. I hadn't had my heart removed and been turned to stone, for example. And we had an idea of where to find our demon creator and handler—that was something to celebrate, not cry over.

Jerome let Magda and I into the house. Then the teen made us coffee while I continued to bawl at my kitchen table.

"I'm sorry, I don't know what's wrong with me," I sobbed.

"Sometimes we just have to release all our emotions at once," Magda said soothingly, and rubbed her hand over my hair like Lilith had done in the Stygian. "When it happens, it usually happens as tears. Also, you were poisoned yesterday. That might be a contributing factor."

"Bah humbug," I sniffled.

"Did you find out anything useful from the trip beyond what a demon executioner is and that you are one?" she asked.

"Yes," Jerome said, setting a cup of coffee down in front of me along with a brand-new bottle of hazelnut creamer. "Azazael's Movement in the Shadow spell was supposed to allow him to breed a demon army. As I understand it, it used Hecate's fertility spell coupled with the death of a supernatural to free up a soul. The person takes the heart from the victim, says some magical words, the demon eats it and becomes pregnant, at which point the soul of the supernatural is taken and given to the growing demon."

"But the first two kills were humans," Magda said. "How the hell does that help angels have more kids?"

"Azazael was going to do it to overthrow Lucifer and the other hell princes," Jerome told her. "If someone believes Lucifer is why angels struggle with fertility, it makes sense."

"Did Azazael tell you who he gave the spell to?" Magda asked.

"He didn't know a name, but he knew they worked at Mission Fertility," Jerome said.

"That is Roderick Felder's clinic," Magda replied.

"Really?" I asked, wiping at my nose with a tissue that had appeared at my elbow with the coffee.

"Well, okay, that's weird." Jerome said.

"Why?" Magda asked.

"Because the Movement in the Shadow spell is listed as being a fertility spell specifically for angels."

"Which is why they killed an angel this time," I asked.

"Possibly," Jerome said. "However, as I understand it, Roderick Felder isn't an angel."

"He's not, he's a vampire," Magda said. "Roderick Felder's sister Bella is married to a wizard."

"Roderick is the brother-in-law of Simon Vance?" I asked, drying my eyes again.

"Yes," Magda said.

"Are any or all of these people good friends?" I asked.

"Yes, Simon's father Robert was coupled for a while with Violet Dunn, Balthazar Leopold's mother, and Violet's sister, Julia, is Roderick and Bella's mother."

"Holy fuck," I muttered. In my head that seemed sorta incestuous, even though biologically I knew it wasn't. "The entire group is related by marriages then?"

"Yes and no. Balthazar was born before Robert and Violet got together, same for Simon. They were kind of step-brothers, albeit Robert and Violet didn't officially marry at any point. However, they were a couple for most of the late 1600s and early 1700s when Simon and Balthazar were growing up. It's how Simon and Bella met."

"Okay, is it Violet and Julia that were angels?" I asked.

"Yes, and Balthazar's father Henry was also an angel. Henry had a bizarre accident when Balthazar was about a year old; he was decapitated in a horse and carriage accident." Decapitation was one of the injuries it was impossible for a supernatural to heal.

"So, Roderick and Bella are part angel, part vampire?" I asked.

"No, they are full vampire. Roderick and Bella were born to Count Vlad Adam and his wife Bianca. Both were captured and beheaded by Ottomans during one of the wars. However, they sent Roderick and Bianca to live with Bianca's brother George, and eventually, he and Julia became a couple. They even married and legally adopted Bella and Roderick, while having a child of their own."

"That is more complicated than my life," I said, trying to convince myself to feel better. "Now, we need evidence."

"You can sense demons, right?" Magda asked.

"Yes," I nodded. "I can also command them to come to me, but I don't know if that's true of genetically engineered demons."

"Why? It's still a demon," Magda said.

"True." I nodded.

"Why don't we go for a drive and you give it a try."

"Sure," I said. I offered to let Magda drive only to learn she didn't know how; she always used portals or teleported when she traveled. This was strange to me, but I was still very young. Maybe in a thousand years, I'd refuse to travel in any fashion other than translocation or portals, too, if I ever learned how to begin with. Instead, she navigated while I drove. She had me circle Roderick Felder's house twice, but I felt nothing there, and when I tried to call a demon, Urziak was summoned instead. I frowned and sent him back to the Stygian. At which point she had me drive to Mission Fertility. I circled the building a half dozen times and felt nothing. She had me park and she, Jerome, and I headed into the clinic. She showed her AESPCA investigator's badge and told the woman at the desk we wanted to look around a bit. Roderick Felder appeared in short order to complain about it, but Magda told me to ignore him.

"Dr. Felder, do you know Soleil Burns?" she asked. He shook his head no. "She's an archangel with a connection to the Stygian which allows her to sense demons," Magda informed him. "She's going to walk around your clinic for a while."

While she argued with Roderick Felder, I took his badge. Jerome and I let ourselves in through another door marked Authorized Personnel Only. I stuck my head in a couple of clinic rooms, apologizing profusely when one was occupied. But I didn't sense anything demonic. After checking nearly every room, Jerome and I exchanged looks. If there was a demon here, I couldn't sense it.

Jerome seemed to be of the same opinion. We did find some stairs that led to a laboratory on the second and third floors, but I didn't sense anything demonic in there, either. Neither did Jerome. However, there were bustling rooms with a dozen people in each.

Outside the second-floor lab, a man came out to yell at us for wandering around a secure area. I told him who I was and why I was there. He looked at me blankly for several moments and then informed me that his lab and the lab on the third floor were not equipped to genetically engineer anything, not a mouse, not a demon. I shrugged and we went back downstairs.

"Nothing," I told Magda.

"His wife is home, we could go back to the house," Magda suggested.

"While I suspect Roderick Felder is involved, I don't think he actually did the genetic engineering," I said with a sigh once we were back in the car. "Let's go to the Divine Blessings Clinic," I told her.

"If you were one of my investigators, I'd tell you to stop being so focused on Balthazar Leopold. It's not illegal to be an asshole," Magda told me. I shrugged and started the drive to Leopold's clinic. I didn't have to circle it. I could feel the demon while we were still a half block away from the clinic.

"Demon," Jerome said, pointing at a building that looked abandoned. I nodded my agreement and parked in a no parking zone in front of the building.

"If someone comes out and complains about us parking here, move the car," I said, giving Jerome the keys.

"Awe man, that's code for stay in the car!" the teen whined. I nodded in agreement again and smiled at him.

"I can't believe this is really about angelic fertility," Magda said.

"It isn't, it's about money," I told her. "Do you have any idea how much angels spend every year on fertility treatments?"

"How would making angels more fertile help Leopold get richer?" Magda asked.

"Because Leopold's clinic offers more than just fertility treatments; it offers angelic prenatal care. I remember my parents getting hundreds of pamphlets in the mail when it was announced Helia was pregnant, offering prenatal care tailored to meet angelic needs. Pregnant angel females are the only race of supernaturals to experience miscarriages without the involvement of demonic possession," I said.

"I didn't know that," Magda said.

"It's not talked about, not even among angels. I only know because of Helia," I replied. "In 2010, a month of prenatal care potions and other services from Divine Blessing Fertility Clinic was $15,000."

"That's close to $140,000 for the duration of the pregnancy," Magda said.

"Yes it is, and Janet told me ages ago, when I was still dating Duke, that if we wanted to try getting pregnant she'd make my prenatal care potions for me, because they were easy and cheap to make and there was no reason for me to spend that kind of money on it when she could do it," I said. "Prenatal care for angels is where all the money really is, I think the fertility clinic is more about getting angels pregnant in order for them to buy the stuff they supposedly need for the pregnancy."

"What all did Helia use during her pregnancies?" Magda asked.

"She didn't," I said, shrugging. "But most angels do. I get coupons for fertility and prenatal aids in my copy of the Cherubim News for all that stuff and have since I was 20."

"Really?" Magda asked as I strode toward a door of the abandoned looking building. I nodded. Magda knocked on the door. It was opened by Balthazar Leopold, who looked very pale and was holding his cell phone at his ear. Magda took it and showed it to me. The caller ID said Roderick.

"Go away, this is private property." Balthazar sneered at Magda.

"I have reason to suspect there's a demon on the property, and since I am currently looking for a demon…" She pushed past him.

"The only demon here is that woman," Balthazar spluttered, pointing at me. I didn't say anything, just stepped in behind Magda.

There were three cambions in the room. A male, a female, and an infant. There were also about a dozen people in the room. Some of them were monitoring the equipment hooked to the cambions, and others were doing things with microscopes and other equipment I couldn't identify. Fan-fucking-tabulous. What the hell was going on.

"I can explain," Balthazar said.

"Let me guess, Roderick said he found a spell that would breed angels in Azazael's grimoire and you've been trying to make angels using it and modern science?" I postulated.

"Yes," Balthazar sputtered.

"Except Azazael's spell makes demons, not angels," I said.

"He said it made angels," he said.

"Demons may not be able to lie, but cambion have no problem with it." I tried not to snarl at him. "Even making angels doesn't give you the right to kill people."

"We need more angels. It is worth all life to get more!" Balthazar told me.

"You're insane. There are three fertility angels, if you'd stop strangling the Angel Council and allow them to serve, we might get more angels." I paused. "Good grief you're a fucking moron."

"I asked Gabriel to come work for me here to help boost the numbers and he refused," Balthazar told me.

"As he should. The impotence of the council is why angel infertility is expanding. Angel children shouldn't just go to angels that can afford your outrageous services, especially because if Gabriel was working here you'd just charge more."

"You don't know what you're talking about. You're too young and all you care about are demons anyway," he said.

"I do care about demons and cambion; they are living beings, not unlike ourselves. However, I am old enough to know that for every year you've run the council has been a year less in births. You have angels believing it's because Lucifer stopped demon breeding, but that was because you needed to cover up that you corrupted the base of throne magic and it is spreading to all of angeldom. When the Witches' Council decided they could no longer back you, you knew the truth would come out if you were voted out. So you took drastic measures by trusting Azazael to provide you with a solution and he did, except his Movement in the Shadows spell is a corruption of Hecate's fertility spell. The point of Movement in the Shadows was to give him a way to create a demon army to overthrow the hell princes and Lucifer, that's why no matter how you tweak it, you still get cambions, not angels."

"I am not the reason for angel infertility!" Balthazar screamed at me.

"Yes, you are. It finally dawned on me today, after meeting the demon Lilith. The archangels started the council to be a democratic institution to allow angels to have a vote in how angeldom is run. Every time it's been run by someone who selflessly gives to angeldom, the birth rates for angels go up. The longer someone corrupt heads the council, the worse the birth rates get," I said. "Lilith told me it was she that wanted Demonation to be sterile so that no demon mother would ever have to feel the joy and guilt of the birth of her child. Her despicable act of murder was done with good intentions; she killed so other demon mothers wouldn't experience what she felt. I could feel her joy and sorrow over it. When we got back, I got overwhelmed and it dawned on me. The demon kings and queens control demon fertility. The Angel Council works the exact same way." Several people at the lab stations had stopped working to look at me. "Jophiel and Zadkiel were building the Stygian when all the archangels got together to make the Angel Council. They would have known the fertility measure of the demons was meant to ensure that during times of cruel demon rulers, the land wouldn't be overrun by demons. Therefore, why not imbue the Angel Council with a similar power. And because the archangels can be a secretive lot, they didn't tell anyone they'd done it. Hell, if they even knew they had. It seems like something Jophiel and Zadkiel would do on their own and not mention to anyone. However, not running the council means angels are free to use other fertility clinics and services, which hits you where it counts; your wallet. Right now, you can bully angels into using Divine Blessings Fertility and Prenatal Clinic. You hook them with those stupid coupons you include in the newsletter and then once you've gotten them here, well, if they go somewhere else they are sure to lose their baby. I suspect that's also your doing," I said.

"This is outrageous!" Balthazar said. "Get off my property."

"Balthazar Leopold, you're under arrest for genetically engineering a hell prince on this plane," Magda stated.

"You have no authority over me and it's not illegal to engineer cambions," Balthazar told her.

"It is if you are using them to kill. Soleil, do you know which one did the killings?" Magda asked. I sadly nodded and looked at the cambion for the first time. They all had the pale skin of the one I had found and given to

Lucifer. The one he'd named Xerxes. "Would a cambion be able to testify to the killings?"

"Yes, with the Rite of Forgiveness they might get their mind back enough to do it," I said. "If not, I'll need to execute him so he can be reincarnated as a full demon and not as a cambion." As if on cue, several people from the AESPCA showed up along with Simon Vance and Roderick Felder. I wondered how Balthazar had managed to raise his first two cambion and how he'd incubated them. The infant and the cambion I had given to Lucifer had been born to the female cambion, I had no doubt, but I wasn't sure how Balthazar had created the first two. I'd have to ask Magda after Batlhazar was interrogated, because I really wanted to know.

"I didn't know he'd use the spell to make a demon," Roderick Felder said.

"You don't look like a moron, but trusting Azazael proves you are," I told him. "I'm not nearly as old as you and I know not to trust Azazael."

"You can't talk to me like that!" Roderick Felder said, hands balled into fists.

"You were told by a cambion about a spell that would make angels fertile and you told your friend not expecting him to use it. Do you think anyone will believe that? Because I think you knew exactly what it was when you gave it to him and I am positive you intended him to use it. I would bet you helped him create the first cambion," I said.

"You don't know what you're talking about," Felder snarled.

"Yes, I do. I remember you from the hospital the night I was nearly eaten by Belial. You're one of the specialists brought in to deal with my wings being poisoned," I told him. "I'll testify that you had access to Belial's DNA, which was used to create the cambion here."

Chapter Twenty-four

The AESPCA was going through Divine Blessings paperwork and all their products for pre-natal care to see if there were hidden interactions with other potions to cause miscarriages if someone changed companies. Balthazar Leopold's bail had been set at four million dollars, cash only, and he was out of jail. Simon Vance, Roderick Felder, and Leopold himself had managed to come up with the money. I found this depressing. He'd spent only two days in jail, which seemed like a miscarriage of justice for three murders.

But there was an emergency vote scheduled for next week to replace the Angel Council. The Witches' Council had come out as endorsing Helia Burns for head of the council. They were endorsing some other candidates for other positions as well. The three cambion Balthazar had created were being kept at the AESPCA for now. They were going to need to learn to be demons. I was scheduled to perform the Rite of Forgiveness on the male cambion involved in the murders. It turned out Hecate's grimoire was very useful, and the spell I used when I performed the Rite of Exorcism had originated from it. Go figure.

Magda had come by yesterday to offer me a job as Division Chief of the Stygian Relations Department. I had declined, but told her I would do what I could to make the imp communication network available to whomever took the job, and suggested my mom for it. After all, she was a descendent of Hecate the Great Witch and had hearth magic. I thought Jerome and I could manipulate it to include imps. Even though she was interested in work, my mom declined. She was pregnant, after all. She instead bought The Handmade Thread. Dad was now converting a room into a workshop for her and her spinning wheel had been taken out of the attic. She was talking about making a special line of yarn that included strands of unicorn hair. I told her we'd have to negotiate that, I wasn't sure Pinkie Pie would be okay with mom plucking her mane and tail for yarn. Unfortunately, for that negotiation I'd mostly be a bystander as Aurora would have to handle Pinkie Pie's half of the communications. Aurora was oddly looking forward to it.

Mom had now been pregnant three weeks. It had been confirmed by both Gabriel and Jerome. And while it was still very early, too early for even a modern-day pregnancy test to show up positive, both were suggesting it was another girl. I was still unsure how I felt about my mom being pregnant. My sister was thrilled. Ariel and Aurora were more like me and unsure. I think Helia was just happy she wasn't going to be the youngest anymore.

Jerome came into the kitchen where I was having coffee and toast. As was becoming my habit, I checked the length of his pants. Jerome was taller than me already, and I swore if I paid enough attention, I'd be able to see him grow. Sure enough, his pants were a little shorter than last week at this time. My eyes found his feet next and I made a mental note that he needed pants and shoes and probably shirts, because if his legs were getting longer, his torso probably was too.

He'd finished school the day before. Next time he went to class, he'd be in high school. This made me happy and sad. After we left the AESPCA today, I was taking him to get his learner's permit to drive. I was feeling nostalgic about this. He'd been so young that day I met him in the streets of Chicago. Then we were meeting up with my parents for a late lunch. The lunch was a surprise, we were going to go look at used cars after lunch to give Jerome an idea of how much he needed to save up, because he was determined to pay half on his first car. Except, knowing my parents, if he found a car that he really liked that they approved of, one of them would buy it after we left. I added a trip to the mall to the list of things that needed to be done today. Tonight, we had a baseball game at six. The Cardinals were playing the Astros and my parents were going to announce the pregnancy to everyone in the family while there. Before the game, Helia was going to be broadcast announcing that she was running for head of the Angel Council and then an angel named Nathan Mitchell was going to announce that Ariel was a fertility angel. Nathan Mitchell had been the Secretary of the Angel Council, and apparently the only one not a complete puppet of Balthazar Leopold. Until the vote was over, he was acting head of the council. Helia had offered to let him run for head and endorse him instead of running herself and he'd told her thank you, but he was happy not running.

"You don't have to come with me," I told Jerome.

"I want to come with you," Jerome replied. "How many times can a kid see the Rite of Forgiveness performed on a cambion?"

"Who knows, although I suspect you won't see much," I told him.

"Maybe not, but just watching it be performed will be nice."

"I feel like life is changing again," I said to him.

"It is, but at least our house didn't have to burn down for the change to occur. You're going to be a big sister all over again. The AESPCA is trying to form a working relationship with the Stygian. Your mom has a job. Magda pulled strings and got you your PI license early. The AESPCA gave you a huge check for solving their demon murder mystery. And they will give you another big check today after you perform the Rite of Forgiveness." The AESPCA had tried the rite on their own several times, and it hadn't worked. Since I'd turned down their other job offer, Magda had offered me a new deal. I wouldn't work for the AESPCA, but if I would be willing to consult with her on things involving demons, I'd be paid for that time. I agreed to this on one condition, that I could get some help with the cambion as needed. Cambions were half demons and needed to understand how to be a demon. After closely examining their DNA, Dr. Lane had pronounced them mostly demon with some angelic and witch DNA thrown in. The female cambion had told us she was the first one created and after every killing, Leopold made her drink a special shake, after which she'd give birth. She told us that killing had happened in the lab and Balthazar had done it himself. Only after Leopold was born did Balthazar start using the cambion to kill, wanting to ensure Leopold would have enough power to challenge Lucifer. She was excited to be reunited with Xerxes and didn't know what had happened to him, only that Leopold and another man she didn't know had taken him from her and he'd never come back.

Lucifer had agreed to take in all three of these cambion. A couple times a week, I summoned Lilith to help them learn to be demons. Oddly, she said the shakes had been fed to her four times, but Magda and her investigators still hadn't found the first victim, the one Balthazar had killed. However, it wouldn't have been turned to stone, so the only clue they had was that it would have been missing its heart. I was surprised by the rapidity of it all. Balthazar had managed to grow a demon to breeding age and get it pregnant three times in the space of six months. Lilith said she wasn't surprised, demon pregnancies rarely lasted more than a month. Which was the other issue, our cambion was due to give birth again any day.

Dr. Lane had taken a special interest in them and was taking very good care of them. She'd even given them all names; the female was Dusana, which meant Soul. The oldest male, who I was providing the Rite of Forgiveness for today, was Ramses, and the two younger male cambions were Alexander and Julius, after the historical leaders. She thought they went well with Xerxes when I told her that's what Lucifer had named the cambion I had already given him. No one had argued with her, which surprised me, since Magda seemed to enjoy arguing. Personally, I thought it was fitting. They all had the demon alpha helix. Surprisingly, Azazael's swab showed only one alpha helix on number 23, the gene he'd inherited from Lilith, because it was the X chromosome.

We arrived at the AESPCA about ten minutes early. I messaged Magda and she met us at the side door the possessed used and we all went straight down to the lab where Dr. Lane and the cambion were spending their time. Magda and the AESPCA had been nice enough to install bunk beds in a room attached to the laboratory. There was also a private bathroom and a small kitchenette attached to the second room. I suspected Dr. Lane was sleeping in her office, although she told me she wasn't. I had also learned that Dr. Lane was trying to figure out if the genes that control magic could be altered in demons so that they didn't draw power from fear. Which is why she'd been so thankful to get demon DNA. She'd been trying to use a combination of all supernatural DNA to solve the puzzle of where demon magic resided in the genome and how it could be altered. My help gave her a huge database of specimens to draw from, although it had raised some questions as well. I hadn't expected Lucifer to have DNA, he was an artificial construct animated by a soul, but he did. Dr. Lane was puzzled because Lucifer and Azazael didn't share any DNA. I had tried to explain it to her by pointing out that Lucifer wasn't Azazael's father, Jophiel was, but the idea of moving a soul from one body to another seemed out of her depth for some reason. On the other hand, Lucifer and Leviathan did share a number of genes. Enough that Dr. Lane said they were closely biologically related, but oddly they didn't seem to be siblings. Which raised a new question for me to ask Leviathan. Although I was only partially convinced he'd have some kind of answers. I was wondering if when he created Lucifer's body, he'd also created Leviathan's. I'd spoken to him once since learning of it, but figuring out how to ask Leviathan if Zadkiel was planning his death even back when they were building the Stygian was awkward and delicate, and I hadn't worked up to it yet.

Chapter Twenty-five

"Ramses, I have never performed this rite before and I'm sorry you are the first, but we need to do it," I said.

"So far, it hasn't worked," Dusana told me, her head down.

"That's because this is the first time they've allowed me to try it. I spoke with a demon that has had it done and he said it hurt a little and tingled a lot," I admitted. "Also, I got permission for Lilith to be with us. She's experienced it before and can tell me if it goes correctly," I told them, at which point I summoned Lilith. Lilith went to stand between Ramses and Dusana, took each of them by the hand and nodded at me. I closed my eyes and concentrated on remembering the words. Hecate had written them in angelic script and I'd had my father go through the pronunciations with me the day before, just in case. I really didn't want to fuck up. I took a couple of deep breaths—all the magic I did came naturally. I wasn't sure this would.

"You got this," Jerome whispered to me. I nodded at him decisively. This was Stygian magic; I could do it. I said the words. Nothing exceptionally interesting happened, except that Ramses collapsed and seemed to pass out.

"This is normal," Lilith said reassuringly. "The spell is soul cleansing as well as mind clarifying. The body needs to reset after it's complete. Just give him a few minutes and he'll come around."

A lab assistant brewed coffee and brought all of us a cup while we waited for Ramses to wake up. I was halfway through my cup when he sat up, gasped, and then started to cry.

"Why is he crying?" I asked Lilith. "I'm a sympathetic crier."

"Soleil, you are a sympathetic everything," Magda said to me with a grin.

"You'd cry too if someone took a huge burden from you," Lilith said. I considered that. No, I'd probably fight it tooth and nail, because I can't do anything the easy way, I thought. However, I kept my mouth shut and closed my eyes to try and stop myself from crying.

"Thank you," Ramses said to me after several minutes of crying. "Thank you so much."

"You're welcome," I said and the cambion suddenly hugged me. At which point Dusana hugged me.

"Now, when do we go to our new home?" Dusana asked after a couple of minutes of hugging, which was far too long for my comfort level. The youngest two cambion were still babies, and I didn't envy the Lucifer household having three demonling cambions running around.

"If this worked, in a few days," Magda Red told her. "Leopold's lawyer has agreed to do a taped interview. What's going to happen is Ramses will be in a room with his attorney. The AESPCA lawyer and Leopold's lawyer will be in the room with him, they will ask him questions on video and it will be recorded like a moving picture. Then that will be played at Leopold's trial for the jury to see." Otherwise, it could take months before we got you to your new home." I nodded my approval.

Gabriel was acting as lawyer for Ramses since the cambion was basically a newborn in an adult body because he'd been killing people to grow his own magic, although it wasn't his fault and he didn't really understand it. Realistically, even though Dusana had given birth to them, she was a baby herself. Magda and the AESPCA would inform me when I was needed to send them to the Stygian. The AESPCA was going to do it, until they realized they couldn't pinpoint the exit for their portal and I could.

We all hugged again and said our goodbyes for a few days. Magda walked Jerome and I out.

"There's still time for you to take the Stygian Relations position," Magda said to me.

"No, thank you. Maybe in a few centuries when I'm bored with exorcisms, lost dogs, and insurance companies," I told her.

"I knew you'd say that, but I had to try one more time." She smiled. "I guess I will return to packing my office."

"Are you leaving the AESPCA?" I asked her. "I'd hire you."

"No, I am taking the job you refused," Magda said. "I had a child with a cambion, so someone above me thinks that makes me qualified for the job. Which means I am probably going to be calling *my* consultant fairly often for advice."

"You have my number, but you might want to text, I'm usually easier to get via text than call." I smiled at her.

"Will do. So I didn't want to be rude and ask, but is Jerome actually growing so fast it's visible?" She pointed at his jeans, which were about two inches above his ankles.

"Sometimes I think so." I nodded.

"Your father was abnormally tall, too. Soleil, go buy the kid some jeans, I know how much you got paid for consulting on that case."

"That is actually on my calendar today after lunch."

"I knew I should have worn shorts today," Jerome said as we got in the car.

"Yeah, because we are less likely to notice that your shorts are above your knees and weren't when we bought them?" I asked him.

"I could probably make a potion to stop me growing," Jerome said.

"Don't you dare, powerful angelic men are always tall," I told him.

"So are powerful demon men," Jerome said.

"This is true, I suspect it's Zadkiel and Jophiel's inside joke that demons grow bigger with more power," I said. "Now, Sophia and Raphael want to take us to lunch at Dolmenco's. Are you up for it?"

"Absolutely," Jerome said. Which was good, because I would have made him go even if he'd said no.

"We'll feed you steak and then take you clothes shopping, because you need new shoes again, I noticed, and I'm sure if your legs and feet are growing your torso must be as well."

I had the lobster tail dinner, and then I begged Eduardo the owner to put a third lobster tail on Dad's bill without the sides and other nonsense. I ate it too. As I did,

289

my mom rudely dug out her cell phone and began texting. I glared at her, and when she finished, she demurely put away her phone.

"Last time you had three lobster tails, Helia was pregnant with Aurora," Dad said with a smile.

"Maybe I binge lobster when all the women in my immediate family get pregnant," I said, looking pointedly at my mother, who had finished off an entire 20 ounce steak, mashed potatoes, a spring vegetable medley, an extra side of fries, two slices of Texas toast, a piece of chocolate mousse pie, and a slice of strawberry cheesecake.

"Are you ready to go car shopping?" Mom asked Jerome.

"I thought we were going clothes shopping?" Jerome replied.

"That too, but first cars. We want to know about what you are expecting to spend and what kind of car you think you'd like," Dad said.

"I have a little over $2,000 saved from my pendant sales. Once I get my practicing wizard license, Remiel said I could sell potions all summer and into the fall to Angel Investigations customers for things like finding your keys and cell phones. He says they would be big sellers." I nodded sagely at this. Remiel had not discussed this with me, but I had expected he had some scheme up his sleeve. "I'm hoping by January I'll have another $1,000 or so saved. I already know that I want an SUV. Nothing too big, but also not too small since I have a family full of winged angels. I just don't think I need an angel edition SUV. I mean it will mostly be Soleil riding with me, and if we need to take others, she might let me use her car."

"Very practical. If you come up with $3,000 that gives you about $6,000. I think you'll get a nice used SUV for that," Dad told him. I did not give either of my parents a look, because I already knew it was a lost cause. If Jerome so much as admired an SUV outside his price range goal, my parents would buy it. Hell, I'd be shocked if it wasn't in their garage by the time the sun set. My parents didn't view it as spoiling a child or overindulging a child, because they had raised Helia and I to be hard workers and hard work was supposed to be rewarded. While I hadn't taught Jerome to be a hard worker, his mom certainly had and Jerome was a straight A student who played sports, helped out around the house, worked, helped out my father whenever with whatever dad needed. For that, he believed Jerome should be rewarded. While I did think my parents were a bit too indulgent, I also didn't disagree with them. Jerome did work his tail off, and he'd earned it.

Jerome found a 14-year-old red Nissan Pathfinder for $5,000, and he was in love. Oddly, my mother arranged to meet with Helia instead of going shopping with us. Even odder, she gave Helia the name of the car lot we were at and told my dad to take their car to the mall. Jerome pointed out that we had plenty of room for Raphael, but my mother was insistent that dad take the car. I tried not to give my mom looks as I got in the car with Jerome.

"Sophia is buying that Pathfinder, isn't she?" Jerome asked Raphael as we walked into the mall.

"No," Raphael said. I believed him, because I knew my dad didn't believe ten-year-old cars were a good deal. My first car had only been six years old, and like the majority of teens, I had wrecked it within the first six months of owning it. Now, in my defense, I wrecked it when a demon was summoned, not by me, while I drove. Gabriel had laughed his ass off about that for months and my second car had been just three years old and I suspected, although no one had confirmed it, that the insurance money had been helped along by the demon-summoning uncle. There was no way my father was going to let Jerome drive around in a 14-year-old car.

"That reminds me; don't let Gabriel ride with you for the first year," I said to Jerome. Gabriel had also been the passenger in Helia's first car wreck, although he hadn't actually been the cause of it like he had been with mine. Unless he'd lied to Helia and told her she was pregnant. I made a mental note to ask Helia about it.

"It took him longer with Helia than you," Raphael said, pursing his lips. "It was nearly seven months before Helia wrecked with him in the car, and she swore it wasn't his fault, but I don't quite believe her."

"I don't get it," Jerome said.

"My brother summoned a demon while Soleil was driving him to work one morning when his car mysteriously broke down. He thought it was hilarious and it totaled the car completely," Raphael said. "He was also riding with Helia when she totaled her car, although Helia told me it wasn't his fault."

"Gabriel is banned from riding with me, got it," Jerome said.

"And Remiel," Dad said. "I can see Gabriel passing the torch on to Remiel with you."

"And Remiel." Jerome nodded. "However, if anyone is going to accidentally summon a demon while I drive, I suspect that would be Soleil."

"That is true, but I think in Missouri you have to have a parent or guardian in the car the first year you drive," Dad said. "I'll have to look it up, it's something weird like that. Now, do you want to start with shoes, shirts, or pants?"

"Let's get the shoes done first," Jerome said. I nodded in agreement. While Jerome and Dad got pants and shirts, I'd get dessert from the fancy popcorn place. This was more for Jerome's comfort than anything else, new pants meant he'd need new underwear too. It turns out when boys get taller, their boxers and jockeys need to get taller too. It also turned out Jerome was horrified to have me shop for his underwear. He didn't seem to notice that most of the time I washed it. An hour later, I was on the phone with my mom who was at a Nissan dealership asking me about red Pathfinders and did I think Jerome would prefer a 2015 or a 2016, they had one of each in red, but not the same red as the 2007. She'd texted me pictures of both of them about 20 minutes earlier and I had said "either," which wasn't the right answer. Immediately after she read the text, she called to lecture me on the safety features of the 2007 compared to the 2016. Finally, I got it.

"If the 2016 is safer than the 2007 or the 2015, get the 2016," I told her.

"Also, the red 2016 is a slightly brighter red than the 2015."

"The real question is, are you going to make Jerome feel bad if you buy the 2016, which is definitely outside what he has budgeted for it."

"It isn't about price, it's about safety," Mom replied.

"Then get the 2016 and explain to Jerome it was about safety," I said. "Also, where are you going to hide it for close to a year?"

"Hide it?" Mom asked.

"Well, you can't give it to him now."

"Why not?" Mom asked.

"He can't drive yet."

"Good point, we'll put it in your garage," Mom said and hung up on me. I sighed. Maybe I wanted ice cream to go with the popcorn. Maybe Jerome would also want ice cream to go with his 2016 Pathfinder that was out of his budget. I got an assortment of fancy popcorn and then meandered over to Target and found Rocky Road ice cream for Jerome and cherry vanilla for me. Ice cream bought, I headed to the angel store my dad liked to shop at. Jerome had two bags from a hip clothing store and two bags with shoes in them. I handed him the bag with the pint of Rocky Road ice cream.

"Uh, why do I need ice cream?" Jerome asked, looking at me. I looked at my father.

"Why does Jerome need ice cream?" Dad asked.

"It's about safety and she's planning to put it in my garage," I told him. Dad looked at me. "You are coming home with me to sort out Jerome's wardrobe and remove all the stuff that doesn't fit anymore so you can explain safety to him," I told him. His phone buzzed. He looked at it, then frowned at me.

"Gotcha, your garage," he said.

"Uh, I know about condoms," Jerome said sheepishly.

"Yes, it's that time," Dad said. "There's so much more you need to know about safety beyond condoms." Poor Jerome. Poor Soleil. I showed Jerome my pint of cherry vanilla ice cream and the fancy popcorn assortment. It had zebra stripes, caramel and almonds, caramel and hazelnuts, chocolate and hazelnuts, white cheddar, and yellow cheddar.

"I know it's Friday, but do you want to watch Disney movies with the girls tonight?" I asked Jerome.

"I think so," Jerome answered. I texted my sister about having a movie night. She agreed and informed me she had tried to talk Mom out of putting it in my garage to no avail and she'd be there to help with the lesson on safe cars. I thanked her and put my phone away.

Chapter Twenty-six

My father parked his SUV at the curb. Helia's car was in her driveway, but she was standing in my yard with my mom when I got home. Jerome looked at me.

"I love everyone, but I do not want to have this discussion with all of you. Raphael, I understand, but Sophia and Helia make me really uncomfortable," Jerome said. "Also, Remiel had this talk with me a while ago. He said you asked him to."

"Yeah, shut up and get out of the car and be prepared to want your ice cream and maybe some popcorn. Also, try to look happy, even if you aren't," I told him.

"What did they do?" Jerome asked me.

"Out," I said opening my door and grabbing the ice cream and popcorn. The moment I got out, Mom banged on the garage door and it started to open. My nieces were giggling so hard as they opened the door, it was a miracle either of them could reach the button, as they were nearly doubled over.

"Jerome, isn't it awesome! Grandma and Grandpa got it for you for next year! You are going to be the coolest kid in high school!" Aurora gasped between giggles as she tried to run out and hug him. Helia and I were pretty sure Aurora had a small crush on Jerome, but we'd also decided it wasn't a bad thing. We'd address it when she got older if it didn't go away.

"Wow, this isn't what I was expecting," Jerome said. He actually did look shocked. My father must be getting better at blocking the teen from reading his thoughts. "I can't afford this, it's newer than the one we looked at."

"We know, but it's about safety. Any car more than ten years old has questionable safety issues. Newer cars have more innovative safety features, because it's an evolving technology," Raphael said. Then he went on and on about how if Jerome was going to be driving, he and Sophia wanted to make sure he had the best safety features available because car accidents accounted for nearly 70 percent of supernatural fatalities. He further explained that nearly all teen drivers have an accident within the first year of driving, which is why they hadn't gotten him a brand-new Pathfinder, with the best security features available, but four or five years was an acceptable risk on the advancement of safety features. Jerome just stood there, stunned. I had already seen this dog and pony show happen twice before; once with me and once with Helia. We'd both picked out unacceptably aged cars when we'd gone shopping, too, and my parents had gotten each of us a newer version of the car we'd picked out in the color we'd picked.

Helia and I stood back and watched.

"Is he angry, sad, happy?" Helia whispered after a moment.

"I'm not sure. I think he's overwhelmed and trying to do the math of how many pendants and potions he needs to sell to pay them back," I whispered.

"Maybe over pizza tonight, we tell him about his secret bank account," Helia told me. I nodded in agreement. Every cent Jerome paid my parents went into a secret bank account in Jerome's name that they intended to give him when he either went off to college or trade school or decided to start his life as an adult in whatever form or fashion that turned out to be. Jerome and my father's relationship had started with Jerome promising to pay Raphael back for some exceptionally gorgeous and expensive pendants that he'd put possession protection on for Valerie and myself. The teen had paid my father back every penny and my father had started him a secret bank account with it. Since then, anytime Raphael has bought something for Jerome that Jerome has paid him back for, my father has just put that money in Jerome's secret bank account.

"It might take me a few years, but if you tell me what my half is, I'll pay you back," Jerome said.

"Don't bother, Jerome," I said.

"It's a gift. It's early, but it's a gift for your birthday," Mom said, hugging Jerome. "I hope you like it; I know it's not exactly the same as the one you picked out, but I hope it's an acceptable replacement. Normally, Raphael would have gone and gotten it, but since you needed new clothes, we figured you were more comfortable buying underwear with him than you would be with me."

"I love it," Jerome told my mom, which made both of my parents incredibly happy. I knew my parents and that was way more important than money or anything else Jerome could have given them in this moment. He loved it. He was happy and that made Sophia and Raphael happy, because at the end of the day that is all they really want out of life, happy kids and happy grandkids, and eventually happy great grandkids. With a little luck they will all be hard workers like they are.

"Ice cream and then you and Dad tackle your closet. You didn't clean it out last time you needed new clothes," I said.

"You didn't buy enough ice cream for everyone," Dad said.

"No, because I have four quarts of ice cream you guys left from the last time you thought we needed ice cream," I said. "I got these two pints special for Jerome and I to deal with you two being overwhelming. The rest of you can eat the non-special ice cream."

"Aunt Asha, I would prefer the special ice cream, if that's okay," Aurora said shyly.

"I had three lobster tails, plus side dishes at lunch, so I would be willing to share my special ice cream with you," I told Aurora. Ariel laughed at me.

"That's why Mom asked me if I was sure I wasn't pregnant!" Helia exclaimed as we walked into my garage.

"I had a craving for lobster tail. I think it's because mom's pregnant." I shrugged.

"It is really odd that you crave lobster when I'm pregnant," Helia said.

"Magda told me I was overly sympathetic today," I told my sister.

"Magda's correct," Helia replied. My phone dinged with a new text. I wondered if Magda's ears were burning and pulled it out fully prepared for the witch to know we'd said her name for some reason. To my surprise it wasn't from Magda, it was from Janet.

Tell your dad thanks! I'll keep in touch. I wanted to tell you how much I enjoyed working with you and learning from you. But I also needed to tell you something I think you need to hear. You are the laziest magic user I have ever met. I can't even use the word practitioner for you, because that implies you practice using magic and you don't. If you practiced even a little, you would be a force to be reckoned with. We're getting married in a few weeks and I'm pregnant. I was hoping you'd allow Jerome to make my prenatal care potions, and I was hoping he could help you learn, because the baby is part angel and I would feel better if the potions had an angelic touch to them.

I considered texting her back that Jerome was also angelic and didn't. Instead, I told her I'd do what I could. Helia bent forward and read the text on my phone.

"Huh, she's right, you definitely don't qualify as a magic practitioner. I'm so excited for her!" Helia gushed. "Are you okay?"

"Fine." I replied.

"You look like you're about to set fire to the yard," Helia responded.

"I don't know why people won't leave me alone about not being able to do magic like that."

"Because you could do magic like that if you tried. You're problem is if you don't get a spell or incantation perfect the first time, you never try again. You just put it in this imaginary category of magic you can't do. You've said yourself over the last few years your magic has really grown, but that isn't true. You've always had these abilities; you were just always too lazy to try using them and god forbid you spend 15 minutes trying to perfect some bit of magic. That would be tragic."

"Magic takes a lot of energy," I said lamely.

"It's like a muscle if you don't use it, it's harder to flex when you do need it," Helia scolded me.

"She's not wrong," Remiel said, walking up to us. "You are an exceptionally lazy magic user. I keep thinking having myself and Jerome around will motivate you to do better with it."

"She's afraid if she gets good with magic, people will expect her to use it all the time and be good with it and something will happen where she'll fail to perform a spell and disappoint everyone. At least this way she can pretend that failure wasn't an aberration, and she thinks everyone will keep their expectations of her magical abilities low," Jerome told them all. I considered opening a portal to the Stygian and going through it, but Jerome would be able to follow me there, so I didn't.

"Oh Soleil, you will never disappoint me," my mom said, hugging me. "Your father and I only expect you to be happy, and if you want to us to continue to ignore how powerful you are because it makes you happy, we will." How does someone respond to that? I was afraid to disappoint my parents, but I knew I wasn't good with magic because I didn't practice it because I was lazy, but looking at my parents, I couldn't tell them that.

"Well shit, now I have to learn to use my magic properly," I sighed.

"If you need help paying for classes to advance your magical skills, we will help you with that. But Soleil, you don't need to use magic to make us happy," Mom said.

"She's right Soleil, if you do want to improve, we'll help you, but do it to make yourself happy. If you're happy, we're happy," Dad told me.

"We can do homework together again!" Jerome said cheerfully. I tried not to groan. I'd done some tutoring after Jerome came to live with me because he was scary powerful. I had hated every second of it. I had no doubt I would hate every second of these lessons too, but Janet was correct, I was the laziest magic user ever and I needed to do something about it, because I was running a business that relied on magic and I was raising a scary powerful wizard. Fan-fucking-tastic, I was going to learn how to use my magic. At least I would be able to make myself a cup of coffee before I got out of bed in the mornings, that would be nice.